Charles Mackay

The Legendary and Romantic Ballads of Scotland

Charles Mackay

The Legendary and Romantic Ballads of Scotland

ISBN/EAN: 9783744777940

Printed in Europe, USA, Canada, Australia, Japan

Cover: Foto ©Andreas Hilbeck / pixelio.de

More available books at **www.hansebooks.com**

LEGENDARY AND ROMANTIC

BALLADS OF SCOTLAND.

EDITED BY

CHARLES MACKAY,

AUTHOR OF "EGERIA," "THE LUMP OF GOLD," ETC.

LONDON:

GRIFFIN, BOHN, & CO., STATIONERS' HALL COURT.

1861.

EDINBURGH:
PRINTED BY BALLANTYNE AND COMPANY,
PAUL'S WORK.

—— Over all this hazy realm is spread
A halo of sad memories of the dead;
Of mournful love-tales—of old tragedies,
Filling the heart with pity, and the eyes
With tears at bare remembrance; and old songs
Of Love's endurance, Love's despair, Love's wrongs,
And triumphs o'er all obstacles at last,
And all the grief and passion of the past.

Voices from the Mountains.

INTRODUCTION.

THIS volume is, for the greater part, a reprint of the valuable collection of Scottish Ballads published by the late William Motherwell under the title of "Ancient and Modern Minstrelsy." The modern ballads, and all that could not fairly be considered either legendary or romantic, have been excluded, as inconsistent with the title adopted for the republication; and several others, from Scott's Minstrelsy of the Scottish Border, and other sources, of which Motherwell neglected, or did not think fit to avail himself, have been added, as being essentially necessary to the completeness of a collection founded upon a broader basis than he had laid down for himself. Mr Motherwell's judicious and accurate notes have been preserved, as well as the greater portion of his learned and sympathetic " Essay on the Origin and History of Scottish Ballad Literature." The subject is so rich and fertile that it has not been possible, within the prescribed limits of one volume, to include more than the very flower or cream of the compositions which the early Scottish ballad writers and singers so profusely scattered over the land, making it musical with the voice of many sorrows; but the Editor believes that the selection, limited as it is, will be found to contain an adequate proportion of the best and most popular of these rude and homely, but hearty and touching lyrics—not as they may have been from time to time "improved" by Percy, Scott, Hogg, and others, sometimes with more taste than reverence, and often without either—but as they came from the mouths of the early singers themselves, long before they were committed to the press. The temptation to "amend" such compositions where the rhythm halts, or the rhyme does not jingle, and where, as in many instances, the correct reading is hopelessly lost, is great and trying to the self-control of most editors; but in this respect Motherwell set an example of fidelity which the Editor of the present volume has scrupulously followed. The only two comparatively modern ballads that have been admitted, are those upon the Yarrow Tragedy by William Hamilton of Bangour, and John Logan—an honour to which their great popularity, and their supersedence of the older versions of the story, seem fairly to entitle them. Wherever, in any ballad, not included in Motherwell's original collection, the Editor has seen reason to believe that Sir Walter Scott, or an inferior hand to his, has tampered with the original version, he has not scrupled to state his opinion—agreeing fully with his predecessor "that such a mode of editing ancient ballads is highly objectionable."

London, *May* 1861.

CONTENTS.

CONTENTS.

PRELIMINARY ESSAY

ON

SCOTTISH BALLAD LITERATURE.

By WILLIAM MOTHERWELL.

As this compilation consists principally of Narrative Ballads, there occurring in it no compositions strictly called Songs, in the sense to which that term is now generally confined, the slight observations with which it has been thought proper to introduce it, are to be understood as referring exclusively to the Ancient Romantic and Historic Ballad of Scotland.

Under the head of ROMANTIC, a phrase we are obliged to employ for lack of something more significant and precise, may be ranged a numerous and highly interesting body of short metrical tales, chiefly of a tragic complexion, which, though possessing all the features of real incident, and probably originating in fact, cannot now, after the lapse of many ages, be with certainty traced to any historical source, public or private. With these may also be classed that description of ANCIENT SONG which treats of incredible achievements, and strange adventures by flood and field,—deals largely with the marvellous in all its multiform aspects,—and occasionally pours a brief but intense glare of supernatural light over those dim and untravelled realms of doubt and dread, whose every nook the giant superstition of elder days has colonised with a prodigal profusion of mysterious and spiritual inhabitants. And, in short, under this comprehensive head, we must include every legend relating to person, place, thing, or occurrence, to establish whose existence it would be vain to seek for other evidence than that which popular tradition supplies.

The other class is much easier described. It embraces all those narrative songs which derive their origin from historical facts, whether of a public or private nature. The subjects of these are national or personal conflicts, family feuds, public or domestic transactions, personal adventure, or local incidents, which, in some shape or other, have fallen under the observation of contemporary and authentic annalists. In general, these compositions may be considered as coeval with the events which they commemorate; but, with this class as with that which has been styled the Romantic ballad, it is not to be expected that, in their progress to our day, they have undergone no modifications of form, and these very considerable, from that in which they were originally produced and promulgated among the people.

This interesting body of popular poetry, part of which, in point of antiquity, may fairly be esteemed equal, if not superior, to the most ancient of our written monuments, has owed its preservation principally to oral tradition. With the exception of a very few pieces, which, more through accident than design, appear to have found their way into old MSS., or early printed volumes, the ancient Ballad Poetry of Scotland must literally be gathered from the lips of

> " The spinsters and the knitters in the sun,
> Who use to chant it."

But fragile and capricious as the tenure may seem by which it has held its existence for centuries, it is worthy of remark how excellently well tradition serves as a substitute for more efficient and less mutable channels of communicating the things of past ages to posterity. In proof of this, it is only necessary to instance the well-known ballad of *Edom o' Gordon*, which is traditionally preserved in Scotland, and of which there is fortunately extant a copy in an English MS., apparently coeval with the date of the subject of the ballad. The title of this copy is *Captain Care*. We owe its publication to the late Mr Ritson, in whose " Ancient Songs " it will be found, printed from a MS. in the Cottonian Library.* Between the text of the traditionary version and that of the MS., a slight inspection will satisfy us that the variations are neither very numerous nor very important. This is taking the MS. as the standard of the original text, although it can scarcely be considered as such, seeing it has been transcribed by an English clerk, who perhaps took it down from the imperfect recitation of some wandering Scottish minstrel, and thereafter altered it to suit

* Ancient Songs, London, 1790, p. 137.—Dr Percy mentions that a fragment of it also occurs in his folio MS.

his own ideas of poetical beauty.*   Could, however, there be MS. copies of other of our ancient ballads recovered, it certainly would be a most desirable and valuable acquisition. If any such exist, and shall at any time hereafter be communicated to the world, it is confidently anticipated that they will establish the fact of tradition being, in all matters relative to popular poetry, a safe and almost unerring guide.

Language, which, in the written literature of a country, is ever varying, suffers no material changes nor corruptions among the lower and uneducated classes of society, by whom it is spoken as their mother tongue. With them, primitive forms of speech, peculiar idiomatic expressions, and antique phrases, are still in use, which we would look for in vain in the literature of the present day, or in its word-books, which are not professedly dedicated to the " restitution of decayed intelligence."   It is not therefore with the unlettered and the rude that oral song suffers vital and irremediable wrong.   What they have received from their forefathers, they transmit in the same shape to their children ; for, as the Pardonere in " The Canterbury Tales " has justly remarked,

> "Lewd peple loven tales olde ;
> Swiche things can they wel report and holde."

---

* Ritson styles it " the undoubted original of the Scottish ballad, and one of the few specimens now extant of the proper old English ballad, as composed, not by a Grub Street author for the stalls of London, but to be chanted up and down the kingdom, by the wandering minstrels of ' the North Countrie.' " But here the critic has gratuitously assumed that the name which appears at the end of it as the copyist is also that of the author.—W. M.

Localities and persons may, it is true, be occasionally shifted to answer the meridian of the reciter, and obsolete terms and epithets be laid aside for others more generally in use ; but what may be called the facts of these compositions are never disturbed, nor are their individual or characteristic features ever lost. The tear and wear of three centuries will do less mischief to the text of an old ballad among the vulgar, than one short hour will effect, if in the possession of some sprightly and accomplished editor of the present day, who may choose to impose on himself the thankless and uncalled-for labour of piecing and patching up its imperfections, polishing its asperities, correcting its mistakes, embellishing its naked details, purging it of impurities, and of trimming it from top to toe with tailor-like fastidiousness and nicety, so as to be made fit for the press. For thus remodelling ancient song, such complacent wights claim as their reward the merest trifle—that of saddling antiquity with the sin of begetting, and the shame of maintaining, a few of the singularly beautiful and delicate growths of their own over-productive fancy. These pernicious and disingenuous practices breed a sickly loathing in the mind of every conscientious antiquary, and would, if not checked and exposed, in a short while lay the broad axe to the root of everything like authenticity in oral song.

The almost total absence of written monuments to support the claims of Scotland to an inheritance of Ancient National Minstrelsy, enforces the stern necessity of not wantonly tampering with the fleeting and precarious memorials tradition has bequeathed to these latter times. Hence it has become of the first importance to collect these songs with scrupulous and unshrinking fidelity. If they are at all worth preserving, and no one who has an unsophisticated and manly taste can deny that they are so, it assuredly must be in the very garb in which they are remembered and known, and can be proved to exist amongst us. It will not do to indulge in idle speculations as to what they once may have been, and to recast them in what we may fancy were their original moulds. We may regret that attention was not earlier bestowed on this neglected though interesting portion of national literature, but the only step we are warranted in taking to remedy what Sir Thomas Browne has denominated "the supinity of elder times," is that of preventing its future dilapidation, by now carefully and accurately gathering what of its wreck we can yet find floating around us. The time may come when even these fragments will also be irretrievably borne beyond our reach.

Collections of these ballads, printed as they orally exist, will to those who succeed us prove a source of peculiar gratification—a record of the most instructive and interesting kind. They convey to posterity, that description of song which is peculiarly national and characteristic; that body of poetry which has inwoven itself with the feelings and passions of the people, and which shadows forth, as it were, an actual embodiment of their universal mind, and of its intellectual and moral tendencies. They communicate, too, another favour, which we would be glad had been conferred on us by any authority a century old; that is, the means of ascertaining what in our day were deemed ancient compositions, and what of more recent or of contemporaneous date with ourselves.

Evident, however, as the importance is of thus collecting our traditionary poetry purely as it is to be found, it unfortunately happens that this has been too often slightingly and slovenly executed. With many of these ballads, liberties of the most exceptionable and flagrant description have occasionally been taken by their respective editors,—liberties as uncalled for as they are unpardonable in the eye of every rigid and honest critic. Some of these offences against truth and correct taste are of a very deep, others of a lighter shade of criminality; but be they what they may in magnitude, all are alike deserving of unmitigated condemnation.

It is perhaps unnecessary to mention, that of every old traditionary ballad known, there exists what may be called different versions. In other words, the same tale is told after a different fashion in one district of the country, from what it is remembered in another. It therefore not unfrequently occurs, that no two copies obtained in parts of the country distant from each other, will be found completely to tally in their texts; perhaps they may not have a single stanza which is mutual property, except certain commonplaces which seem an integrant portion of the original mechanism of all our ancient ballads, and the presence of which forms one of their most peculiar and distinctive characteristics, as contrasted with the modern ballad. Both of these copies, however, narrate the same story. In that particular, their identity with each other cannot be disputed; but in many minute circumstances, as well as in the way by which the same catastrophe is brought out, sensible differences exist. By selecting the most beautiful and striking passages which present themselves in the one copy, and making these cohere as they best may with similar extracts detached from the other copy, the editor of oral poetry succeeds in producing from the conflicting texts of his various authorities a third version, more perfect and ornate than any individual one as it originally stood. This improved version may contain the quintessence—the poetic elements of each copy consulted, but in this general resemblance to all it loses its particular affinity to any one. Its individuality entirely disappears, and those features by which each separate copy proved its authenticity, in the collated version become faint and dubious, confused and undistinguishable. Such copies, however, are those which find their way readiest into our every-day compilations of such things, as well on account of their superior poetical merit, as of the comparative distinctness and fulness of their narrative; and to readers not accustomed to inquire into the nature of traditionary poetry, they thus convey very inaccurate impressions of the state in which these compositions are actually extant among us.

This mode, then, of editing ancient ballads, by subjecting them to the process of refinement now described, though it be more conscientious and less liable to censure than another method also resorted to, is nevertheless highly objectionable, as effectually marring the venerable simplicity of early song, destroying in a great measure its characteristic peculiarities, and as being the means of introducing erroneous conceptions regarding our vernacular poetry which has been recovered from tradition.

All versions of a ballad so preserved by oral transmission from one age to another, are entitled to be considered as of equal authenticity, and coeval production, one with the other, although among them wide and irreconcilable discrepancies exist. Indeed, the differences between some copies of the same ballad are so important, that their existence can be accounted for in no other way than by supposing these different versions the productions of so many distinct minstrels, each of whom obtained the story, which he versified from a channel foreign to that accessible by his fellow-poets. Some of these diversities, it is true, may be attributable to the interpolations and corruptions acquired in the course of time, through the ignorance of reciters. Some are inaccurately committed to memory at first, and are thus in an incomplete form delivered. Others are in part forgotten, and the defects of the memory may be supplied by the invention of the reciter, or the limb of some other similar composition substituted for that which is lost. But allowing the utmost latitude for the many mutations incident to this species of literature, still it cannot account for all the variations we find in these copies, several of which ought to be elevated to the rank of distinct ballads, in place of being regarded as mere variations from one original text.

Under the pressure of such circumstances, then, it surely is the duty of the collector and editor of traditionary ballads to avoid the perilous and frequently abortive task of uniting discordant and essentially incohesive texts, and to content himself with merely selecting that one of his copies which appears the most complete and least vitiated, and to give it purely and simply as he obtained it, without hazarding any emendation whatsoever.

If this comparatively innocent mode of restoring our ancient ballads be obnoxious to censure, they are still more culpable as editors who, under no authority of written or recited copy, but merely to gratify their own insatiate rage for innovation and improvement, recklessly and injudiciously cut and carve as they list on these productions, and, in some cases, entirely re-write them. Where the narrative is poor in incident, where it is wholly barren of imagery, there they most thickly plant their own bastard inventions, and strew the delicate blossoms of their own precious conceit; where the ancient song breaks forth in the earnest, simple, and downright language of passion and of nature, there our ballad renovator must dilute it to the slip-slop sentiment of his own day, and garnish it with the artificial brilliancies of his own style of writing; introducing throughout a current of feeling, and a tissue of allusions, (poetical, very poetical, we shall be charitable enough to suppose they are,) wholly at issue with the cast of thought, the manners, and the modes of expression peculiar to the age which produced the original poem. And, where the ancient minstrel, true in his delineations of society and of manners to the times in which he flourished, faithfully and vigorously sketches, *ad vivam*, nor hesitates, in the rush and tide of his song, to call a spade a spade, the modern affects to shudder at the grossness and vulgarity of antiquity, and diligently weaves his own gossamer web of sensuality around the nakedness of ancient simplicity, and then gloats over his seductive handiwork with the complacency of the merest voluptuary. They who choose to stigmatise the muse of antiquity as being rather "high-kilted," do no service either to letters or to morality by apparelling her in a "trailing gown," or giving her a "side tail" of their own fashioning. In truth, it is by such impertinent and pernicious labours that the obscenities of early writers become disgustingly obtruded on the public eye. Had they been allowed to pass uncommented on, they would never have called a blush to the innocent cheek, or in the unaffectedly pure mind have wakened one unhallowed thought. For the curious and important knowledge, then, which enables us to detect and understand the gross witticisms and licentious allusions of our ancestors, we stand indebted to the tasteful emendations, the delicate and minute criticism of these singularly sensitive and moral editors. But in their bitter wrath, and in their lachrymose exclamations against the licentiousness of ancient song, and the times which produced and could relish such foul dainties, and in the pains they take to detect the presence of indelicate inuendo, though never so cunningly wrapped up in some dark allegory, and in the skill they shew for its purification by kindly paraphrasing every objectionable passage, these well-meaning individuals not unfrequently manifest a lurking affection for their task, and a perfect acquaintance with its subject, seldom to be found in conjunction with that unspotted purity and extraordinary refinement and maiden-like delicacy which they profess.

There is yet another description of old-song editors, whose mischievous and dishonest propensities cannot be too severely reprobated. It consists of those gentlemen who deem themselves fully better poets than ever earlier times produced, but who cannot persuade the public to think so, or even prevail on it to read their compositions till they have given them a slight sprinkling of olden phraseology, and stoutly maintained that they were genuine specimens of ancient song. Some trash accounted as ancient, they have by sheer impudence thus succeeded in forcing down the throat of a credulous and gaping public ; but sooner or later these paltry forgeries are laid bare, to the shame and confusion of the utterer. The attempt to poison the sources of history, and to confound truth by such fabrications, is despicable and unprincipled. It is much to be regretted, however, that some men of undeniable talents have occasionally lent themselves to such ignoble ends, and bartered an honest fame for a worthless and shadowy triumph. But with all their ingenuity in the manufacture of these antique gems, they can at best only gull the rabble,—a poor and mean gratification,—while on every hand they encounter the risk of being roughly handled by those who know the studies in which they traffic much better than themselves, and who by a solitary scratch of their pen can dissipate the idle fabrications thus painfully reared on falsehood and imposition, and expose their authors to the contempt and derision of that public whose credulity and confidence they have abused.

When we look around us and find so voluminous a body of vernacular poetry traditionally preserved among the patriotic children of an ancient and heroic race, for a period of time to which imagination can assign no definite limits, but whose origin seems as remote, and involved in as much darkness, as the early history of the people themselves—a body of poetry, breathing at one time of " high erected thoughts seated in a heart of courtesie," and at another, overflowing with pathos and tenderest feeling ; at one time swelling into all the pomp of chivalric circumstance, and full of unmingled joy and triumph ; at another, moment narrowing itself into the intense interest of the deepest tragedy ;—a series of compositions, terse and unlaboured, but supplying in their details satisfactory and striking illustrations of the manners, habits, feelings, superstitions, and prejudices of days deep hidden in the gloom of hoar antiquity, and whose peculiarities of style so completely distinguish them from those productions of more recent times which embrace a similar range of topics : and when we find this curious and interesting species of national literature transmitted even to the present day, with a copiousness and fidelity almost rivalling the certainty and authenticity of written monuments, we are naturally led to inquire, not only into the causes which have so linked it with the affections of each succeeding race, but our attention is also directed to the times which first cherished so remarkable a class of compositions, and to the poets by whom it was produced. Ample though such a field of inquiry be, it nevertheless is one wherein little progress can be made with any degree of historical certainty; and, in an investigation whose object is professed to be the elucidation of truth, it would be idle to substitute conjecture for facts.

To point out what truly are the most ancient of these compositions cannot be attempted with any success. Though tradition may faithfully transmit to us the narrative uninjured and unshorn of any part of its circumstance—nay, even give the sentiments of the poet unaltered, and preserve the character of the piece precisely as at first portrayed, yet it alters the language so completely, that not a word may be preserved which originally was there. The phraseology of one age, as it becomes obsolete and strange, is in oral literature ever supplanted by equivalent terms which are better understood, or are in daily use; and these again, in their turn, at some future period, yield to the same inexorable law of perpetual mutation. Thus the distinguishing features of different ages, so far as these are indicated by language, become so thoroughly blended, that to fix the antiquity of traditionary song by any evidence which its diction supplies, is a hopeless, and, at best, an unsatisfactory endeavour.

" There are in Scotland," says Ritson, " many ballads, or legendary and romantic songs, composed in a singular style, and preserved by tradition among the country people. It must, however, be confessed that none of these compositions

bear satisfactory marks of the antiquity they
pretend to, while the expressions or allusions
occurring in some would seem to fix their origin to
a very modern date."* The opinions of a writer
of so much acuteness and information in poetic
archæology as Ritson, however hastily and in-
considerately delivered, are deserving of attention; but in this quotation it is to be observed
that he only refers to the "expressions and allusions" interspersed through the ballads he had
an opportunity of studying, not to their general
structure, and to those commonplaces and curious
burdens they frequently have, which serve as
landmarks and helps to the memory of the
reciter, while they secure the stream of the narrative from being broken or interrupted by the
innovations of time, and the mutations of language. It is granted at once that the "expressions
and allusions" of these compositions fluctuate,
and that frequently; but these changes never
alter entirely the venerable aspect of the whole
ballad. It is like repairing gradually the weather-
worn face of an ancient cathedral by the inser-
tion here and there of a freshly-hewn stone, as
need may require. The outline of the building
and the effect of the whole remain unchanged.
Though the comparatively modern look of ballad
phraseology, so far as dependent on certain allusions and expressions, is admitted to greater latitude than what is truly the fact, it is well known
to those acquainted with the subject, that they still
retain many "aureat termes," struck in the mint
of the olden time, amply sufficient to vouch for

* Historical Essay prefixed to "Scottish Song," Lond.
1794, p. lxxx.

their remote extraction and gentle blood, even were there no other evidence at hand of a less questionable and suspicious kind. That evidence is contained in the bosom of the ballads themselves. They enjoy peculiar features, which not only distinguish them from the like sort of compositions produced in more recent times, but certain characteristics which separate them from the written poetry of their own day, and identify them with each other as belonging to one body and family of national minstrelsy. These features, it will be found, are common also to the early traditionary poetry of the Scandinavian provinces of Europe; and constitute, in fact, the boundary line which exists between what is the oral and what is the written poetry of a people, or of that poetry which is equally intelligible to the unlettered as to the learned. We shall endeavour partially to sketch some of these distinctive and unalterable features of the ancient traditionary ballad of Scotland, although we feel that to do complete justice to the subject is neither in our power, nor is it compatible with the limits of this essay. Besides, there grows up an intuitive and auxiliary sense in all who are familiar with this study, which enables them at once, without any laboured process of induction or critical analysis, to discriminate between what is ancient and what is modern, or the imitation of the ancient; but this kind of intuitive perception cannot be communicated by words to another; and it is now merely mentioned to obviate any appearance of dogmatism, if, in the course of our observations, we should at any time call this old or that new, this genuine or that a forgery, without condescending to detail the grounds upon which such brief censures are founded.

The first thing that solicits our notice in the romantic ballad is the almost uniform dramatic cast of its structure. The action of the piece commences at once. It does not, like the metrical romance, proceed after craving the attention of lord and lady, and invoking the aid of the Virgin Mary, &c., to give a sketch of the parentage, education, and promising qualities of the doughty knight or gentle squire who is to figure in it. There is no pompous announcement of the exquisite enjoyment to be derived from the carping of such noble *gestes*. If such particulars are at all alluded to, they are noticed merely incidentally, and dashed off perhaps in a single line. The characters and the destinies of those who form the subject of such tales are learned from their actions, not by the description of the poet. They generally open with some striking and natural picture, pregnant with life and motion. The story runs on in an arrowlike stream, with all the straightforwardness of unfeigned and earnest passion. There is no turning back to mend what has been said amiss, to render more clear that which may have been dimly expressed, or slightly hinted ; and there is no pause made to gather on the way beautiful images or appropriate illustrations. If these come naturally and unavoidably as it were, good and well, but there is no loitering and winding about and about as if unwilling to move on till these should suggest themselves. The charm of the composition lies in the story which it evolves. Strained and artificial feeling has no place in it, and rhetorical embellishments are equally unknown. Descriptions of natural scenery are never attempted, and sentiment is almost unheard of. Much is always left for imagination to fancy, and for the feelings of the auditors to supply, roused, as they cannot fail to be, by the scenic picture rapidly and distinctly traced before the mind's eye. In his narrative, the poet always appears to be acting in good faith with his audience. He does not sing to another what he discredits himself, nor does he appeal to other testimony in support of his statements. There is no reference to "as the boke tells," or "as in romans I rede," for a corroboration of what he affirms. He always speaks as if the subject which he handles were one quite familiar to those whom he addresses, and touching which nothing but a perfectly honest and circumstantial statement of facts could be relished. If fifteen stalworth foresters are slain by one stout knight, single-handed, he never steps out of his way to prove the truth of such an achievement by appealing to the exploits of some other notable manslayer. If a mermaid should, from a love of solitude and the picturesque, haunt some lone and lovely river, and there, while kembing her yellow locks, peradventure fascinate some unhappy wight, the poet never apologises for the appearance of the water-woman, by covertly insinuating how marvellous be the inhabitants of the ocean. And though an elfin knight should unceremoniously adopt for his paramour some young lady whom he meets of a summer's evening, while rambling through the gay greenwood, and whose taste for the loveliness of nature is certainly more remarkable than her prudence—he never betrays any surprise at the circumstance, but treats it as a matter of every-day occurrence and historical notoriety. Should an unhappy ghost wander back to earth, the poet is perfectly master of the dialogue he holds with the maid he left behind him : nor is he at a loss accurately to describe how the fiend can, with a single kick of his cloven foot, sink a goodly bark, although reasonable doubts may well be entertained how such facts could have transpired, seeing none of its crew ever reached the land to sing of such an "unhappy voyage," more terrific by a deal than that performed under the melancholy auspices of that "brisk and tall young man," hight "William Glen," who was bound for, but, alas, never returned from, "New Barbarie."

But be the subject of the narrative what it may, whether it be of real life fraught with an interest deeply tragical, or one of wild superstition and romantic incident, it will ever be found clearly, succinctly, and impressively told. There is no unnecessary waste of words—no redundancy of circumstances, nor artful involution of plot— and no laying of colour above colour, to give a body and brilliancy to the picture. It stands out in simple and severe beauty—a beauty arising not from the loveliness of any one individual feature, but from the perfect harmony and wholeness subsisting among and sustaining all.

From the dramatic structure of these songs, we are naturally led to infer that when the singing or recitation of them was the business of minstrels, they were prefaced with some account of the previous history of the several individuals whom they respectively commemorate ; and that many minute circumstances elucidatory of them were detailed, not only for the purpose of interesting their hearers, but likewise to make the abrupt transitions occurring in some of these ballads more easy of apprehension to such as were strangers in the company. That this was the fact, admits of little doubt. Traces of such a custom still remain in the lowlands of Scotland, among those who have stores of these songs upon their memory. Reciters frequently, when any part of the narrative appears incomplete, supply the defect in prose. Where the ballad naturally terminates, they can tell what became of some inferior or subordinate character mentioned in it, whom the minstrel has passed over in silence, as interfering with the interest which should be exclusively concentrated around the principal personages. Some pieces, too, are prose and rhyme intermixed; the dialogue and those parts purely lyrical are in metre, while the narrative and descriptive portions are given in such humble prose as the reciter can furnish.

That many of these ballads had certain frames in which they were set, and which, like the chorus of the ancient drama, discussed the motives of the characters, or entered more minutely into their history than was consistent with the limits and action of the metrical piece, derives corroboration from the fact that a few of them still retain in their initial stanzas, matter of an explanatory description. And, acting upon this principle, it would appear that the writers and printers of our modern ballads have, in the introductory verses of these ditties, or in the formidable titles with which they are prefixed, endeavoured to communicate to the reader that information which the ancient minstrel in all probability announced orally to his audience before he smote his harp with the hand of power.

There is another feature which the ancient ballads have in common with each other, and which constitutes a material distinction between them and those written purposely for the press. They are much more licentious and incorrect in their metres, according to the present standards of taste in these matters: the accent not unfrequently falls on syllables at variance with our present mode of pronunciation, and they have throughout the marks of a composition not meant for being committed to writing, but whose music formed an essential part of it, and from which it could not well be separated without sensibly interfering with its unity and injuring its effect. And indeed it is pretty evident, that many of them would require both the voice and instrument to be humoured, so as to conceal the many irregularities of measure and rhyme, or other accidental harshness into which the poet had fallen. It is well observed by the father of this kind of literature, in his learned "Essay on the Ancient Minstrels," that, "in the more ancient ballads in that collection, the reader would observe a cast of style and measure very different from that of contemporary poets of a higher class; many phrases and idioms which the minstrels seem to have appropriated to themselves, and a very remarkable licence of varying the accent of words at pleasure, in order to humour the flow of the verse, particularly in the rhyme, as

Countriè, harpèr, battèl, morning,
Ladiè, singèr, damsèl, living,

instead of country, lády, hárper, sínger, &c. This
liberty is but sparingly assumed by the classical
poets of the same age, or even by such as professedly wrote for the press. For it is to be
observed, that so long as the minstrels subsisted,
they seemed never to have designed their rhymes
for literary publication, and probably never committed them to writing themselves; what copies
are preserved of them were doubtless taken down
from their lips. But as the old minstrels gradually wore out, a new race of ballad-writers succeeded—an inferior sort of minor poets—who wrote
narrative songs merely for the press. Instances
of both may be found in the reign of Elizabeth.
The old minstrel ballads are in the northern
dialect, abound with antique phrases, are extremely
incorrect, and run into the utmost licence of
metre; they have also a romantic wildness, and
are in the true spirit of chivalry. The other sort
are written in exacter measure, have a low or
subordinate correctness, sometimes bordering on
the insipid, yet often well adapted to the pathetic;
these are generally in the southern dialect, exhibit
a more modern phraseology, and are commonly
descriptive of more modern manners."* These
observations, which refer to the English ballad,
are equally applicable to the ancient and modern
ballad of Scotland. For it need scarcely be mentioned, that in their character both resemble each
other so much, that it becomes impossible to say
to which country a great number of them belong.
Indeed the most of our old ballads appear to
have been equally well known on the south, as

* Reliques of English Poetry. 5th edit. Lond. 1812.

on the north of the Tweed; but in the Scottish ballads there never occurs any mention of "harpers of the North Countrie," which silence, taken in conjunction with the admission of the English ballads, may be twisted into something like a proof that Scotland was looked on as the accredited source of minstrel song. We know her poets did not scruple to acknowledge their obligations to Chaucer as "flour of rethoris al," and even "Dan Lydgate" came in for a share of their approbation, along with "moral Gower;" and had her minstrels owed anything to their brethren of the south, that debt, no doubt, would have been as gratefully remembered.

But one of the most striking, and we may add, never-varying features of these compositions, is their ever agreeing in describing certain actions in one uniform way—their identity of language, epithet, and expression, in numerous scenes where the least resemblance of incident occurs. Instances of this fact are familiar to the student of old ballads as household words; but, as it is not every one who pays attention to these curious relics of early poetry, it may be excusable to dwell a little on this singularity of their composition. It would seem that these common-places are so many ingenious devices, no doubt suggested by the wisdom and experience of many ages, whereby oral poetry is more firmly imprinted on the memory, more readily recalled to it, when partially obliterated, and, in the absence of letters, the only efficacious means of preserving and transmitting it to after-times. Besides, it is in them that we not unfrequently recognise those epithets and allusions which carry the compositions to which they appertain to a remote age—epithets and allusions to which the reciter of modern times does not and cannot well attach any distinct meaning, but which he nevertheless repeats as he got them; because he finds they occur in all such songs as uniformly as its burden perhaps of "derry down, down, hey derry down." In no modern, or comparatively modern, ballad do they ever present themselves, except in a few which may be considered as framed on the ancient models, or in those which immediately succeeded to the ancient ones, whose features in part they must have retained, in order to win their way to vulgar favour. For a sudden departure from those forms which use had rendered familiar, and age venerable, would not be tolerated by the body of the people; but a silent and imperceptible change might be gradually introduced without exciting disgust, or openly warring with the overwhelming power of ancient prepossessions and long-cherished associations. The snake does not cast off its slough at once, but slowly, and part by part, it peals off and wears away; nor did the ballad part all at once with the livery grave antiquity had clothed it in. Thus to very recent times, indeed, we can distinctly follow out the traces of the ancient ballad style of writing; and it is remarkable enough that the compositions which so retain the characteristics of an earlier body of song, though never so faintly apparent, are those which have become most extensively diffused over the country, and have been most perfectly committed to memory.

Shakspeare has sung that "the course of true love never did run smooth," and many of our ancient ballads confirm the sad tale. In those ballads whose interest is derived from this fruitful source of human misery, we find a perfect uniformity of expression in all cases where the death of the lovers is described. The very hour of this mournful event is pointed out with a painful precision, that would defy the utmost chronological accuracy of the minutest obituarist; and when they are interred, as always happens, the one in the chancel, and the other in the quire, the miracle of the rose-bush, springing from the one grave, and growing and entwining itself with the briar, which shoots up with a fond eagerness from the other, till they reached the roof, where they shape themselves into a true-love knot, follows as a matter of course. This beautiful and pleasing fiction casts a soft and tender light over the moral history of that people whose popular poetry cherishes such amiable creations; and who in their hearts believe this emblematic triumph of imperishable constancy and true passion over death itself. The lovers in these compositions are ever found in "their lives lovely, and in their death undivided."

In cases where a message is to be run, a letter or token to be delivered, the same identity of expression, or but slightly varied, according to circumstances, obtains. The message itself is delivered word for word as it was communicated, and, if a letter happens to be the medium of intelligence, we find it uniformly has the effect of exciting very opposite emotions in the individual to whom it is addressed. Like the fatal mandate delivered to Sir Patrick Spens, the first line provokes a "loud lauch," but at the second, "the saut tear blinds his ee;" and those ballads which go the length of describing the further effects produced, generally mention that of the third line, "a word he could not see."

Gentle dames, who choose to undergo a voluntary penance, as a mark of their sorrow for the loss of their paramours, cannot content themselves with a less period than seven years for enduring privations which would shock any sensitive lady of the present day. These privations consist in denying themselves the use of coal and candle—neglect to comb their hair—to glove their hand—or put a shoe on their foot, or a smock on their back. After enduring these hardships they not unfrequently have the satisfaction, on some chill moonshiny night, of meeting their lover's spirit, with whom they enjoy an edifying conversation, and to whom they then render back his plighted troth, in order that he may sleep at peace in his cold and narrow home. Indeed, there is not an action, nor an occurrence of any sort, but what has its appropriate phraseology, and to enumerate all these would, in effect, be to give the principal portion of all our ancient ballads. For in all cases where there is an identity of incident, of circumstance, of action, each ballad varies not from the established mode of clothing these in language. This simplicity of narrative and undeviating recurrence of identical expressions in analogous cases, is one never-failing mark of the antiquity of these songs, and their absence the best argument to the contrary. When a lover comes to his true-love's bower, he uniformly makes use of but one argument to gain admittance :—

> "O rise, O rise, Lady Margerie,
>   O rise and let me in,
> For the rain rains on my yellow hair,
>   And the dew draps on my chin."

And, much to the credit of the tender hearts that then held the world in gentle thrall, we seldom find that the shivering gallant was long excluded, for, as the minstrel has it,

> "With her feet as white as sleet,
>   She strode her bower within,
> And with her fingers lang and sma',
>   She loot sweet Willie in."

A combat, though never so toughly and tediously maintained, is very briefly handled by the poet. There is a sort of brachigraphy, or shorthand, used in the description, quite startling to the prosing of a modern versifier. The "nut-brown sword," which, at this moment, "hung low down by the gair" of the one duellist, is, in the next, sheathed "betwixt the short rib and the lang" of the other. When swords were at every one's thigh, it was of use to know how to wield them effectively. And it may be remarked, that the expressions of *wiping on the sleeve, drying on the grass,* and *sluiting owre the strae,* always occur in such ballads as indicate a dubious and protracted and somewhat equal combat; and I take it these expressions were meant to convey that idea to the mind, as opposed to cases in which an individual has been overpowered by superior numbers, or assassinated unawares.

This uniformity of phraseology in describing incidents of a similar nature, which pervades all our ancient ballads, might appear to argue a poverty both of expression and invention in these

minstrel poets ; but if the compositions were narratives of real facts produced on the spur of the
occasion, as in most cases we have ventured to
suppose them to be, the use of such commonplaces becomes abundantly obvious. They not
only assisted the memory in an eminent degree,
but served as a kind of groundwork on which the
poem could be raised. With such commonplaces
indelibly fixed in his memory, the minstrel could
with ease to himself, and with the rapidity of
extemporaneous delivery, rapidly model any event
which came under his cognisance into song.
They were like inns or baiting-places on a journey, from one to the other of which he could
speedily transport himself. They were the general outlines of every class of human incident and
suffering then appropriated to song, and could be
fitted easily to receive individual interest as circumstances might require, and that without any
painful stretch of fancy or invention. Indeed the
original production of these commonplaces be-
tokens no slender ingenuity on the part of these
song-inditers. They were like a commodious gar-
ment that could be wrapped expeditiously round
every subject of whatever nature or dimensions.
Something of the same sort, though in a less
marked degree, may be discovered in the con-
struction of the longer metrical romances—all
arguing that the composition of these pieces had
been reduced to a certain system, and subjected
to a peculiar mechanism necessarily arising out
of the circumstances under which they were produced—and the incessant craving of the popular
taste for novel incident and fresh excitement.
Besides these peculiar forms of expression, estab-

lished epithets, and variety of commonplaces, another means of assisting the memory, and preserving the character of the melody unchanged, was adopted. This consisted in the burthens attached to the songs, many of which certainly in our day appear totally unmeaning and extravagant. But it is not unlikely that these "stiff burdouns," though abundantly curious and incomprehensible to us, had a significance, and were a key to a whole family of associations and feelings, of which we can form little or no conception.* It is probable they may have been fragments of still more ancient songs, to which the Ramsays and Cunninghams of these times had fitted new words for the nonce. This seems to be the fact with regard to the Danish ballads; and it is known, that it was a common practice with the old French poets to make a particular line of an old song the *refrain* or burden of a new.†

In the popular poetry of the Northern nations the same remarkable features are all to be found. Not only these, but the very subjects of some of the ballads appear to be the same with those of our ancient ballads. Of this interesting fact, many instances will be found in those pieces of traditionary poetry which Mr Jamieson has translated from the Kæmpe Viser. In the work

---

* If we are to credit Jones, (see his "Welsh Bards," p. 128,) the common burden of "hey derry down," signified, "Let us hie to the green oak," and was the burden of our old song of the Druids, sung by the bards inviting the people to their religious assemblies in the groves.

† Illustrations of Northern Antiquities. Burney's History of Music, vol. ii. Pinkerton's Tragic Ballads.

where most of these translations appear, that ingenious writer observes, " There may be remarked in all the Scottish and Danish traditionary ballads a frequent and almost unvaried recurrence of certain terms, epithets, metaphors, and phrases, which have obtained general currency, and seem peculiarly dedicated to this kind of composition. The same ideas, actions, and circumstances, are almost uniformly expressed in the same form of words ; and whole lines, and even stanzas, are so hackneyed among the reciters of popular ditties, that it is impossible to give them their due appropriation, and to say to which they originally belonged." To these peculiarities, in what may be styled the mechanism of the ancient ballad, and which appear to be thus common to the traditionary poetry of other countries, may be attributed the purity and integrity with which a great body of it has been transmitted to the present day, notwithstanding the many causes which, for centuries, have been vigorously at work to corrupt and annihilate it. " Time, which antiquates antiquities, and hath an art to make dust of all things, hath yet spared these minor monuments."

The greater bulk of the ancient pieces with which we are acquainted, neither in their names nor in the incidents which they relate, contain anything romantic or extravagant. Their heroines have homely enough sounding names, seldom indulging in a larger variety than what this slender catalogue of Lady Margaret, Lady Marjorie, or fair Janet affords. The same remark applies with equal justice to the lords and knights, who enact the parts of lovers or persecutors—Sweet

William, Lord Thomas, Earl Richard or John,
are the favourite appellations. The subjects of
which they treat are evidently pictures drawn
from a state of society comparatively rude, in
which the distinctions of rank were few, but
deeply marked. The personages, however, who
figure in them move in the higher classes, which
is another proof of their antiquity, and places
them anterior to those circumstances that over-
threw the institutions of chivalry, and sapped
the foundations of feudal aristocracy, thereby introducing the mixed aspect and form of society
now known in this country. In general they
present a series of domestic tragedies, which,
without any violation of truth, may be considered
as painted from actual life and every-day occur-
rences. The minstrel had no inducement to feign
a narrative calculated to awaken the dormant
sensibilities of his auditors, when the unsophisticated material was ready made to his hand, and
that of a description, too, much more pregnant
with interest and variety than invention could
supply. Indeed, this appetite in the vulgar mind
for true incident is, in our time, remarkably
apparent in the avidity with which the miserable
rhymes hawked about the streets, and palmed off
as the poetic effusions of notorious criminals
under sentence of death, are perused, and the
facility with which easy melodies are fitted to
them for the purpose of singing. And it is a
received proverb in our language, no doubt de-
derived from the times when minstrelsy was in
its meridian glory, that there is no *geste* like a
real *geste ;* in other words, that there is no tale
like a true tale.

While there is an ample store of ballads which appear to be referable to real incident and matter of fact, those which record what Gawin Douglas has characterised as

> " Wilde auentouris monstouris and quent affrayis
>   Of uncouth dangeris,"

are comparatively few. But whether this class of ballads be, as we have imagined them to be, no more than metrical relations of certain passages occurring at different times in the great drama of human life, or whether they be the veriest creations of the poet and the fabulist, it matters little, for whichever way the fact stands, this much is certain, that their popularity has arisen from, and their permanency among us been owing, in no partial degree, to the received and general impression that has obtained among the people of their original derivation from historical sources. This, independently of the other attractions which many of them possess, as simple and effective pieces of poetic composition, has seated them firmly in the hearts and affections of the people, and secured them for centuries from being swept away by the more elaborated and artificial strains, which recent and succeeding times have accumulated.

It is well known by all who have personally undergone the pleasant drudgery of gathering our traditionary song, that the old people who recite these legends attach to them the most unqualified and implicit belief. To this circumstance may be ascribed the feeling and pathos with which they are occasionally chanted; the audible sorrow that comes of deep and honest sympathy with the fates and fortunes of our fellow kind. In the spirit, too, with which such communications are made, in the same spirit must they be received and listened to. The audacious sceptic, who, in the plenitude of his shallow worldly wisdom, dared to question their being matter of incontrovertible fact, I may state, for the information of those who may hereafter choose to amuse themselves in the quest of olden song, would eventfully find the lips of every venerable sybil in the land most effectually sealed to his future inquiries. Reciters, moreover, frequently assign special localities to the ancient ballads, which they gladly indicate to the inquisitive, and to these they appeal as a triumphant refutation of every objection which learned scepticism may urge to the accuracy of the facts thus traditionally preserved. The wood or the water, the tower or the town, the castle or the kirk, the bridge or the bower, nay, even the good oak-tree to which some doughty hero of elder times hath leaned his back, and resolutely made good his quarrel against tremendous odds, can all be singled out and shewn to be in perfect accordance with the history as delivered in the ballad. It must be admitted, however, that these localities are very accommodating, and that the evidence which they afford is entitled to little or no weight. For a ballad, when it has become a favourite of the people in any particular district, is soon fitted with localities drawn from the immediate neighbourhood. This is more particularly the case with any one which represents a class of similar compositions. Thus Tomalin or Tamlane, which may be looked on as the representative of the whole class of ballads relative to "Faerye," and which is claimed by the editor of "The Border Minstrelsy" as a Selkirkshire ballad, in which district it is stated to be completely located, will be found clothed with every particular of local habitation and name in many other counties far distant from that which has sought to attach it as exclusive property.

It has been usual to ascribe the composition of this large body of traditionary poetry to the minstrels,—an order of professional poets and musicians, whose history from various causes is necessarily somewhat obscure, and which, till the time of Dr Percy, had been wholly neglected. The wide diffusion of our ballads over every part of the country, both north and south of the Tweed, and the various sets which are extant of these, would (were there no intrinsic evidence afforded by these compositions themselves) be amply corroborative and confirmatory of such an opinion. The minstrels were, as one of their number informs us, accustomed to

> "—— walken fer and wyde,
> Her and ther in every syde,
> In mony a diverse londe,"

with harp in hand, and thereto singing or reciting, not only the *Romance of price*, but those more succinct and veracious narratives which have reached to our time in the form of ballads.

But when the age of chivalry passed away, and the minstrel profession declined in importance, or gradually assimilated itself to other callings, and at length sunk into neglect and opprobrium, through the influence of causes too numerous and foreign from our purpose to trace ; the lower ranks of the people became, as is always the case,

the rightful and undisputed heirs of the cast-off
tastes and literature of the higher orders. It was
not to be supposed, however, that all at once they
could either keenly relish or appreciate the more
refined and elaborated productions of the minstrel
muse. In fact, they could not understand them.
At least, we have the authority of Robert de
Brunne for hazarding this conjecture, who mentions expressly that he undertook his translation

> "For the luf of symple men,
> That strange Inglis cannot ken,"

and that he made it

> "—— noght for no disours,
> Ne for seggours, nor harpours,"

whereas, had he indulged himself in the "quainte
Inglis" of the minstrels, who addressed their
productions "for pride and nobleye,"

> "—— fele men that it herde,
> Suld not witte how that it ferde;"

and he concludes his introduction by stating that

> "— men besoght me many a tyme,
>   To turne it bot in *light* ryme;
>   Thai seyd if I in *strange* ryme it turne,
>   To here it many on suld skurne;
>   For in it ere names fulle selcouthe
>   That ere not vsed now in *mouthe;*
>   And therefore for the *comonalte,*
>   That blithely wild listen to me;
>   On light lange I it began,
>   For luf of the lewed man."

Neither could the "comonalte" spare so
much leisure as sufficed for the recitation of
pieces distinguished for prolixity, nor could their
circumstances enable them to remunerate the
disour, seggour, or harpour for such prolonged

enjoyments. A simpler intellectual fare was required for the palate of a rude audience, and this the historical ballad supplied. Their stubborn sensibilities could only be excited by narratives of real incident, suffering, or adventure, distinctly, plainly, and artlessly told. With confessedly fictitious woes, or fabulous deeds, however brilliantly detailed, they could not sympathise ; and a long period elapsed after the romance had ceased to be heard in the halls of the great, before it found its way to the fireside of the hind and the artisan. When it did find its way, however, it lived long in their remembrance —traces of which can be discovered as late as the middle of last century.

THE LEGENDARY AND ROMANTIC BALLADS OF SCOTLAND.

SIR PATRICK SPENS.

This ballad lays claim to a high and remote antiquity. It is supposed by Bishop Percy to be founded on some event of real history; but in what age the hero of it lived, or when the fatal expedition which it records happened, he confesses himself unable to determine. Sir Walter Scott and Mr Finlay, in their respective collections, concur in assigning it a like foundation, though they disagree as to the historical incident whence it has originated; while, on the other hand, Mr Ritson asserts that "no memorial of the subject of the ballad exists in history." Sir Walter Scott inclines to think that the ballad may record some unsuccessful attempt to bring home Margaret, commonly called "the Maid of Norway," previous to that embassy despatched for her by the Regency of Scotland, after the death of her grandfather, Alexander III. And, though no account of such an expedition appears in history, it is nevertheless ingeniously contended, that its silence cannot invalidate tradition, or form any argument against the probability of such an event—more especially when the meagre materials whence Scottish history is derived, are taken into view. Mr

Finlay objects to giving the ballad, as it stands, so high a claim to antiquity, but suggests that if it be referred to the time of James III., who married Margaret, daughter of the King of Denmark, it would be brought a step nearer probability.

To both these opinions, however, Ritson's observation applies with overwhelming force. There is no historical evidence of this disastrous shipwreck, either in the embassy for the Maiden of Norway, or in that for the wife of James III. And meagre as the sources of our history may be, it seems improbable that an expedition which terminated so fatally, and to which so many of the choicest gallants of the day, and highest nobles of the land, must necessarily have been attached, should fail to be chronicled. Had they fallen in the field of battle, would all memory of them have been lost? Certainly not. If they perished on the ocean, why is history oblivious of their names? The very circumstance of a national calamity like this happening by shipwreck being of more rare occurrence than one of equal magnitude in time of war, would, we think, be a very mean of securing it a more prominent place in the histories of the times. The ballad must therefore be either wholly fabulous, or it must refer to some other event than any yet spoken of.

Our own opinion is, that the ballad is founded on authentic history, and that it records the melancholy and disastrous fate of the gallant band which followed in the suite of Margaret, daughter of Alexander III., when she was espoused to Eric of Norway. According to Fordun, in this expedition many distinguished nobles accompanied her to Norway to grace her nuptials, several of whom perished in a storm while on their return to Scotland. Whoever studies the ballad attentively, and makes due allowance for the transpositions, corruptions, and interpolations which must unavoidably have crept into its text, must ultimately become a convert to the opinion we have now advanced. The bitter taunt of the Norwegians to Sir Patrick—

> "Ye Scottishmen spend a' our king's gowd
> And a' our *queenis* fee,"

was without meaning and point formerly—its application is now felt.—MOTHERWELL.

It has been asserted that Elizabeth Halkett, Lady Wardlaw, who died in the eighteenth century, and is known as
the author of "Hardyknute," inserted in Percy's Reliques,
was the author of Sir Patrick Spens.   The assertion is not
supported by proof.

THE king sits in Dunfermline town,
    Drinking the blude-red wine :
" O where will I get a skeely skipper
    To sail this ship of mine ?"

It's up and spake an eldern knight,
    Sat at the king's right knee :
" Sir Patrick Spens is the best sailor
    That ever sailed the sea."

The king has written a braid letter,
    And sealed it with his hand,
And sent it to Sir Patrick Spens,
    Was walking on the strand.

"To Noroway, to Noroway,
    To Noroway o'er the faem ;
The king's daughter of Noroway,
    'Tis thou maun bring her hame !"

The first word that Sir Patrick read,
    Sae loud, loud laughèd he ;
The neist word that Sir Patrick read,
    The tear blinded his ee.

"O wha is this has done this deed,
    And tauld the king o' me,
To send us out at this time of the year,
    To sail upon the sea ?

"Be 't wind, be 't weet, be 't hail, be 't sleet,
  Our ship must sail the faem ;
The king's daughter of Noroway,
  'Tis we must fetch her hame."

They hoysed their sails on Monenday morn,
  Wi' a' the speed they may ;
They hae landed in Noroway
  Upon a Wodensday.

They hadna been a week, a week
  In Noroway, but twae,
When that the lords o' Noroway
  Began aloud to say :

"Ye Scottishmen spend a' our king's gowd
  And a' our queenis fee."
"Ye lie, ye lie, ye liars loud !
  Fu' loud I hear ye lie !

"For I hae brought as much white monie
  As gane* my men and me—
And I hae brought a half-fou † o' gude red
    gowd
  Out owre the sea wi' me.

"Mak ready, mak ready, my merry men a' !
  Our gude ship sails the morn."
"Now, ever alake ! my master dear,
  I fear a deadly storm !

"I saw the new moon, late yestreen,
  Wi' the auld moon in her arm ;
And if we gang to sea, master,
  I fear we 'll come to harm."

* "Gane :" suffice.
† "Half-fou :" the eighth part of a peck.

They hadna sailed a league, a league,
  A league but barely three,
When the lift grew dark, and the wind blew
    loud,
  And gurly grew the sea.

The ankers brak, and the topmasts lap,
  It was sic a deadly storm ;
And the waves came o'er the broken ship
  Till a' her sides were torn.

"O where will I get a gude sailor
  To take my helm in hand,
Till I get up to the tall topmast
  To see if I can spy land ?"

"O here am I, a sailor gude,
  To take the helm in hand,
Till you go up to the tall topmast—
  But I fear you 'll ne'er spy land."

He hadna gane a step, a step,
  A step but barely ane,
When a bout* flew out of the goodly ship,
  And the saut sea it came in.

" Gae fetch a web o' the silken claith,†
  Another o' the twine,
And wap them into our ship's side,
  And let na the sea come in."

* "Bout :" a bolt.

† In Finlay's collection appear two stanzas, not else-
where to be found, that add the befitting incident of
superstitious belief to the tragedy recorded.

    " Then up an' cam' a mermaid,
      Wi' a siller cup in her han':

They fetched a wab o' the silken claith,*
  Another o' the twine,
And they wapped them roun' that gude
    ship's side,
  But still the sea came in.

O laith, laith were our gude Scots lords
  To weet their cork-heeled shoon !
But lang or a' the play was played
  They wat their hats aboon.

And mony was the feather bed
  That floated on the faem ;
And mony was the gude lord's son
  That never mair cam' hame.

The ladyes wrang their fingers white—
  The maidens tore their hair ;
A' for the sake of their true loves—
  For them they 'll see na mair.

O lang, lang may the ladyes sit,
  Wi' their fans into their hand,
Before they see Sir Patrick Spens
  Come sailing to the strand !

'Sail on, sail on, my gude Scotch lords,
  For ye sune will see dry lan'.'

'Awa', awa', ye wild woman,
  And let your fleechin' be ;
For, sen your face we 've seen the day,
  Dry lan' we 'll never see.'"

* In Buchan's collection of Ancient Ballads is this additional stanza, which appears justified by a subsequent
allusion :—

" There are five-and-fifty feather beds
  Well packèd in ae room,
And ye 'll get as muckle gude canvass
  As wrap the ship a' roun'."

And lang, lang may the maidens sit,
  Wi' their gowd kaims in their hair,
A' waiting for their ain dear loves—
  For them they 'll see na mair.

Half owre, half owre to Aberdour,*
  'Tis fifty fathoms deep,
And there lies gude Sir Patrick Spens,
  Wi' the Scots lords at his feet.

* In Scott's "Border Minstrelsy," this line reads—

  "O forty miles off Aberdeen;"

but we are inclined to favour the reading—

  "Half owre, half owre to Aberdour."

For, with submission to the opinion of Sir W. Scott, the meaning of this line is not that the shipwreck took place in the Frith of Forth, but midway between Aberdour and Norway. And, as it would seem from the narrative at the commencement of the ballad that Sir Patrick sailed from the Forth, it is but fair to infer that, in his disastrous voyage homeward, he would endeavour to make the same port. This opinion will be corroborated if we are correct in assigning the ballad to the historical event mentioned in the introductory remarks.—MOTHERWELL.

THE BATTLE OF OTTERBOURNE.

The following edition of the Battle of Otterbourne is essentially different from that which is published in the "Reliques of Ancient Poetry," and is obviously of Scottish composition. The particulars of that noted action are related by Froissart, with the highest encomium upon the valour of the combatants on each side. This song was first published from Mr Herd's "Collection of Scottish Songs and Ballads," 2 vols. 8vo, Edin. 1774, but two recited copies have fortunately been obtained from the recitation of old persons residing at the head of Ettrick forest, by which the story is brought out and completed in a manner much more correspondent to the true history. —Sir Walter Scott.

It fell about the Lammas tide,
   When the muir-men win their hay,
The doughty Earl of Douglas rode
   Into England, to catch a prey.

He chose the Gordons and the Græmes,
   And the Lindesays, light and gay;
But the Jardines would not with him ride,
   And they rue it to this day.

And he has burned the dales of Tyne,
   And part of Bambrough shire;
And three good towers on Roxburgh fells,
   He left them all on fire.

"Yet I will stay at Otterbourne,
   Where you shall welcome be;
And, if ye come not at three days' end,
   A fause lord I 'll ca' thee."

"Thither will I come," proud Percy said,
   "By the might of Our Ladye!"
"There will I bide thee," said the Douglas,
   "My troth I plight to thee."

They lighted high on Otterbourne,
  Upon the bent sae brown ;
They lighted high on Otterbourne,
  And threw their pallions down.

And he that had a bonnie boy,
  Sent out his horse to grass ;
And he that had not a bonnie boy,
  His ain servant he was.

But up then spake a little page,
  Before the peep of dawn—
"O waken ye, waken ye, my good lord,
  For Percy's hard at hand."

"Ye lie, ye lie, ye liar loud !
  Sae loud I hear ye lie ;
For Percy had not men yestreen,
  To dight my men and me.

"But I hae dreamed a dreary dream,
  Beyond the Isle of Sky ;
I saw a dead man win a fight,
  And I think that man was I."

He belted on his good braid sword,
  And to the field he ran ;
But he forgot the helmet good,
  That should have kept his brain.

When Percy wi' the Douglas met,
  I wat he was fu' fain !
They swakked* their swords, till sair they
    swat,
  And the blood ran down like rain.

* "Swakked:" to throw violently ; to cross.

But Percy with his good broadsword,
  That could so sharply wound,
Has wounded Douglas on the brow,
  Till he fell to the ground.

Then he called on his little foot-page,
  And said—"Run speedilie,
And fetch my ain dear sister's son,
  Sir Hugh Montgomery."

"My nephew good," the Douglas said,
  "What recks the death of ane!
Last night I dreamed a dreary dream,
  And I ken the day's thy ain.

"My wound is deep; I fain would sleep;
  Take thou the foremost three,
And hide me by the braken bush,
  That grows on yonder lee.

"O bury me by the braken bush,
  Beneath the blooming brier,
But let not living mortal ken,
  That a kindly Scot lies here."

He lifted up that noble lord,
  Wi' the saut tear in his ee;
He hid him in the braken bush,
  That his merrie men might not see.

The moon was clear, the day drew near,
  The spears in flinders flew,
But mony a gallant Englishman
  Ere day the Scotsmen slew.

The Gordons good, in English blood,
   They steeped their hose and shoon ;
The Lindsays flew like fire about,
   Till all the fray was done.

The Percy and Montgomery met,
   That either of other were fain ;
They swapped swords, and they twa swat,
   And the blude ran down between.

" Yield thee, O yield thee, Percy !" he said,
   " Or else I 'll lay thee low !"
" To whom shall I yield," said Earl Percy,
   " Sin' I see it must be so ?"

" Thou shalt not yield to lord nor loun,
   Nor yet shalt yield to me ;
But yield thee to the braken * bush,
   That grows on the lilye lee !"

" I will not yield to a braken bush,
   Nor yet will I yield to a brier ;
But I would yield to Earl Douglas,
   Or Montgomery, if he were here."

As soon as he knew 'twas Montgomery,
   He stuck his sword in the gronde ;
And the Montgomery was a courteous knight,
   And quickly took him by the honde.

This deed was done at Otterbourne,
   At the breaking of the day ;
Earl Douglas was buried at the braken bush,
   And the Percy led captive away.

   *   *   *   *   *   *

* "Braken :" fern.

CHILD NORYCE

Of the many ancient ballads which have been preserved
by tradition among the peasantry of Scotland, none has
excited more interest in the world of letters than the
beautiful and pathetic tale of "Gil Morice;" and this no
less on account of its own intrinsic merits as a piece of
exquisite poetry, than of its having furnished the plot of
the justly-celebrated tragedy of Douglas.* It has likewise supplied Mr Langhorne with the principal materials
from which he has woven the fabric of his sweet though
prolix poem of "Owen of Carron;" and Mr Jamieson
mentions that it has also been "made the subject of a
dramatic entertainment with songs, by Mr Rennie of
Aberdeen."† Perhaps the list could be easily increased
of those who have drawn their inspiration from this
affecting strain of olden minstrelsy.

If any reliance is to be placed on the traditions of that
part of the country where the scene of the ballad is laid,
we shall be enforced to believe that it is founded on facts
which occurred at some remote period of Scottish history.
The "green wood" of the ballad was the ancient forest
of Dundaff in Stirlingshire, and Lord Barnard's castle is
said to have occupied a precipitous cliff overhanging the
water of Carron, on the lands of Halbertshire. A small
burn which joins the Carron, about five miles above these
lands, is named the Earlsburn, and the hill near the source
of that stream is called the Earlshill, both deriving their
appellations, according to the unvarying traditions of the
country, from the unfortunate Earl's son who is the hero
of the ballad. He, also, according to the same respectable
authority, was "beautiful exceedingly," and especially
remarkable for the extreme length and loveliness of his yellow hair, which shrouded him as it were with a golden mist.
To these floating traditions we are probably indebted for
the attempts which have been made to improve and em-

* "When this tragedy was originally produced at Edinburgh, in
1756, the title of the heroine was Lady Barnard : the alteration to
Lady Randolph was made on its being transplanted to London." It
was acted in Covent Garden in 1757.—*Biographia Dramatica*, vol. ii.
p. 175.
† *Popular Ballads and Songs.* Edinburgh, 1806, vol. i. p. 5.

bellish the ballad by the introduction of various new stanzas since its first appearance in a printed form.

Of the early printed editions of this ballad the Editor has been unable to procure any copy.* In Percy's Reliques it is mentioned that it had run through two editions in Scotland, the second of which appeared at Glasgow in 1755, 8vo, and that to both there was prefixed an advertisement setting forth that the preservation of the poem was owing "to a lady who favoured the printers with a copy, as it was carefully collected from the mouths of old women and nurses," and requesting "that any reader who could render it more perfect and complete would oblige the public with such improvements." This was holding out too tempting a bait not to be greedily snapped at by some of those "ingenious hands" who have corrupted the purity of legendary song in Scotland by manifest forgeries and gross impositions. Accordingly, sixteen additional verses soon appeared in manuscript, which the editor of the Reliques has inserted in their proper places, though he rightly views them in no better light than that of an ingenious interpolation. Indeed, the whole ballad of *Gil Morice*, as the writer of the present notice has been politely informed by the learned and elegant editor of "The Border Minstrelsy," underwent a total revisal about the period when the tragedy of Douglas was in the zenith of its popularity; and this improved copy, it seems, embraced the "ingenious interpolation" above referred to. Independent altogether of this positive information, any one familiar with the state in which traditionary poetry has been transmitted to the present times, can be at no loss to detect many more "ingenious interpolations" as well as paraphrastic additions in the ballad as now printed. But though it has been grievously corrupted in this way, the most scrupulous inquirer into the authenticity of ancient

* Since writing this he has been kindly favoured by Mr David Laing of Edinburgh with an edition which, though it has neither place, date, nor printer's name, may, from its title, be considered as the first Edinburgh edition, and printed probably in 1756. The title is given at length, "Gil Morice, an ancient Scots poem. The foundation of the tragedy called Douglas, as it is now acted in the Concert-hall, Canongate." Except some slight variations in orthography, and in its omitting the sixteen additional verses which are mentioned by Bishop Percy as having been subsequently added to the ballad, there is no other material difference between this edition and that which is reprinted in the Reliques.

song can have no hesitation in admitting that many of its verses, even as they now stand, are purely traditionary, and fair and genuine parcels of antiquity, unalloyed with any base admixture of modern invention, and in nowise altered, save in those changes of language to which all oral poetry is unavoidably subjected in its progress from one age to another.

With much deference to the opinion of others skilled in these matters, the Editor has, in point of antiquity, to challenge for *Child Noryce* a precedence far above any of its fellows; indeed, in his judgment, it has every appearance of being the prime root from which the *Gil Morice* of Percy, and all the variations of the ballad heretofore known, have originated. That the reader may have no room to doubt its genuineness, the Editor thinks it right to mention, that it is given verbatim as it was taken down from the singing of Widow M'Cormick, of Paisley, in January 1825.—MOTHERWELL.

CHILD NORYCE is a clever young man,
　　He wavers wi' the wind;
His horse was silver shod before,
　　With the beaten gold behind.

He called to his little man John,
　　Saying, "You don't see what I see;
For, oh, yonder I see the very first woman
　　That ever loved me.

"Here is a glove, a glove," he said,
　　"Lined with the silver grey;
You may tell her to come to the merry green wood,
　　　　To speak to Child Nory.

"Here is a ring, a ring," he says,
　　"It's all gold but the stane;
You may tell her to come to the merry green wood,
　　　　And ask the leave o' nane."

"So well do I love your errand, my master,
　But far better do I love my life;
O would ye have me go to Lord Barnard's castel,
　To betray away his wife?"

"O don't I give you meat," he says,
　"And don't I pay you fee?
How dare you stop my errand," he says,
　"My orders you must obey."

Oh, when he came to Lord Barnard's castel,
　He tinkled at the ring;
Who was as ready as Lord Barnard himself,*
　To let this little boy in.

"Here is a glove, a glove," he says,
　"Lined with the silver grey;
You are bidden to come to the merry green wood,
　To speak to Child Nory.

"Here is a ring, a ring," he says,
　"It's all gold but the stane:
You are bidden to come to the merry green wood,
　And ask the leave o' nane."

Lord Barnard he was standing by,
　And an angry man was he:
"Oh, little did I think there was a lord in this
　　world
　My lady loved but me!"

* This unquestionably should be Lady Barnard, instead
of her lord—see third stanza under; but as it was so
recited, this obvious error the Editor did not conceive
himself warranted to correct, more especially as he has
found it out of his power to obtain another copy of the
ballad from any different quarter.—MOTHERWELL.

Oh, he dressed himself in the holland smocks,
   And garments that was gay;
And he is away to the merry green wood,
   To speak to Child Nory.

Child Noryce sits on yonder tree,
   He whistles and he sings;
"O wae be to me," says Child Noryce,
   "Yonder my mother comes!"

Child Noryce he came off the tree,
   His mother to take off the horse;
"Och alas, alas," says Child Noryce,
   "My mother was ne'er so gross."

Lord Barnard he had a little small sword
   That hung low down by his knee;
He cut the head off Child Noryce,
   And put the body on a tree.

And when he came to his castel,
   And to his lady's hall,
He threw the head into her lap,
   Saying, "Lady, there is a ball!"

She turned up the bloody head,
   She kissed it frae cheek to chin;
"Far better do I love this bloody head,
   Than all my royal kin.

"When I was in my father's castel,
   In my virginitie;
There came a lord into the north,
   Gat Child Noryce with me."

'O wae be to thee, Lady Margaret," he said,
  "And an ill death may you die;
For if you had told me he was your son,
  He had ne'er been slain by me."

————

THE YOUNG TAMLANE.

A fragment of this singular story appeared in Herd's
Collection, 1776.   It was inserted complete in Scott's
"Minstrelsy of the Scottish Border, ' prefaced by an ad-
mirable essay on the Fairy Mythology of Scotland.   But
Scott either interpolated himself, or adopted the interpolations by others, of at least a dozen stanzas—bearing
the stamp of "modern antiquity" so visibly and palpably
about them, as not only to spoil the charm of the ballad,
but to fail in deceiving the most careless reader.   Professor Aytoun, in his recent collection, presents the public
with a version amended by and collated with several
others; but I have preferred to republish that of Sir
Walter Scott, with the omission of the modern stanzas,
that add nothing to the story, and that have the additional
demerit of weakening the strength and diluting the sturdy
beauty of the original.—C. M.

O I FORBID ye, maidens a',
  That wear gowd on your hair,
To come or gae by Carterhaugh,
  For young Tamlane is there.

There 's nane, that gaes by Carterhaugh,
  But maun leave him a waud,
Either goud rings, or green mantles,
  Or else their maidenheid.

Now, gowd rings ye may buy, maidens,
    Green mantles ye may spin;
But, gin ye lose your maidenheid,
    You'll ne'er get that agen.

But up then spak her fair Janet,
    The fairest o' a' her kin;
"I'll cum and gang to Carterhaugh,
    And ask nae leave o' him."

Janet has kilted her green kirtle,*
    A little abune her knee;
And she has braided her yellow hair,
    A little abune her bree.

And when she came to Carterhaugh,
    She gaed beside the well;
And there she fand his steed standing,
    But away was himsel'.

She hadna pu'd a red, red rose,
    A rose but barely three;
Till up and starts a wee, wee man,
    At Lady Janet's knee.

Says—"Why pu' ye the rose, Janet?
    What gars ye break the tree?
Or why came ye to Carterhaugh,
    Withouten leave o' me?"

"Oh I will pu' the flowers," she said,
    "And I will break the tree,
For Carterhaugh it is mine ain;
    I'll ask nae leave o' thee."

---

* The ladies are always represented, in Dunbar's poems, with green mantles and yellow hair.—*Maitland Poems,* vol. i. p. 45.

He 's ta'en her by the milk-white hand,
   Amang the leaves sae green ;
And what they did I cannot tell—
   The green leaves were between.

He 's ta'en her by the milk-white hand,
   Amang the roses red ;
And what they did I cannot say—
   She ne'er returned a maid.

When she cam to her father's ha',
   She lookèd pale and wan ;
They thought she 'd dreed some sair
     sickness,
   Or been wi' some leman.

She didna comb her yellow hair,
   Nor make meikle o' her heid ;
And ilka thing that lady took
   Was like to be her deid.

It 's four and twenty ladies fair
   Were playing at the ba' ;
Janet, the wightest of them anes,
   Was faintest o' them a'.

Four and twenty ladies fair
   Were playing at the chess ;
And out there came the fair Janet,
   As green as any grass.

Out and spak an auld gray-headed knight,
   Lay o'er the castle wa'—
" And ever alas ! for thee, Janet,
   But we 'll be blamed a' ! "

"Now haud your tongue, ye auld gray
        knight,
    And an ill death may ye die,
Father my bairn on whom I will,
    I 'll father nane on thee."

Out then spak her father dear,
    And he spak meek and mild—
"And ever, alas! my sweet Janet,
    I fear ye gae with child."

"And if I be with child, father,
    Mysel' maun bear the blame;
There 's ne'er a knight about your ha'
    Shall hae the bairnie's name.

"And if I be with child, father,
    'Twill prove a wondrous birth;
For well I swear I 'm not wi' bairn
    To any man on earth.

"If my love were an earthly knight,
    As he 's an elfin gray,
I wadna gie my ain true love
    For nae lord that ye hae."

She prineked hersel' and prinned hersel',
    By the ae light of the moon,
And she 's away to Carterhaugh,
    To speak wi' young Tamlane.

And when she cam' to Carterhaugh,
    She gaed beside the well;
And there she saw the steed standing,
    But away was himsel'.

She hadna pu'd a double rose,
   A rose but only twae,
When up and started young Tamlane,
   Says—Lady, thou pu's nae mae!

" Why pu' ye the red, red rose, Janet,
   Within this garden green,
And a' to kill the bonny babe,
   That we got us between?"

" The truth ye 'll tell to me, Tamlane;
   A word ye mauna lie;
Gin e'er ye was in holy chapel,
   Or sained* in Christentie."

" The truth I 'll tell to thee, Janet,
   A word I winna lie ;
A knight me got, and a lady me bore,
   As well as they did thee.

" Randolph, Earl Murray, was my sire,
   Dunbar, Earl March, is thine ;
We loved when we were children small,
   Which yet you well may mind.

" When I was a boy just turned of nine,
   My uncle sent for me,
To hunt, and hawk, and ride with him,
   And keep him companie.

" There came a wind out of the north,
   A sharp wind and a snell ;
And a dead sleep came over me,
   And frae my horse I fell.

        * " Sained :" hallowed.

" The Queen of Fairies keppit me,
   In yon green hill to dwell;
And I 'm a fairy, lyth and limb;
   Fair lady, view me well.

" But we, that live in Fairy-land,
   No sickness know, nor pain;
I quit my body when I will,
   And take to it again.

" And I would never tire, Janet,
   In elfish land to dwell;
But aye at every seven years,
   They pay the teind to hell;
And I am sae fat, and fair of flesh,
   I fear 'twill be mysel'.

" This night is Hallowe'en, Janet,
   The morn is Hallowday;
And, gin ye dare your true love win,
   Ye hae na time to stay.

" The night it is good Hallowe'en,
   When fairy folk will ride;
And they that wad their true love win,
   At Miles Cross they maun bide."

" But how shall I thee ken, Tamlane?
   Or how shall I thee knaw,
Amang so mony unearthly knights,
   The like I never saw?"

" The first company that passes by,
   Say na, and let them gae;
The next company that passes by,
   Say na, and do right sae;
The third company that passes by,
   Then I 'll be ane o' thae.

"First let pass the black, Janet,
  And syne let pass the brown;
But grip ye to the milk-white steed,
  And pu' the rider down.

"For I ride on the milk-white steed,
  And aye nearest the town;
Because I was a christened knight,
  They gave me that renown.

"My right hand will be gloved, Janet,
  My left hand will be bare;
And these the tokens I gie thee,
  Nae doubt I will be there.

"They'll turn me in your arms, Janet,
  An adder and a snake;
But haud me fast, let me not pass,
  Gin ye wad be my make.

"They'll turn me in your arms, Janet,
  An adder and an ask;
They'll turn me in your arms, Janet,
  A bale that burns fast.

"They'll turn me in your arms, Janet,
  A red-hot gad o' airn;
But haud me fast, let me not pass,
  For I'll do you no harm.

"First dip me in a stand o' milk,
  And then in a stand o' water;
But haud me fast, let me not pass—
  I'll be your bairn's father.

"And, next, they'll shape me in your arms,
    A tod, but and an eel;
But haud me fast, nor let me gang,
    As you do love me weel.

"They'll shape me in your arms, Janet,
    A dove, but and a swan;
And, last, they'll shape me in your arms,
    A mother-naked man:
Cast your green mantle over me—
    I'll be myself again."

Gloomy, gloomy, was the night,
    And eiry was the way,
As fair Janet, in her green mantle,
    To Miles Cross she did gae.

And first gaed by the black, black steed,
    And then gaed by the brown;
But fast she gript the milk-white steed,
    And pu'd the rider down.

She pu'd him frae the milk-white steed,
    And loot the bridle fa';
And up there raise an eldritch cry—
    "He's won among us a'!"

They shaped him in fair Janet's arms,
    An ask, but and an adder;
She held him fast in every shape—
    To be her bairn's father.

They shaped him in her arms at last,
    A mother-naked man;
She wrapt him in her green mantle,
    And sae her true love wan.

Up then spake the Queen o' th' Fairies,
  Out o' the bush o' broom—
"She that has borrowed young Tamlane,
  Has gotten a stately groom."

Up then spake the Queen o' th' Fairies,
  Out o' the bush of rye—
"She's ta'en away the bonniest knight
  In a' my cumpanie.

"But had I kenn'd, Tamlane," she says,
  "A lady wad borrowed thee—
I wad ta'en out thy twa gray een,
  Put in twa een o' tree.

"Had I but kenn'd, Tamlane," she says,
  "Before ye came frae hame—
I wad tane out your heart o' flesh,
  Put in a heart o' stane.

"Had I but had the wit yestreen,
  That I hae coft* the day—
I'd hae paid my kane seven times to hell,
  Ere you'd been won away!"

* "Coft:" bought.

ERLINTON.

This ballad is published from the collation of two copies, obtained from recitation.   It seems to be the rude original, or perhaps a corrupted and imperfect copy, of *The Child of Elle*, a beautiful legendary tale, published in Percy's "Reliques of Ancient Poetry."   It is singular that this charming ballad should have been translated or imitated by the celebrated Bürger, without acknowledgment of the English original.   As *The Child of Elle* avowedly received corrections, we may ascribe its greatest beauties to the poetical taste of the ingenious editor.—SIR WALTER SCOTT.

ERLINTON had a fair daughter,
  I wat he weired her in a great sin ;*
For he has built a bigly bower,
  An' a' to put that lady in.

An' he has warned her sisters six,
  An' sae has he her brethren se'en,
Either to watch her a' the night,
  Or else to seek her morn and e'en.

She hadna been i' that bigly bower,
  Not a night, but barely ane,
Till there was Willie, her ain true love,
  Chapped at the door, crying, " Peace within !"

" O whae is this at my bower door,
  That chaps sae late, or kens the gin ?"†
" O it is Willie, your ain true love,
  I pray you rise an' let me in !"

* " Weired her in a great sin :" placed her in danger of committing a great sin.—W. S.
† " Gin :" the slight or trick necessary to open the door.

"But in my bower there is a wake,
　An' at the wake there is a wane ;*
But I 'll come to the green-wood the morn,
　Whar blooms the brier, by mornin' dawn."

Then she 's gane to her bed again,
　Where she has layen till the cock crew thrice,
Then she said to her sisters a',
　" Maidens, 'tis time for us to rise."

She pat on her back a silken gown,
　An' on her breast a siller pin,
An' she 's tane a sister in ilka hand,
　An' to the green-wood she is gane.

She hadna walked in the green-wood,
　Na not a mile but barely ane,
Till there was Willie, her ain true love,
　Whae frae her sisters has her ta'en.

He took her sisters by the hand,
　He kissed them baith, an' sent them hame,
An he 's ta'en his true love him behind,
　And through the green-wood they are gane.

They hadna ridden in the bonnie green-wood,
　Na not a mile but barely ane,
When there came fifteen o' the boldest knights,
　That ever bare flesh, blood, or bane.

The foremost was an aged knight,
　He wore the gray hair on his chin,
Says, " Yield to me thy lady bright,
　An' thou shalt walk the woods within."

* " Wane :" a number of people.

“ For me to yield my lady bright
　　To such an aged knight as thee,
People wad think I war gane mad,
　　Or a’ the courage flown frae me.”

.But up then spake the second knight,
　　I wat he spake right boustouslie,
“ Yield me thy life, or thy lady bright,
　　Or here the tane of us shall die.”

“ My lady is my world’s meed,
　　My life I winna yield to nane ;
But, if ye be men of true manhood,
　　Ye ’ll only fight me ane by ane.”

He lighted off his milk-white horse,
　　And gae ’m his lady by the head,
Saying, “ See ye dinna change your cheer,
　　Until you see my body bleed.”

He set his back into an aik,
　　He set his feet against a stane ;
And he has fought these fifteen men,
　　And killed them a’ but barely ane ;
For he has left the aged knight,
　　But to carry the tidings hame.

When he gaed to his lady fair,
　　I wot he kissed her tenderlie :
“ Thou ’rt mine ain love, I have thee bought ;
　　And we shall walk the green-wood free.”

COSPATRICK.

A copy of this ballad, materially different from that which follows, appeared in "Scottish Songs," 2 vols., Edinburgh, 1792, under the title of *Lord Bothwell.* Some stanzas have been transferred from thence to the present copy, which is taken down from the recitation of a lady, nearly related to the Editor. Some readings have been also adopted from a third copy, in Mrs Brown's MS., under the title of *Child Brenton.* Cospatrick (Comes Patricius) was the designation of the Earl of Dunbar in the days of Wallace and Bruce.—SIR WALTER SCOTT.

Herd published, in 1775, a version of this story, under the title of *Bothwell*—which Professor Ayton adopts in his recent collection. Another version was published, in 1827, by Mr P. Buchan, under the title of *Lord Dingwall.* In Cromek's "Remains of Nithsdale and Galloway Song," is a poem—"We were sisters, sisters seven"—drawn from the same source, and in some respects a finer composition than *Cospatrick.*—C. M.

COSPATRICK has sent o'er the faem;
Cospatrick brought his ladye hame;
And fourscore ships have come her wi',
The ladye by the green-wood tree.

There were twal' and twal' wi' baken bread,
And twal' and twal' wi' gowd sae red,
And twal' and twal' wi' bouted flour,
And twal' and twal' wi' the paramour.

Sweet Willy was a widow's son,
And at her stirrup he did run;
And she was clad in the finest pall,
But aye she loot the tears down fall.

"O is your saddle set awrye?
Or rides your steed for you owre high?
Or are you mourning, in your tide,
That you suld be Cospatrick's bride?"

"I am not mourning, at this tide,
That I suld be Cospatrick's bride;
But I am sorrowing, in my mood,
That I suld leave my mother good."

"But, gentle boy, come tell to me,
What is the custom of thy countrie?"
"The custom thereof, my dame," he says,
"Will ill a gentle ladye please.

"Seven king's daughters has our lord wedded,
  And seven king's daughters has our lord
      bedded;
But he's cutted their breasts frae their breast-
      bane,
And sent them mourning hame again.

"Yet, gin you're sure that you're a maid,
Ye mae gae safely to his bed;
But gif o' that ye be na sure,
Then hire some damsel o' your bour."

The ladye's called her bour-maiden,
That waiting was into her train.
"Five thousand merks I'll gie to thee,
To sleep this night with my lord for me."

When bells were rung, and mass was sayne,
And a' men unto bed were gane,
Cospatrick and the bonny maid,
Into ae chamber they were laid.

"Now speak to me, blankets, and speak to me,
      bed,
And speak, thou sheet, enchanted web;
And speak, my sword, that winna lie,
Is this a true maiden that lies by me?"

"It is not a maid that you hae wedded,
But it is a maid that you hae bedded;
It is a leal maiden that lies by thee,
But not the maiden that it should be."

O wrathfully he left the bed,
And wrathfully his claes on did;
And he has ta'en him through the ha',
And on his mother he did ca'.

"I am the most unhappy man,
That ever was in Christen land!
I courted a maiden, meik and mild,
And I hae gotten naething but a woman
    wi' child."

"O stay, my son, into this ha',
And sport ye wi' your merry men a';
And I will to the secret bour,
To see how it fares wi' your paramour."

The carline she was stark and sture,
She aff the hinges dang the dure.
"O is your bairn to laird or loun,
Or is it to your father's groom?"

"O hear me, mother, on my knee,
Till my sad story I tell to thee:
O we were sisters, sisters seven,
We were the fairest under heaven.

"It fell on a summer's afternoon,
When a' our toilsome work was done,
We coost the kevils us amang,
To see which suld to the green-wood gang.

"Ohon! alas, for I was youngest,
And aye my weird it was the strongest!
The kevil it on me did fa',
Whilk was the cause of a' my woe.

"For to the green-wood I maun gae,
To pu' the red rose and the slae;
To pu' the red rose and the thyme,
To deck my mother's bour and mine.

"I hadna pu'd a flower but ane,
When by there came a gallant hinde,
Wi' high colled hose and laigh colled shoon,
And he seemed to be some king's son.

"And be I maid, or be I nae,
He kept me there till the close o' day;
And be I maid, or be I nane,
He kept me there till the day was done.

"He gae me a lock o' his yellow hair,
And bade me keep it ever mair;
He gae me a carknet* o' bonny beads,
And bade me keep it against my needs.

"He gae to me a gay gold ring,
And bade me keep it abune a' thing."
"What did ye wi' the tokens rare,
That ye gat frae that gallant there?"

* "Carknet:" a necklace.   Thus—

"She threw away her rings and *carknet* cleen."

—Harrison's translation of "Orlando Furioso," Notes on book 37th.

“O bring that coffer unto me,
And a’ the tokens ye sall see.”
“Now stay, daughter, your bour within,
While I gae parley wi’ my son.”

O she has ta’en her thro’ the ha’,
And on her son began to ca’:
“What did ye wi’ the bonny beads,
I bade ye keep against your needs?

“What did you wi’ the gay gold ring,
I bade you keep abune a’ thing?”
“I gae them to a ladye gay,
I met in green-wood on a day.

“But I wad gie a’ my halls and tours,
I had that ladye within my bours;
But I wad gie my very life,
I had that ladye to my wife.”

“Now keep, my son, your ha’s and tours;
Ye have that bright burd in your bours;
And keep, my son, your very life;
Ye have that ladye to your wife.”

Now, or a month was come and gane,
The ladye bore a bonny son;
And ’twas weel written on his breast-bane,
“Cospatrick is my father’s name.”

TRUE THOMAS.

True Thomas, Thomas the Rhymer, or Thomas of Ercildoune, in the Eildon Hills, is a personage almost as mythological as Merlin or King Arthur. He is supposed —if he ever existed at all, which is doubtful—to have flourished early in the thirteenth century, and to have been the author of "The Romance of Sir Tristrem." Sir Walter Scott was at some pains to collect particulars about him, and has gathered into a focus all the facts and suppositions on which he could lay hands. True Thomas is believed in popular superstition to have come back at the end of seven years, delivered his prophecies, and then returned to his captivity among the fairies.—C. M.

TRUE Thomas lay on Huntly bank,
   A ferlie* he spied wi' his ee,
And there he saw a lady bright
   Come riding down by the Eildon tree.

Her shirt was o' the grass-green silk,
   Her mantle o' the velvet fine;
At ilka tett† of her horse's mane
   Hung fifty siller bells and nine.

True Thomas he pulled off his cap,
   And louted low down to his knee:
"All hail, thou mighty Queen of Heaven,
   For thy peer on earth I never did see!"

"O no, O no, Thomas," she said,
   "That name does not belong to me;
I am but the Queen of fair Elfland,
   That am hither come to visit thee.

* "Ferlie:" something wonderful, or marvellous.
† "Tett:" lock.

"Harp and carp, True Thomas," she said,
 "Harp and carp along wi' me;
And if ye dare to kiss my lips,
 Sure of your body I will be."

"Betide me weal, betide me woe,
 That weird shall never daunton me!"
Since he has kissed her rosy lips,
 All underneath the Eildon tree.

"Now ye maun go wi' me," she said,
 "True Thomas, ye maun go wi' me;
And ye maun serve me seven years,
 Through weal or woe, as chance may be."

She mounted on her milk-white steed,
 She's ta'en true Thomas up behind;
And aye, whene'er her bridle rung,
 The steed flew swifter than the wind.

O they rode on, and farther on,
 The steed gaed swifter than the wind,
Until they reached a desert wide,
 And living land was left behind.

"Light down, light down, now, true Thomas,
 And lean your head upon my knee;
Abide and rest a little space,
 And I will show you ferlies three.

"O see ye not yon narrow road,
 So thick beset with thorns and briers?
That is the path of righteousness,
 Though after it but few enquires.

"And see ye not that braid, braid road,
    That lies across that lily leven?
That is the path of wickedness,
    Though some call it the road to heaven.

"And see ye not that bonny road,
    That wins about the fernie brae?
That is the road to fair Elfland,
    Where thou and I this night maun gae.

"But, Thomas, ye maun hold your tongue,
    Whatever ye may hear or see;
For if ye speak word in Elflyn land,
    Ye'll ne'er get back to your ain countrie."

O they rode on and further on,
    And they waded through rivers aboon the knee,
And they saw neither sun nor moon,
    But they heard the roaring of the sea.

It was mirk, mirk night, and there was nae stern
        light,
    And they waded through red blude to the knee;
For a' the blude that's shed on earth
    Rins through the springs o' that countrie.

Sine they came on to a garden green,
    And she pu'd an apple frae a tree:
"Take this for thy wages, true Thomas,
    It will give thee the tongue that can never lie."

"My tongue is mine ain," true Thomas said,
    " A gudely gift ye wast gie to me;
I neither dought to buy nor sell,
    At fair or tryst where I may be.

> "I dought neither speak to prince or peer,
>   Nor ask of grace from fair ladye."
> "Now hold thy peace!" the lady said,
>   "For as I say, so it must be."
>
> He has gotten a coat of the even cloth,
>   And a pair of shoes of velvet green;
> And till seven years were gone and past,
>   True Thomas on earth was never seen.

SIR CAULINE.

This ancient and beautiful romantic ballad is given from Percy's Reliques, in which it was first published, from that folio MS. about whose existence the late Mr Ritson was so sceptical. Percy confessed that he was tempted to add several stanzas to the first part, and still more in the second, to connect and complete the story in the manner which appeared to him most interesting and affecting. How much it owes to his taste and genius we have not the means of ascertaining; but that his interpolations and additions have been very considerable, any one acquainted with ancient minstrelsy will have little room to doubt. We suspect, too, that the original ballad had a less melancholy catastrophe, and that the brave Sir Cauline, after his combat with the "hend Soldan," derived as much benefit from the leechcraft of fair Christabelle, as he did after winning the Eldritch sword.

Between this ballad and some parts of the metrical romance of *Sir Tristrem*, the late Mr Finlay of Glasgow affects to discover a resemblance, but he has not condescended to trace a parallel between them. Indeed, we cannot help thinking, for all he says to the contrary, that his reasoning is no whit superior to Fluellin's: "There is a river at Macedon, and there is also moreover a river at Monmouth:" and, according to Mr Finlay, "There is an Irish king and his daughter in Sir Cauline;" and there is "also moreover an Irish king and his daughter in *Sir Tristrem.*" The concealed love of Sir Cauline for one so much above him in station will remind the reader of the gentle

> "—— Squyer of lowe degrè
> That loved the king's doughter of Hungre."

—Motherwell.

THE FIRST PART.

In Ireland, ferr over the sea,
    There dwelleth a bonnye kinge;
And with him a yong and comlye knighte,
    Men call him Sir Cauline.

The kinge had a ladye to his daughter,
    In fashyon she hath no peere;
And princely wightes that ladye wooed,
    To be theyr wedded feere.

Sir Cauline loveth her best of all,
    But nothing durst he saye;
Ne descreeve his counsayl to no man,
    But deerlye he loved this may.

Till on a day it so befell
    Great dool to him was dight;
The mayden's love removde his mynd,
    To care-bed went the knighte.

One while he spred his armes him fro,
    One while he spred them nye;
" And aye! but I winne that ladyes love,
    For dole now I mun dye."

And when our parish mass was done,
   Our king was bowne to dyne:
He says, "Where is Sir Cauline,
   That is wont to serve the wyne?"

Then aunswerde him a courteous knighte,
   And fast his handes gan wringe:
"Sir Cauline is sicke, and like to dye,
   Without a good leechinge."

"Fetche me downe my daughter deere,
   She is a leeche fulle fine;
Goe take him doughe and the baken bread,
And serve him with the wyne so red;
   Lothe I were him to tine."

Fair Christabelle to his chamber goes,
   Her maydens following nye;
"O well," she saith, "how doth my lord?"
   "O sicke, thou fair ladye."

"Now ryse up, wightyle man, for shame,
   Never lye soe cowardlee,
For it is told in my father's halle
   You dye for love of me."

"Fayre ladye, it is for your love,
   That all this dill I drye.
For if you wold comfort me with a kisse,
Then were I brought from bale to blisse,
   No longer would I lye."

"Sir knight, my father is a kinge,
   I am his onlye heire;
Alas! and well you knowe, sir knighte,
   I never can be your fere."

"O ladye, thou art a kinge's daughter,
    And I am not thy peere ;
But let me do some deeds of armes,
    To be your bacheleere."

"Some deeds of armes, if thou wilt doe,
    My bacheleere to be,
(But ever and aye my heart wold rue,
    Giff harm should happe to thee.)

"Upon Eldritch hill there groweth a thorne
    Upon the mores brodinge ;*
And dare ye, sir knight, wake there all
        night,
    Until the fayre morning?

"For the Eldritch knight, so mickle of
        might,
    Will examine you beforne ;
And never man bare life awaye,
    But he did him scaith and scorne.

"That knight he is a foul paynim,
    And large of limb and bone ;
And but if Heaven may be thy speede,
    Thy life it is but gone."

"Now on the Eldritch hill I 'll walk
    For thy sake, fair ladye ;
And I 'll either bring you a ready token,
    Or I 'll never more you see."

* "Mores brodinge :" This phrase is obscure. Motherwell supposes that it means "a thorn broading, or spread-
ing on the moors."

The lady has gone to her own chaumbere,
　　Her maidens following bright;
Sir Cauline lope from care-bed soone,
And to the Eldritch hills is gone,
　　For to walk there all night.

Unto midnight, that the moone did rise,
　　He walked up and down;
Then a lightsome bugle heard he blowe
　　Over the bents so brown;
Quoth he, "If cryance come till my heart,
　　I am far from any good town."

And soon he spied on the mores so broad,
　　A furious wight and fell;
A ladye bright his brydle led,
　　Clad in a fayre kyrtle:

And soe faste he called on Sir Cauline,
　　"O man I rede thee fly,
For but if cryance comes till thy heart,
　　I weene but thou mun dye."

He saith, "No cryance comes till my heart,
　　Nor in faith, I will not flee;
For cause thou minged not Christ before,
　　The less me dreadeth thee."

The Eldritch knighte, he pricked his steed;
　　Sir Cauline bold abode:
Then either shooke his trustye speare,
And the timber these two children bare,
　　Soe soone in sunder slode.

Then took they out theyr two good swordes,
　　And layden on full faste,
Till helme and howberke, mail and shield,
　　They all were well-nye brast.

The Eldritch knight was mickle of might,
    And stiffe in stower did stande;
But Sir Cauline, with a "backward" stroke,
    He smote off his right hand;
That soone he, with pain, and lacke of bloud,
    Fell down on that lay-land.

Then up Sir Cauline lift his brande,
    All over his head so hye:
"And here I sweare by the holy roode,
    Nowe, caytiffe, thou shalt dye."

Then up and came that ladye bright,
    Fast wringing of her hand:
"For the mayden's love, that most you love,
    Withhold your deadlye brand.

"For the mayden's love, that most you love,
    Now smite no more, I pray;
And aye whatever thou wilt, my lord,
    He shall thy hests obey."

"Now sweare to me, thou Eldritch knighte,
    And here on this lay-land,
That thou wilt believe on Christ his laye,*
    And thereto plight thy hand:

"And that thou never on Eldritch come
    To sport, gamon, or playe;
And that thou here give up thy armes
    Until thy dying daye."

The Eldritch knighte gave up his armes,
    With many a sorrowfulle sighe;
And sware to obey Sir Cauline's hest,
    Till the tyme that he should die.

* "Laye:" law.

And he then up, and the Eldritch knighte,
  Sett him in his saddle anone;
And the Eldritch knight, and his ladye,
  To theyr castle are they gone.

Then he tooke up the bloudy hand,
  That was so large of bone,
And on it he founde five ringes of gold,
  Of knightes that had been slone.

Then he took up the Eldritch sword,
  As hard as any flint;
And he took off those ringes five,
  As brighte as fyre and brent.

Home then pricked Sir Cauline,
  As light as leafe on tree;
I wis he neither stint ne blanne,*
  Till he did his ladye see.

Then down he knelt upon his knee,
  Before that ladye gay;
"O ladye, I have bin on Eldritch hills,
  These tokens I bring away."

"Now welcome, welcome, Sir Cauline,
  Thrice welcome unto mee,
For now, I perceive, thou art a true knighte,
  Of valour bolde and free."

"O ladye, I am thy own true knight,
  Thy hests for to obey;
And mought I hope to win thy love!"—
  No more his tonge colde say.

* "Blanne:" ceased.

The ladye blushéd scarlette red,
   And fette a gentill sigh ;
" Alas ! sir knight, how may this be,
   For my degree's soe high ?

" But sith thou hast hight, thou comely
      youth,
   To be my batchelere,
I 'll promise, if thee I may not wed,
   I will have none other fere."

Then she held forth her lily-white hand,
   Towards that knight so free ;
He gave to it one gentill kiss,
His heart was brought from bale to bliss,
   The teares sterte from his ee.

" But keep my counsayl, Sir Cauline,
   Ne let no man it know ;
For and ever my father sholde it ken,
   I wot he wolde us sloe."*

From that daye forthe, that ladye fayre
   Lovèd Sir Cauline the knight ;
From that day forth, he only joyde
   When she was in his sight.

Yea, and oftentimes they met
   Within a fair arboure,
Where they, in love, and sweet daliaunce,
   Past many a pleasaunt houre.

* " Sloe :" slay.

THE SECOND PART.

Everye white will have its blacke,
　And everye sweet its soure :
This founde the ladye Christabelle
　In an untimely houre.

For so it befelle, as Sir Cauline
　Was with that ladye fair,
The kinge her father walked forthe
　To take the evenyng air :

And into the arboure as he went
　To rest his wearye feet,
He found his daughter and Sir Cauline
　There sette in daliaunce sweet.

The kinge he started forthe, i-wys,
　And an angrye man was he :
"Nowe, traytoure, thou shalt hang or drawe,
　And rewe shall thy ladye."

Then forthe Sir Cauline he was ledde,
　And thrown in dungeon deep :
And the ladye into a towre so hye,
　There left to wayle and weep.

The queene she was Sir Cauline's friend,
　And to the kinge said she :
"I praye you save Sir Cauline's life,
　And let him banisht be."

"Now, dame, that traitor shall be sent
　Across the salt sea foam :
But here I will make thee a band,
If ever he come within this land,
　A foule death is his doom."

All woe-begone was that gentill knight
　To part from his ladye ;
And many a time he sighed sore,
　And cast a wistfulle eye :
"Fair Christabelle, from thee to part,
　Far liefer had I dye."

Fair Christabelle, that ladye bright,
　Was had forthe of the towre ;
But ever shee droopeth in her minde,
As nipt by an ungentle winde
　Doth some faire lilye flowre.

And ever she doth lament and weep,
　To tine* her lover soe :
"Sir Cauline, thou little think'st on me,
　But I will still be true."

Many a king, and many a duke,
　And lord of high degree,
Did sue to that faire ladye of love ;
　But never she wolde them nee.†

When many a day was past and gone,
　No comfort she could find,
The king proclaimed a tournament,
　To cheer his daughter's mind.

And there came lords, and there came knights,
　From many a far countrye,
To break a spear for their ladye's love,
　Before that fair ladye.

* "Tine :" lose.　　　† "Nee :" near, or come near.

And many a ladye there was sette,
　　In purple and in pall ;
But fair Christabelle, so woe-begone,
　　Was the fairest of them all.

Then many a knighte was mickle of might
　　Before his ladye gay ;
But a stranger knighte whom no man knew,
　　He wan the prize each day.

His acton it was all of black,
　　His hawberke and his shield ;
And no man wist whence he did come,
And no man knew whence he did gone,
　　When they came from the field.

And now three days were prestlye* past
　　In feats of chivalrye,
When lo, upon the fourth morninge,
　　A sorrowful sight they see :

A hugye giant stiffe and starke,
　　All foule of limbe and lere,
Twa goggling eyen, like fire farden,
　　A mouth from eare to eare.

Before him came a dwarf full low,
　　That waited on his knee ;
And at his back five heads he bore,
　　·All wan and pale of blee.

" Sir," quoth the dwarf, and louted low,
　　" Behold that hend† Soldain !
Behold these heads I bear with me !
　　They are knights which he hath slain.

* " Prestlye :" quickly.　　† " Hend :" courteous.

" The Eldritch knight is his own cousine,
    Whom a knight of thine hath shent ;
And he is to come to avenge his wrong :
And to thee, all thy knights among,
    Defiance here hath sent.

" But yet he will appease his wrath,
    Thy daughter's love to win ;
And but thou yield him that fayre mayde,
    Thy halls and towers must brenne.*

" Thy head, sir king, must go with me,
    Or else thy daughter dear :
Or else within these lists soe broad,
    Thou must find him a peer."

The king he turned him round about,
    And in his heart was woe :
" Is there never a knighte of my round table
    This matter will undergo ?

" Is there never a knight amongst ye all
    Will fight for my daughter and me ?
Whoever will fight yon grim Soldan,
    Right fair his meede shall be.

" For he shall have my broad lay-lands,
    And of my crown be heyre ;
And he shall win fair Christabelle
    To be his wedded fere."

But every knight of his round table
    Did stand both still and pale ;
For, whenever they look'd on the grim Soldan,
    It made their hearts to quail.

* "Brenne :" burn.

All woe-begone was that fayre ladye,
  When she saw no help was nigh:
She cast her thought on her own true love,
  And the tears gusht from her eye.

Up then stert the stranger knighte,
  Sayde, " Ladye, be not afraid;
I 'll fight for thee with this grim Soldan,
  Though he 's unmacklye * made.

" And if thou wilt lend me the Eldritch sword
  That lyeth within thy bowre,
I trust in Christ for to slaye this fiend,
  Though he be stiff and stowre."

" Goe fetch him down the Eldritch sword,"
  The king he cried, " with speed :
.Nowe, Heaven assist thee, courteous knight;
  My daughter is thy meed."

The giant, he stepped into the lists,
  And said, " Away ! away !
I sweare, as I am the hend Soldan,
  Thou lettest † me here all day !"

Then forth the stranger knight he came,
  In his black armour dight;
The ladye sighed a gentle sigh,
  " That this were my true knight !"

And now the giant and knight be met,
  Within the lists sae broad;
And now, with swords soe sharp of steel,
  They gan to lay on load.

* " Unmacklye : " misshapen.   † " Lettest : " hinderest.

The Soldan struck the knight a stroke
    That made him reel aside ;
Then woe-begone was that fayre ladye,
    And thrice she deeply sighd.

The Soldan struck a second stroke,
    And made the bloude to flow ;
All pale and wan was that ladye fayre,
    And thrice she wept for woe.

The Soldan struck a third fell stroke,
    Which brought the knight on his knee :
Sad sorrow pierced that ladye's heart,
    And she shriekt loud shriekings three.

The length he leapt upon his feet,
    All reckless of the pain ;
Quoth he, "But Heaven be now my speede,
    Or else I shall be slain."

He grasped his sword with mayne and mighte,
    And spying a secret part,
He drove it into the Soldan's side,
    And pierced him to the heart.

Then all the people gave a shout,
    When they saw the Soldan fall ;
The ladye wept and thankèd Christ,
    That had rescued her from thrall.

And now the king, with all his barons,
    Rose up from off his seat,
And down he stepped into the lists,
    That courteous knighte to greet :

But he, for pain and lacke of bloude,
   Was fallen into a swound,
And there, all waltering in his gore,
   Lay lifeless on the ground.

"Come down, come down, my daughter dear,
   Thou art a leech of skill;
Far liefer had I lose half my lands,
   Than this good knight should spille."

Down then steppeth that fayre ladye,
   To help him if she may;
But when she did his beaver raise,
"It is my life, my lord!" she says,
   And shriekt and swound away.

Sir Cauline just lift up his eyes,
   When he heard his ladye cry:
"O ladye, I am thine own true love;
   For thee I wisht to dye."

Then giving her one parting look,
   He closed his eyes in death,
Ere Christabelle, that ladye mild,
   Began to draw her breath.

But when she found her comelye knight
   Indeed was dead and gone,
She laid her pale, cold cheek to his,
   And thus she made her moan:

"O stay, my dear and only lord,
   For me, thy faithfulle feere;
'Tis meet that I sholde follow thee,
   Who hast bought my love soe dear!"

> Then faintinge in a deadly swoune,
>   And with a deep fetch'd sigh,
> That burst her gentle heart in twain,
>   Fayre Christabelle did dye.

HYND HORN.

An imperfect copy of this very old ballad appeared in "Select Scottish Songs, Ancient and Modern," edited by Mr Cromek ; but that gentleman seems not to have been aware of the jewel he had picked up, as it is passed over without a single remark. We have been fortunate enough to recover two copies from recitation, which, joined to the stanzas preserved by Mr Cromek, have enabled us to present it to the public in its present complete state. Though *Hynd Horn* possesses no claims upon the reader's attention on account of its poetry, yet it is highly valuable, as illustrative of the history of Romantic Ballad. In fact, it is nothing else than a portion of the ancient English metrical romance of *Kyng Horn*, which some benevolent pen, peradventure "for luf of the lewed man," hath stripped of its "quainte Inglis," and given

> "In symple speche as he couthe,
>   That is lightest in manne's mouthe."

Of this the reader will be at once convinced, if he compares it with the romance alluded to, or rather with the fragment of the one preserved in the Auchinleck MS., entitled, *Horne Childe and Maiden Riminild*, both of which ancient poems are to be found in Ritson's Metrical Romances.

It is perhaps unnecessary to remind the reader that Hend or Hynd means "courteous, kind, affable," &c., an epithet which, we doubt not, the hero of the ballad was fully entitled to assume.—MOTHERWELL.

A different version, omitting altogether the alternately-repeated lines, that spoil the reading, but add grace to the singing of this ballad—

> "With a hey lillelu and a how lo lan,
>   And the birk and the brume blooms bonnie,"

appears in Buchan's Ancient Ballads, and has been repeated, with a few variations, in Professor Aytoun's collection.

NEAR Edinburgh was a young child born,
  With a hey lillelu and a how lo lan;
And his name it was called young Hynd Horn,
  And the birk and the brume blooms bonnie.

Seven lang years he served the king,
And it's a' for the sake of his dochter Jean.

The king an angry man was he,
He sent young Hynd Horn to the sea.

"Oh, I never saw my love before,
Till I saw her thro' an augre bore.

" And she gave to me a gay gold ring,
With three shining diamonds set therein.

" And I gave to her a silver wand,
With three singing lavrocks set thereon.

" What if those diamonds lose their hue,
Just when my love begins for to rue?

" For when your ring turns pale and wan,
Then I 'm in love with another man."

He 's left the land, and he 's gone to the sea,
And he 's stayed there seven years and a day.

Seven lang years he has been on the sea,
And Hynd Horn has looked how his ring may be.

But when he looked this ring upon,
The diamonds were both pale and wan.

Oh ! the ring it was both black and blue,
And she 's either dead or married now.

He 's left the seas, and he 's come to the land,
And the first he met was an auld beggar man.

“ What news, what news, my silly auld man—
For it 's seven years since I have seen land.

“ What news, what news, thou auld beggar man,
What news, what news, by sea or land ?”

“ No news at all,” said the auld beggar man,
“ But there is a wedding in the king’s hall.

“ There is a king’s dochter in the west,
And she has been married thir nine nights past.

“ Into the bride-bed she winna gang,
Till she hears tell of her ain Hynd Horn.”

“ Wilt thou give to me thy begging-coat,
And I ’ll give to thee my scarlet cloak.

“ Wilt thou give to me thy begging-staff,
And I ’ll give to thee my good grey steed.”

The auld beggar man cast off his coat,
And he 's ta’en up the scarlet cloak.

The auld beggar man threw down his staff,
And he has mounted the good grey steed.

The auld beggar man was bound for the mill,
But young Hynd Horn for the king’s hall.

The auld beggar man was bound for to ride,
But young Hynd Horn was bound for the bride.

When he came to the king's gate,
He asked a drink for young Hynd Horn's sake.

These news unto the bonnie bride came,
That at the yett there stands an auld man.

"There stands an auld man at the king's gate,
He asketh a drink for young Hynd Horn's sake."

"I'll go through nine fires so hot,
But I'll give him a drink for young Hynd Horn's
    sake."

She went to the gate where the auld man did
    stand,
And she gave him a drink out of her own hand.

She gave him a cup out of her own hand,
He drunk out the drink, and dropt in the ring.

"Got thou it by sea, or got thou it by land,
Or got thou it off a dead man's hand?"

"I got it not by sea, but I got it by land,
For I got it out of thine own hand."

"I'll cast off my gowns of brown,
And I'll follow thee from town to town."

"I'll cast off my gowns of red,
And along with thee I'll beg my bread."

"Thou need not cast off thy gowns of brown,
For I can make thee lady of many a town.

"Thou need not cast off thy gowns of red,
For I can maintain thee with both wine and
    bread."

The bridegroom thought he had the bonnie bride
    wed,
But young Hynd Horn took the bride to the bed.

BONNIE GEORGE CAMPBELL

Is probably a lament for one of the adherents of the house
of Argyle, who fell in the battle of Glenlivat, on Thurs-
day, the 3d of October 1594. Of this ballad Mr Finlay had only recovered three stanzas, which he has given
in the preface to his "Scottish Historical and Romantic
Ballads," page xxxiii., introduced by the following remarks :—"There is another fragment still remaining,
which appears to have belonged to a ballad of adventure,
perhaps of real history. I am acquainted with no poem of
which the lines, as they stand, can be supposed to have
formed a part."—MOTHERWELL.

There exists a cotemporary ballad on this battle, which
has been published by Graham Dalzell, in his "Scottish
Poems of the Sixteenth Century." It begins thus :—

> "M'Callum More came from the west,
>   With many a brow and brand,
> To work the Rinnes he thought it best—
>   The Earl of Huntly's land."

It appears, however, highly probable that the poem here
given commemorates the assassination of John Campbell
of Calder, which was the result of the same conspiracy
which effected the murder of the "Bonnie Earl of Murray."
—C. M.

HIE upon Hielands
  And low upon Tay,
Bonnie George Campbell
  Rade out on a day.

Saddled and bridled
  And booted rade he ;
Hame cam' his gude horse,
  But never cam' he !

Out cam' his auld mither
  Greeting fu' sair,
And out cam' his bonnie bride
  Rivin' her hair.
Saddled and bridled
  And booted rade he ;
Toom hame cam' the saddle,
  But never cam' he !

"My meadow lies green,
  And my corn is unshorn ;
My barn is to bigg,
  And my babie's unborn."
Saddled and bridled
  And booted rade he ;
Toom hame cam' the saddle,
  But never cam' he !

YOUNG BENJIE.

First printed, from recitation, by Sir Walter Scott, in
the "Border Minstrelsy." The first two lines are almost
identical with the chorus of the Scottish version of *Old
King Cole* :—

> "Of all the maids in fair Scotland,
>   There 's nane to compare wi' Marjorie."

OF a' the maids o' fair Scotland,
  The fairest was our Marjorie ;
And young Benjie was her ae true love,
  And a dear true love was he.

And wow! but they were lovers dear,
　And loved fu’ constantlie ;
But aye the mair when they fell out,
　The sairer was their plea.

And they hae quarrelled on a day,
　Till Marjorie’s heart grew wae,
And she said she ’d chuse another love,
　And let young Benjie gae.

And he was stout and proud hearted,
　And thought o ’t bitterlie :
And he ’s gane by the wan moonlight
　To meet his Marjorie.

“ O open, open, my true love !
　O open and let me in !”
“ I dare na open, young Benjie,
　My three brothers are within.”

“ Ye lie, ye lie, my bonnie burd,
　Sae loud ’s I hear ye lie ;
As I came by the Lowden banks,
　They bade gude e’en to me.

“ But ’fare ye well, my ae fause love,
　That I have loved sae lang ;
It sets ye chuse another love,
　And let young Benjie gang.”

Then Marjorie turned her round about,
　The tear blinding her ee,
“ I dare na, dare na let thee in,
　But I ’ll come down to thee.”

Then saft she smiled, and said to him,
  "O what ill hae I dune?"
He took her in his armis twa,
  And threw her o'er the linn.

The stream was strang, the maid was stout,
  And laith, laith to be dang;
But ere she wan the Lowden's banks
  Her fair colour was wan.

Then up an' spak her eldest brother,
  "O see na ye what I see?"
And out then spak her second brother,
  "It's our sister Marjorie!"

Out then spak her eldest brother,
  "O how shall we her ken?"
And out then spak her youngest brother,
  "There's a honey-mark on her chin."

Then they've ta'en up the comely corpse
  And laid it on the ground:
"O wha has killed our ae sister,
  And how can he be found?

"The night it is her low lykewake,
  The morn her burial day,
And we maun watch at mirk midnight,
  And hear what she will say."

Wi' doors ajar, and candle light,
  And torches burning clear,
The streiket corpse, till still midnight,
  They wake, but naething hear.

About the middle o' the night
  The cocks began to craw,
And at the dead hour o' the night
  The corpse began to thraw.

"O wha has done thee wrang, sister,
  Or dared the deadly sin?
Wha was sae stout, and feared nae dout,
  As throw ye o'er the linn?"

"Young Benjie was the first ae man
  I laid my love upon;
He was sae stout and proud hearted
  He threw me o'er the linn."

"Shall we young Benjie head, sister,
  Shall we young Benjie hang,
Or shall we pike out his twa grey een,
  And punish him ere he gang?"

"Ye mauna Benjie head, brothers,
  Ye mauna Benjie hang,
But ye maun pike out his twa grey een,
  And punish him ere he gang.

"Tie a green gravat about his neck,
  And lead him out and in,
And the best ae servant about your house
  To wait young Benjie on.

"And aye, at every seven years' end,
  Ye 'll tak him to the linn;
For that 's the penance he maun dree,
  To scug* his deadly sin."

* "Scug:" expiate.

THE SONG OF THE OUTLAW MURRAY.

"This ballad appears to have been composed about the reign of James V.   It commemorates a transaction, supposed to have taken place betwixt a Scottish monarch and an ancestor of the ancient family of Murray of Philiphaugh, in Selkirkshire.

"The merit of this beautiful old tale, it is thought, will be fully acknowledged.   It has been, for ages, a popular song in Selkirkshire.   The scene is, by the common people, supposed to have been the Castle of Newark upon Yarrow.   This is highly improbable, because Newark was always a royal fortress.   Indeed, the late excellent antiquarian, Mr Plummer, Sheriff-depute of Selkirkshire, remembered the *insignia* of the unicorns, &c., so often mentioned in the ballad, in existence upon the old tower in Hanginshaw, the seat of the Philiphaugh family; although, upon first perusing a copy of the ballad, he was inclined to subscribe to the popular opinion.   The tower of Hargingshaw has been demolished for many years. It stood in a romantic and solitary situation, on the classical banks of the Yarrow.   When the mountains around Hangingshaw were covered with the wild copse which constituted a Scottish forest, a more secure stronghold for an outlawed baron can hardly be imagined.

"The tradition of Ettrick Forest bears, that the Outlaw was a man of prodigious strength, possessing a baton or club, with which he laid *lee* (*i.e.*, waste) the country for many miles round; and that he was at length slain by Buccleuch, or some of his clan, at a little mount, covered with fir-trees, adjoining to Newark Castle, and said to have been a part of the garden.   A varying tradition bears the place of his death to have been near to the house of the Duke of Buccleuch's gamekeeper, beneath the castle; and that the fatal arrow was shot by Scott of Haining, from the ruins of a cottage on the opposite side of the Yarrow.   There were extant, within these twenty years, some verses of a song on his death.   The feud between the Outlaw and the Scotts may serve to explain the asperity with which the chieftain of that clan is handled in the ballad.

G

"In publishing the following ballad, the copy principally resorted to is one apparently of considerable antiquity, which was found among the papers of the late Mrs Cockburn of Edinburgh, a lady whose memory will be long honoured by all who knew her. Another copy, much more imperfect, is to be found in Glenriddel's MSS. The names are in this last miserably mangled, as is always the case when ballads are taken down from the recitation of persons living at a distance from the scenes in which they are laid. Mr Plummer also gave the editor a few additional verses, not contained in either copy, which are thrown into what seemed their proper place. There is yet another copy, in Mr Herd's MSS., which has been occasionally made use of. Two verses are restored in the present edition, from the recitation of Mr Mungo Park, whose toils, during his patient and intrepid travels in Africa, have not eradicated from his recollection the legendary lore of his native country.

"The arms of the Philiphaugh family are said by tradition to allude to their outlawed state. They are indeed those of a huntsman, and are blazoned thus : Argent, a hunting horn sable, stringed and garnished gules, on a chief azure, three stars of the first. Crest, a Demi Forester, winding his horn, proper. Motto, *Hinc usque superna venabor*."—SIR WALTER SCOTT.

ETTRICKE Forest is a fair forest,
  In it grows many a seemly tree;
There's hart and hynd, and doe and roe,
  And of a' wild beasts great plentie.

There's a fair castelle, bigged wi' lime and stane;
  O! gin it stands not pleasantlie!
In the forefront o' that castelle fair,
  Twa unicorns are braw to see;
There's the picture of a knight, and a ladye bright,
  And the grene hollin abune their bree.*

* "Bree:" brow.

There an Outlaw keeps five hundred men ;
　He keeps a royal companie !
His merrymen are a' in ae liverye clad,
　O' the Linkome grene sae gay to see ;
He and his ladye in purple clad,
　O ! gin they lived not royallie !

Word is gane to our noble king,
　In Edinburgh, where that he lay,
That there was an Outlaw in Ettricke Forest,
　Counted him nought, nor his courtrie gay.

"I make a vow," then the gude king said,
　"Unto the man that deir bought me,
I'se either be king of Ettricke Forest,
　Or king of Scotlande that Outlaw shall be !"

Then spake the lord, hight Hamilton,
　And to the noble king said he,
"My sovereign prince, some counsel take,
　First at your nobles, syne at me.

"I rede ye, send yon braw Outlaw till,
　And see gif your man come will he :
Desire him come and be your man,
　And hold of you yon Forest free.

"Gif he refuses to do that,
　We'll conquer baith his lands and he !
Or else, we'll throw his castell down,
　And make a widow o' his ladye."

The king then call'd a gentleman,
　James Boyd, (the earl of Arran his brother
　　　was he)
When James he came before the king,
　He kneelit before him on his knee.

"Welcome, James Boyd!" said our noble king;
  "A message ye maun gang for me;
Ye maun hye to Ettricke Forest,
  To yon Outlaw, where bideth he;

"Ask him of whom he holds his lands,
  Or man, who may his master be,
And desire him come, and be my man,
  And hold of me yon Forest free.

"To Edinburgh to come and gang,
  His safe warrant I sall gie;
And gif he refuses to do that,
  We'll conquer baith his lands and he.

"Thou may'st vow I'll cast his castell down,
  And mak a widow o' his ladye;
I'll hang his merrymen, pair by pair,
  In ony frith where I may them see."

James Boyd tuik leave o' the noble king,
  To Ettricke Forest fair cam he;
Down Birkendale Brae when that he came
  He saw the fair Forest wi' his ee.

Baith doe and roe, and hart and hinde,
  And of a' wild beastis great plentie;
He heard the bows that bauldly rang,
  And arrows whidderan' him near by.

Of that fair castell he got a sight;
  The like he neir saw wi' his ee!
On the forefront o' that castell fair,
  Twa unicorns were gay to see;
The picture of a knight, and lady bright,
  And the green hollin abune their bree.

Thereat he spyed five hundred men,
  Shooting with bows on Newark Lee ;
They were a' in ae livery clad,
  O' the Lincome green sae gay to see.

His men were a' clad in the green,
  The knight was armed capapie,
With a bended bow, on a milk-white steed ;
  And I wot they ranked right bonilie.

Therby Boyd kend he was master man,
  And served him in his ain degree.
"God mot thee save, brave Outlaw Murray !
  Thy ladye, and all thy chivalrie !"
"Marry, thou's welcome, gentleman,
  Some king's messenger thou seems to be."

"The king of Scotlande sent me here,
  And, gude Outlaw, I am sent to thee ;
I wad wot of whom ye hold your lands,
  Or man, wha may thy master be ?"

"Thir lands are MINE !" the Outlaw said ;
  "I ken nae king in Christentie ;
Frae Soudron * I this Forest wan,
  Whan the king nor his knightis were not to
    see."

"He desires you 'll come to Edinburgh,
  And hold of him this Forest free ;
And, gif ye refuse to do this,
  He 'll conquer baith thy lands and thee.
He hath vow'd to cast thy castell down,
  And mak a widow o' thy ladye ;

<hr>

* "Soudron :" Southern, or English.

" He 'll hang thy merrymen, pair by pair,
  In ony frith where he may them find."
" Aye, by my troth !" the Outlaw said,
  "Than wald I thinke me far behind.

" Ere the king my fair countrie get,
  This land that 's nativest to me !
Mony o' his nobles sall be cauld,
  Their ladyes sall be right wearie."

Then spak his ladye, fair of face,
  She said, " Without consent of me,
That an Outlaw suld come before a king ;
  I am right rad * of treasonrie.
Bid him be gude to his lords at hame,
  For Edinburgh my lord sall never see."

James Boyd tuik his leave o' the Outlaw keen,
  To Edinburgh boun is he ;
When James he cam before the king,
  He knelt lowlie on his knee.

" Welcome, James Boyd !" said our noble king ;
  What Forest is Ettricke Forest free ?"
" Ettricke Forest is the fairest forest
  That ever man saw wi' his ee.

" There 's the doe, the roe, the hart, the hynde,
  And of a' wild beasts great plentie ;
There 's a pretty castell of lyme and stane,
  O gif it stands not pleasauntlie !

" There 's in the forefront o' that castell,
  Twa unicorns, sae bra' to see ;
There 's the picture of a knight, and a ladye bright,
  Wi' the green hollin abune their bree.

* "Rad :" afraid.

"There the Outlaw keeps five hundred men,
  He keeps a royal companie!
His merrymen in ae livery clad,
  O' the Linkome green sae gay to see:
He and his ladye in purple clad;
  O! gin they live not royallie!

"He says, yon forest is his own;
  He wan it frae the Southronie;
Sae as he wan it, sae will he keep it,
  Contrair all kings in Christendie."

"Gar warn me Perthshire, and Angus baith;
  Fife up and down, and Lothians three,
And graith my horse!" said our noble king,
  "For to Ettricke Forest hie will I me."

Then word is gane the Outlaw till,
  In Ettricke Forest, where dwelleth he,
That the king was coming to his cuntrie,
  To conquer baith his lands and he.

"I mak a vow," the Outlaw said,
  "I mak a vow, and that trulie,
Were there but three men to tak my pairt,
  Yon king's coming full dear suld be!"

Then messengers he called forth,
  And bade them hie them speedilye—
"Ane of ye gae to Halliday,
  The laird of the Corehead is he.

"He certain is my sister's son;
  Bid him come quick and succour me!
The king comes on for Ettricke Forest,
  And landless men we a' will be."

"What news? What news?" said Halliday,
  "Man, frae thy master unto me?"
"Not as ye wad; seeking your aide;
  The king's his mortal enemie."

"Aye, by my troth!" said Halliday,
  "Even for that it repenteth me;
For gif he lose fair Ettricke Forest,
  He'll tak fair Moffatdale frae me.

"I'll meet him wi' five hundred men,
  And surely mair, if mae may be;
And before he gets the Forest fair,
  We a' will die on Newark Lee!"

The Outlaw call'd a messenger,
  And bid him hie him speedilye,
To Andrew Murray o' Cockpool—
  "That man's a dear cousin to me;
Desire him come, and mak me aid,
  With a' the power that he may be."

"It stands me hard," Andrew Murray said,
  "Judge gif it stand na hard wi' me ·
To enter against a king wi' crown,
  And set my lands in jeopardie!
Yet if I come not on the day,
  Surely at night he sall me see."

To Sir James Murray of Traquair,
  A message came right speedilye—
"What news? What news?" James Murray said,
  "Man, frae thy master unto me?"

"What needs I tell? for weel ye ken,
  The king's his mortal enemie;
And now he is coming to Ettricke Forest,
  And landless men ye a' will be."

"And, by my troth," James Murray said,
  "Wi' that Outlaw will I live and die ;
The king has gifted my lands lang syne—
  It cannot be nae warse wi' me."

The king was coming thro' Caddon Ford,*
  And full five thousand men had he ;
They saw the dark Forest them before,
  They thought it awsome for to see.

Then spak the lord, hight Hamilton,
  And to the noble king said he,
"My sovereign liege, some counsel take,
  First at your nobles, syne at me.

"Desire him meet thee at Permanscore,
  And bring four in his companie,
Five earls sall gang yoursell before,
  Gude cause that you suld honour'd be.

"And gif he refuses to do that,
  We 'll conquer baith his lands and he ;
There sall never a Murray, after him,
  Hold land in Ettricke Forest free."

Then spak the keen laird of Buckscleuth,
  A stalworth man, and stern was he—
"For a king to gang an Outlaw till,
  Is beneath his state and his dignitie.

"The man that wons you Forest intill,
  He lives by reif and felonie !
Wherefore, brayd on, my sovereign liege !
  Wi fire and sword we 'll follow thee ;
Or, gif your courtrie lords fa' back,
  Our borderers sall the onset gie."

* A ford on the Tweed, at the mouth of the Caddon
Burn, near Yair.

Then out and spak the noble king,
  And round him cast a wilie ee—
" Now had thy tongue, Sir Walter Scott,
  Nor speak of reif nor felonie :
For, had every honest man his ain,
  A right puir clan thy ain wad be!"

The king then call'd a gentleman,
  Royal banner-bearer there was he ;
James Hop Pringle of Torsonse, by name ;
  He came and kneelit upon his knee.

" Welcome, James Pringle of Torsonse !
  A message ye maun gang for me ;
Ye maun gae to yon Outlaw Murray,
  Surely where bauldly bideth he.

" Bid him mete me at Permanscore,
  And bring four in his companie ;
Five earls sall come wi' mysel,
  Gude reason I suld honour'd be.

" And, gif he refuses to do that,
  Bid him look for nae good o' me ;
There sall never a Murray, after him,
  Have land in Ettricke Forest free."

James cam before the Outlaw keen,
  And served him in his ain degree—
" Welcome, James Pringle of Torsonse !
  What message frae the king to me ?"

" He bids ye meet him at Permanscore,
  And bring four in your companie ;
Five earls sall gang himsell before,
  Nae mair in number will he be.

" And, gif you refuse to do that,
    (I freely here upgive wi' thee)
He 'll cast yon bonny castle down,
    And make a widow o' that gaye ladye.

" He 'll loose yon bluidhound borderers,
    Wi' fire and sword to follow thee ;
There will never a Murray, after thysell,
    Have land in Ettricke Forest free."

" It stands me hard," the Outlaw said ;
    "Judge gif it stands na hard wi' me,
Wha reck not losing of mysell,
    But a' my offspring after me.

" My merrymen's lives, my widow's tears—
    There lies the pang that pinches me,
When I am straught in bluidie card,
    Yon castell will be right drearie.

" Auld Halliday, young Halliday,
    Ye shall be twa to gang wi' me ;
Andrew Murray, and Sir James Murray,
    We 'll be nae mae in companie."

When that they came before the king,
    They fell befor him on their knee—
" Grant mercie, mercie, noble king !
    E'en for His sake that died on trie."

" Siccan like mercie sall ye have ;
    On gallows ye sall hangit be !"
" Our God forebode," quoth the Outlaw then,
    " I hope your grace will better be !
Else, ere you come to Edinburgh port,
    I trow thin guarded sall ye be :

"Thir lands of Ettricke Forest fair,
  I wan them from the enemie;
Like as I wan them, sae will I keep them,
  Contrair a' kings in Christendie."

All the nobles the king about,
  Said pitie it were to see him die—
"Yet grant me mercie, sovereign prince!
  Extend your favour unto me!

"I 'll give thee the keys of my castell,
  Wi' the blessing o' my gay ladye,
Gin thou 'lt make me sheriffe of this Forest,
  And a' my offspring after me."

"Wilt thou give me the keys of thy castell,
  Wi' the blessing of thy gaye ladye?
I'se make thee sheriffe of Ettricke Forest,
  Surely while upward grows the tree;
If you be not traitour to the king,
  Forfauted sall thou never be."

"But, prince, what sall come o' my men?
  When I gae back, traitour they 'll ca' me.
I had rather lose my life and land,
  Ere my merrymen rebuked me."

"Will your merrymen amend their lives?
  And a' their pardons I grant thee—
Now, name thy landis where'er they lie,
  And here I render them to thee."

"Fair Philiphaugh is mine by right,
  And Lewinshope still mine shall be;
Newark, Foulshiells, and Tinnies baith,
  My bow and arrow purchased me.

"And I have native steads to me,
  The Newark Lee and Hangingshaw;
I have mony steads in the Forest shaw,
  But them by name I dinna knaw."

The keys o' the castell he gave the king,
  Wi' the blessing o' his fair ladye;
He was made sheriffe of Ettricke Forest,
  Surely while upward grows the tree;
And if he was na traitour to the king,
  Forfauted he suld never be.

Wha ever heard, in ony times,
  Siccan an Outlaw in his degree,
Sic favour get before a king,
  As the OUTLAW MURRAY of the Forest
    free?

JOHNNIE OF BREADISLEE.

History is silent with regard to this young Nimrod.
"He appears," says the Editor of the Border Minstrelsy,
"to have been an outlaw and deer-stealer,—probably one
of the broken men residing upon the border. It is sometimes said that this outlaw possessed the old castle of
Morton, in Dumfriesshire, now ruinous." Another tradition assigns Braid, in the neighbourhood of Edinburgh, to
have been the scene of his "woeful hunting."—MOTHER-
WELL.

Another version of this ballad, under the title of *Johnnie
o' Cocklesmuir*, has been reprinted in "Scottish Ancient
Traditional Ballads," by the Percy Society; but it is of
inferior merit.—C. M.

JOHNNIE rose up in a May morning,
  Called for water to wash his hands—
"Gar loose to me the gude graie dogs
  That are bound wi' iron bands."

When Johnnie's mother gat word o' that,
  Her hands for dule she wrang—
"O Johnnie! for my benison,
  To the grenewood dinna gang!

"Eneugh ye hae o' the gude wheat bread,
  And eneugh o' the blude-red wine;
And therefore, for nae venison, Johnnie,
  I pray ye, stir frae hame."

But Johnnie's busk't up his gude bend bow,
  His arrows, ane by ane;
And he has gane to Durrisdeer
  To hunt the dun deer down.

As he came down by Merriemass,
  And in by the benty line,
There has he espied a deer lying
  Aneath a bush of ling.*

Johnnie he shot, and the dun deer lap.
  And he wounded her on the side;
But, atween the water and the brae,
  His hounds they laid her pride.

And Johnnie has bryttled† the deer sae weel,
  That he's had out her liver and lungs;
And wi' these he has feasted his bludy hounds,
  As if they had been earl's sons.

They eat sae much o' the venison,
  And drank sae much o' the blude,
That Johnnie and a' his bludy hounds
  Fell asleep, as they had been dead.

* "Ling:" heath.
† "Bryttled:" to cut up venison.

And by there came a silly auld carle,
   An ill death mote he die!
For he's away to Hislinton,
   Where the Seven Foresters did lie.

"What news, what news, ye gray-headed carle,
   What news bring ye to me?"
"I bring nae news," said the gray-headed carle,
   Save what these eyes did see.

"As I came down by Merriemass,
   And down amang the scroggs,*
The bonniest childe that ever I saw
   Lay sleeping amang his dogs.

"The shirt that was upon his back
   Was o' the Holland fine;
The doublet which was over that
   Was o' the lincome † twine.

"The buttons that were on his sleeve
   Were o' the goud sae gude;
The gude graie hounds he lay amang,
   Their mouths were dyed wi' blude."

Then out and spak the First Forester,
   The heid man ower them a'—
"If this be Johnnie o' Breadislee,
   Nae nearer will we draw."

But up and spak the Sixth Forester,
   (His sister's son was he)
"If this be Johnnie o' Breadislee,
   We soon shall gar him die!"

* "Scroggs:" stunted trees.　　† "Lincome:" Lincoln.

The first flight of arrows the Foresters shot,
  They wounded him on the knee;
And out and spak the Seventh Forester,
  "The next will gar him die."

Johnnie's set his back against an aik,
  His fute against a stane;
And he has slain the Seven Foresters,
  He has slain them a' but ane.

He has broke three ribs in that ane's side,
  But and his collar bane;
He 's laid him twa-fald ower his steed,
  Bade him carry the tidings hame.

"O is there na a bonnie bird,
  Can sing as I can say;
Could flee away to my mother's bower,
  And tell to fetch Johnnie away?"*

The starling flew to his mother's window-stane,
  It whistled and it sang;
And aye the ower word o' the tune
  Was—"Johnnie tarries lang!"

They made a rod o' the hazel bush,
  Another o' the slae-thorn tree,
And mony, mony were the men
  At fetching our Johnnie.

* Perhaps, after this stanza should be inserted the beautiful one preserved by Mr Finlay, so descriptive, as he justly remarks, of the languor of approaching death :—

    "There 's no a bird in a' this forest
      Will do as meikle for me,
    As dip its wing in the wan water,
      And straik it on my ee bree "

Then out and spak his auld mother,
    And fast her tears did fa'—
"Ye wad nae be warned, my son Johnnie,
    Frae the hunting to bide awa.

"Aft hae I brought to Breadislee
    The less gear and the mair,
But I ne'er brought to Breadislee
    What grieved my heart sae sair!

"But wae betyde that silly auld carle!
    An ill death shall he die!
For the highest tree in Merriemass
    Shall be his morning's fee."

Now Johnnie's gude bend bow is broke,
    And his gude graie dogs are slain;
And his body lies dead in Durrisdeer,
    And his hunting it is done.

———

SIR HUGH; OR, THE JEW'S DAUGHTER.

Two copies of this ballad appeared in Herd's Collection, Edin., 1776, under the above title; a third is printed in Dr Percy's Reliques; and Mr Jamieson has given another copy of the same ballad, taken down from recitation. To this last, which differs in a few particulars from those already published, its learned Editor has prefixed some interesting notices, which may be consulted with advantage. The present edition is likewise given as taken down from the recitation of a lady; and as it contains some additional circumstances not to be found in any of the copies mentioned above, it has been deemed proper to publish it as it stands, without attempting to incorporate it with any other version.—MOTHERWELL.

Yesterday was brave Hallowday,
　And, above all days of the year,
The schoolboys all got leave to play,
　And little Sir Hugh was there.

He kicked the ball with his foot,
　And kepped it with his knee,
And even in at the Jew's window
　He gart the bonnie ba' flee.

Out then came the Jew's daughter—
　"Will ye come in and dine?"
"I winna come in, and I canna come in,
　Till I get that ball of mine.

"Throw down that ball to me, maiden,
　Throw down the ball to me."
"I winna throw down your ball, Sir Hugh,
　Till ye come up to me."

She pu'd the apple frae the tree,
　It was baith red and green,
She gave it unto little Sir Hugh,
　With that his heart did win.

She wiled him into ae chamber,
　She wiled him into twa,
She wiled him into the third chamber,
　And that was warst o't a'.

She took out a little penknife,
　Hung low down by her spare,
She twined this young thing o' his life,
　And a word he ne'er spak mair.

And first came out the thick, thick blood,
   And syne came out the thin,
And syne came out the bonnie heart's blood—
   There was nae mair within.

She laid him on a dressing-table,
   She dress'd him like a swine,*
Says, "Lie ye there, my bonnie Sir Hugh,
   Wi' ye're apples red and green."

She put him in a case of lead,
   Says, "Lie ye there and sleep ;"
She threw him into the deep draw-well
   Was fifty fathom deep.

A schoolboy walking in the garden,
   Did grievously hear him meen,
He ran away to the deep draw-well
   And fell down on his knee,

Says, "Bonnie Sir Hugh, and pretty Sir Hugh,
   I pray you speak to me ;
If you speak to any body in this world,
   I pray you speak to me."

When bells were rung and mass was sung,
   And every body went hame,
Then every lady had her son,
   But Lady Helen had nane.

* "She dressed him like a 'Swan'" was the reading
we got; but, in deference to former editions, we have
substituted "Swine," though it is questionable how far a
Jewess could be skilled in the cookery of an animal abo-
minated by her people.—W. M.

She rolled her mantle her about,
    And sore, sore did she weep ;
She ran away to the Jew's castle
    When all were fast asleep.

She cries, "Bonnie Sir Hugh, O pretty Sir
      Hugh,
    I pray you speak to me ;
If you speak to any body in this world,
    I pray you speak to me."

"Lady Helen, if ye want your son,
    I 'll tell ye where to seek ;
Lady Helen, if ye want your son,
    He 's in the well sae deep."

She ran away to the deep draw-well,
    And she fell down on her knee,
Saying, "Bonnie Sir Hugh, O pretty Sir Hugh,
    I pray ye speak to me,
If ye speak to any body in the world,
    I pray ye speak to me."

"Oh ! the lead it is wondrous heavy, mother,
    The well it is wondrous deep,
The little penknife sticks in my throat,
    And I downa to ye speak.

"But lift me out o' this deep draw-well,
    And bury me in yon churchyard ;
Put a Bible at my head," he says,
    "And a Testament at my feet,
And pen and ink at every side,
    And I 'll lie still and sleep.

"And go to the back of Maitland town,
   Bring me my winding sheet;
For it's at the back of Maitland town
   That you and I shall meet."

O the broom, the bonny, bonny broom,
   The broom that makes full sore;
A woman's mercy is very little,
   But a man's mercy is more.*

THE LAIRD O' LOGIE;

OR, MAY MARGARET,

Appears to be founded on an incident which is detailed at
some length in Spottiswoode's History of the Church of
Scotland, see ed. Lond. 1668, b. vi. p. 389; and also in
"The Historic of King James the Sext," quoted by the
editor of "The Border Minstrelsy." The common
printed edition of this ballad goes under the title of *The
Laird of Ochiltree*, but the copy here followed is that
recovered by Sir Walter Scott, which is preferable to the
other, as agreeing more closely, both in the name and in
the circumstance, with the real fact. The third stanza
in the present copy was obtained from recitation; and, as
it describes very naturally the agitated behaviour of a
person who, like May Margaret, had high interests at
stake, it was considered worthy of being preserved.—
MOTHERWELL.

I WILL sing, if ye will hearken,
   If ye will hearken unto me;
The king has ta'en a poor prisoner,
   The wanton laird o' young Logie.

* This stanza, though meant for a moral, seems to have
little business here, and we are at a loss to make sense of
the second line.—W. M.

Young Logie's laid in Edinburgh chapel,
    Carmichael's the keeper o' the key;
And May Margaret's lamenting sair,
    A' for the love of young Logie.

May Margaret sits in the Queen's bower,
    Kinking her fingers ane by ane,
Cursing the day that she ere was born,
    Or that she ere heard o' Logie's name.

"Lament, lament na, May Margaret,
    And of your weeping let me be,
For ye maun to the king himsel,
    To seek the life o' young Logie."

May Margaret has kilted her green cleiding,
    And she has curl'd back her yellow hair—
"If I canna get young Logie's life,
    Farewell to Scotland for evermair."

When she came before the king,
    She kneelit lowly on her knee.
"O what 's the matter, May Margaret?
    And what needs a' this courtesie?"

"A boon, a boon, my noble liege,
    A boon, a boon, I beg o' thee!
And the first boon that I come to crave,
    Is to grant me the life o' young Logie."

"O na, O na, May Margaret,
    Forsooth, and so it manna be;
For a' the gowd o' fair Scotland
    Shall not save the life o' young Logie."

But she has stown the king's reddling kaim,
   Likewise the queen her wedding knife;
And sent the tokens to Carmichael,
   To cause young Logie get his life.

She sent him a purse o' the red gowd,
   Another o' the white monie;
She sent him a pistol for each hand,
   And bade him shoot when he gat free.

When he came to the Tolbooth stair,
   There he let his volley flee;
It made the king in his chamber start,
   E'en in the bed where he might be.

"Gae out, gae out, my merrymen a',
   And bid Carmichael come speak to me,
For I'll lay my life the pledge o' that,
   That yon's the shot o' young Logie."

When Carmichael came before the king,
   He fell low down upon his knee;
The very first word that the king spake,
   Was—"Where's the laird of young Logie?"

Carmichael turn'd him round about,
   (I wat the tear blinded his eye,)
"There came a token frae your grace,
   Has ta'en away the laird frae me."

"Hast thou play'd me that, Carmichael?
   And has thou play'd me that?" quoth he;
"The morn the Justice Court's to stand,
   And Logie's place ye maun supplie."

Carmichael's awa to Margaret's bower,
  E'en as fast as he may drie—
"O if young Logie be within,
  Tell him to come and speak with me!"

May Margaret turn'd her round about,
  (I wat a loud laugh laughed she,)
"The egg is chipped, the bird is flown,
  Ye'll see nae mair of young Logie."

The tane is shipped at the pier of Leith,
  The tother at the Queen's Ferrie;
And she's gotten a father to her bairn,
  The wanton laird of young Logie.

THE TWA BROTHERS.

The domestic tragedy which this affecting ballad commemorates is not without a precedent in real history; nay, we are almost inclined to believe that it originated in the following melancholy event :—

"This year, 1589, in the moneth of July, ther falls out a sad accident, as a further warncing that God was displeased with the familie. The Lord Sommervill haveing come from Cowthally, earlie in the morning, in regaird the weather was hott, he had ridden hard to be at the Drum be ten a clock, which haveing done, he laid him down to rest. The servant, with his two sones, William Master of Sommervill, and John his brother, went with the horses to ane Shott of land, called the Prety Shott, directly opposite the front of the house where there was some meadow ground for grassing the horses, and willowes to shaddow themselves from the heat. They had not long continued in this place, when the Master of Somervill efter some litle rest awakeing from his sleep, and finding his pistolles that lay hard by him wett with the dew he began to rub and dry them, when unhappily one of them went off the ratch, being lying upon his knee, and the muzel turned syde-ways, the ball strocke his brother John directly in the head, and killed him outright, soe that his sorrowful brother never had one word from him, albeit he begged it with many teares."—*Memorie of the Somervilles*, vol. i. p. 467.—W. M.

There were twa brothers at the scule,
   And when they got awa'—
"It's will ye play at the stane-chucking?
   Or will ye play at the ba'?
Or will ye gae up to yon hill head,
   And there we'll warsle a fa'?"

"I winna play at the stane-chucking,
   Nor will I play at the ba',
But I'll gae up to yon bonnie green hill,
   And there we'll warsle a fa'."

They warsled up, they warsled down,
   Till John fell to the ground;
A dirk fell out of William's pouch,
   And gave John a deadly wound.

"O lift me, lift me on your back,
   Take me to yon well so fair;
And wash my bloody wounds o'er and o'er,
   And they'll ne'er bleed ony mair."

He's lifted his brother upon his back,
   Ta'en him to yon well so fair;
He's wash'd his bluidy wounds o'er and o'er;
   But aye they bleed an' mair and mair.

"Tak ye aff my Holland sark,
   And rive it gair by gair,
And row it in my bluidy wounds,
   And they'll ne'er bleed ony mair."

He's taken aff his Holland sark,
    And torn it gair by gair;
He's rowit it in his bluidy wounds,
    But aye they bleed an' mair and mair.

"Tak now aff my green cleiding,
    And row me saftly in;
And tak me up to yon kirk style,
    Whare the grass grows fair and green."

He's taken aff the green cleiding,
    And rowed him saftly in;
He's laid him down by yon kirk style,
    Whare the grass grows fair and green.

"What will ye say to your father dear,
    When ye gae hame at e'en?"
"I'll say ye're lying at yon kirk style,
    Whare the grass grows fair and green."

"O no, O no, my brother dear,
    O you must not say so;
But say that I'm gane to a foreign land,
    Whare nae man does me know."

When he sat in his father's chair
    He grew baith pale and wan.
"O what blude's that upon your brow?
    O dear son, tell to me."
"It is the blude o' my gude gray steed;
    He wadna ride wi' me."

"O thy steed's blude was ne'er sae red,
    Nor e'er sae dear to me:
O what blude's this upon your cheek?
    O dear son, tell to me."
"It is the blude of my greyhound;
    He wadna hunt for me."

"O thy hound's blude was ne'er sae red,
   Nor e'er sae dear to me :
O what blude 's this upon your hand?
   O dear son, tell to me."
"It is the blude of my gay goss hawk;
   He wadna flee for me."

"O thy hawk's bluid was ne'er sae red,
   Nor e'er sae dear to me :
O what blude 's this upon your dirk?
   Dear Willie, tell to me."
"It is the blude of my ae brother;
   O dule and wae is me."

"O what will ye say to your father?
   Dear Willie, tell to me."
"I 'll saddle my steed, and awa I 'll ride,
   To dwell in some far countrie."

"O when will ye come hame again?
   Dear Willie, tell to me."
"When sun and mune leap on yon hill,
   And that will never be."

She turn'd hersel' right round about,
   And her heart burst into three :
"My ae best son is deid and gane,
   And my tother ane I 'll ne'er see !"

FINE FLOWERS I' THE VALLEY.

This favourite ballad—which exists in a variety of forms, both in Scotland and England—first appeared in Herd's Collection.   Jamieson, who calls it *The Cruel Brother*, printed it with the burden chorus—

> "With a heigho and a lily gay,
> And the primrose blooms sae sweetly,"

instead of the burden more commonly used—

> "Fine flowers in the valley,
> The red, the green, and the yellow."

The following is taken from Gilchrist's Collection.

THERE were three ladies in a ha',
 Fine flowers i' the valley,
There came three lords amang them a',
 The red, green, and the yellow.

The first o' them was clad in red,
"O! lady fair, will ye be my bride?"

The second o' them was clad in green,
"O! lady fair, will ye be my queen?"

The third o' them was clad in yellow,
"O! lady fair, will ye be my marrow?"

"O! ye maun ask my father dear,
Likewise the mother that did me bear;

"And ye maun ask my sister Ann,
And not forget my brother John."

"O! I have asked thy father dear,
Likewise the mother that did thee bear;

"And I have asked thy sister Ann ;
But I forgot thy brother John."

Now when the wedding day was come,
The knight would take his bonny bride home.

And mony a lord, and mony a knight,
Cam' to behold that lady bright.

There was nae man that did her see,
But wished himsel bridegroom to be.

Her father led her through the ha',
Her mother danced before them a'.

Her sister Anne led her through the close,
Her brother John put her on her horse.

"You are high, and I am low,
Give me a kiss before you go."

She was louting down to kiss him sweet,
When wi' his penknife he wounded her deep.

"Ride up, ride up," said the foremost man,
"I think our bride looks pale and wan."

"O lead me over into yon stile,
That I may stop and breathe awhile.

"O lead me over into yon stair,
For there I'll lie and bleed nae mair."

"O! what will you leave to your mother dear?"
"The silken gown that I did wear."

"What will you leave to your father dear?"
"The milk-white steed that brought me here."

"What will you leave to your sister Ann ?"
"My silken snood and golden fan."

"What will you leave to your brother John?"
"The highest gallows to hang him on."

"And what will you leave to your brother
    John's wife ?"
"Grief and sorrow to end her life."

"And what will you leave to your brother
    John's bairns ?"
"The world wide for them to range."

SON DAVIE! SON DAVIE!

The following, which is given from the recitation of an
old woman, will strike the reader as resembling the ballad
of *The Twa Brothers*. But it resembles more the ballad
given in Percy's Reliques, beginning—

> "Why does zour brand sae drap wi' blood ?
>   Edward ! Edward !"

and which was communicated by Lord Hailes. Indeed,
there is reason to believe that his lordship made a few
slight verbal improvements on the copy he transmitted,
and altered the hero's name to Edward ; a name which,
by the by, never occurs in a Scottish ballad, except where
allusion is made to an English king. This, then, may be
looked upon as the *genuine* traditionary version.—MOTHER-
WELL.

"WHAT bluid's that on thy coat lap ?
   Son Davie ! son Davie !
What bluid's that on thy coat lap ?
   And the truth come tell to me, O."

"It is the bluid of my great hawk,
   Mother lady! mother lady!
It is the bluid of my great hawk,
   And the truth I hae tald to thee, O."

"Hawk's bluid was ne'er sae red,
   Son Davie! son Davie!
Hawk's bluid was ne'er sae red,
   And the truth come tell to me, O."

"It is the bluid of my grey hound,
   Mother lady! mother lady!
It is the bluid of my grey hound,
   And it wudna rin for me, O."

"Hound's bluid was ne'er sae red,
   Son Davie! son Davie!
Hound's bluid was ne'er sae red,
   And the truth come tell to me, O."

"It is the bluid o' my brother John,
   Mother lady! mother lady!
It is the bluid o' my brother John,
   And the truth I hae tald to thee, O."

"What about did the plea begin?
   Son Davie! son Davie!"
"It began about the cutting o' a willow wand,
   That would never hae been a tree, O."

"What death dost thou desire to die?
   Son Davie! son Davie!
What death dost thou desire to die?
   And the truth come tell to me, O."

"I 'll set my foot in a bottomless ship,
  Mother lady! mother lady!
I 'll set my foot in a bottomless ship,
  And ye 'll never see mair o' me, O."

"What wilt thou leave to thy poor wife?
  Son Davie! son Davie!"
"Grief and sorrow all her life,
  And she 'll never get mair frae me, O."

"What wilt thou leave to thy young son?
  Son Davie! son Davie!"
"The weary warld to wander up and down,
  And he 'll never get mair o' me, O."

"What wilt thou leave to thy mother dear?
  Son Davie! son Davie!"
"A fire o' coals to burn her wi' hearty cheer,
  And she'll never get mair o' me, O."

———

EDWARD! EDWARD!

This has been well called a "terrible ballad." It is
here reprinted from Percy's Reliques—somewhat modernised in the spelling, but not otherwise altered from the
form in which it was communicated by Lord Hailes, its
supposed adapter.

"WHY does your brand sae drap wi' blude?
                Edward! Edward!
Why does your brand sae drap wi' blude,
And why sae sad gang ye, O?"

"O! I hae killed my hawk sae gude,
                    Mither! mither!
O! I hae killed my hawk sae gude
And I hae nae mair but he, O."

"Your hawk's blude was never so red,
                    Edward! Edward!
Your hawk's blude was never so red,
My dear son, I tell thee, O."

"O! I hae killed my red roan steed,
                    Mither! mither!
O! I hae killed my red roan steed,
That erst was fair and free, O."

"Your steed was auld, and ye hae got mair,
                    Edward! Edward!
Your steed was auld, and ye hae got mair,
Some other dule ye drie, O."

"O! I hae killed my father dear,
                    Mither! mither!
O! I hae killed my father dear,
Alas, and wae is me, O."

"And whatten penance will ye drie for that?
                    Edward! Edward!
And whatten penance will ye drie for that?
My dear son, now tell me, O."

"I 'll set my feet in yonder boat,
                    Mither! mither!
I 'll set my feet in yonder boat.
And I 'll fare over the sea, O."

"And what will ye do wi' your towers and your
          ha' ?
                         Edward ! Edward !
And what will ye do wi' your towers and your ha',
That were sac fair to see, O ?"

"I 'll let them stand till they doun fa',
                         Mither ! mither !
I 'll let them stand till they doun fa',
For here never mair maun I be, O."

" And what will ye leave to your bairns and your
          wife ?
                         Edward ! Edward !
And what will ye leave to your bairns and your
          wife,
When ye gang over the sea, O ?"

"The warld's room, let them beg through life,
                         Mither ! mither !
The warld's room, let them beg through life,
For them never mair will I see, O."

" And what will ye leave to your ain mither dear ?
                         Edward ! Edward !
And what will ye leave to your ain mither dear,
My dear son, now tell me, O ?"

"The curse of hell frae me shall ye bear,
                         Mither ! mither !
The curse of hell frae me shall ye bear,
Sic counsels ye gave to me, O ! "

EDOM O' GORDON.

The stronghold of the Gordons was in Berwickshire;
and Edom or Adam Gordon, deputy for his brother the
Earl of Huntly, in one of his ravaging forays, killed
Arthur Forbes, brother to Lord Forbes. Not long afterwards he "summoned" the house of Rodes, near Dunse,
in Berwickshire, which belonged to Alexander Forbes,
then absent from home. The lady refused to surrender,
without the sanction of her husband; upon which Adam
Gordon set fire to the castle. The lady, together with
her children and servants, twenty-seven persons in all,
perished in the flames. The facts are related by Spottiswoode in his "History of the Church of Scotland."

It fell about the Martinmas,
   When the wind blew shrill and cauld,
Said Edom o' Gordon to his men,
   "We maun draw till a hauld.*

"And what a hauld sall we draw till,
   My merry men and me?
We wull gae to the house o' the Rodes,
   To see that fair ladie."

The lady stood on her castle wa',
   Beheld baith dale and down:
There she was 'ware of a host of men
   Came riding to the toun.

"O see ye not, my merry men a'?
   O see ye not what I see?
Methinks I see a host of men:
   I marvel wha they be."

* "Hauld:" hold.

She weened it had been her luvely lord,
   As he cam riding hame;
It was the traitor Edom o' Gordon,
   Wha reckt nae sin nor shame.

She had nae sooner buskit hirsel,
   And putten on her goun,
But Edom o' Gordon and his men
   Were round about the toun.

They had nae sooner supper set,
   Nae sooner said the grace,
Than Edom o' Gordon and his men
   Were light about the place.

The lady ran up to her tower head,
   So fast as she could hie,
To see if by her fair speechès
   She could wi' him agree.

But whan he saw this lady safe
   And her gates all lockèd fast,
He fell into a rage of wrath,
   And his look was all aghast.

"Come down to me, ye lady gay,
   Come down, come down to me;
This night sall ye lig within mine arms,
   To-morrow my bride sall be."

"I winna come down, ye false Gordon,
   I winna come down to thee;
I winna forsake my ain dear lord,
   That is sae far frae me."

"Give owre your house, ye lady fair,
  Give owre your house to me,
Or I sall bren yoursel therein,
  Bot and your babies three."

"I winna give owre, ye false Gordòn,
  To nae sik traitor as ye;
And if ye bren my ain dear babes,
  My lord sall make ye drie.

"But reach my pistol, Glaud, my man,
  And charge ye weil my gun;
For, but an I pierce that bluidy butchèr,
  My babes we been undone."

She stood upon her castle wa',
  And let twa bullets flee;
She mist that bluidy butcher's heart,
  And only razed his knee.

"Set fire to the house!" quo' false Gordòn,
  All wud* wi' dule and ire;
"False lady, ye sall rue this deed,
  As ye bren in the fire."

"Wae worth, wae worth ye, Jock, my man,
  I paid ye weil your fee;
Why pu' ye out the ground-wa' stane,
  Lets in the reek to me?

"And e'en wae worth ye, Jock, my man,
  I paid ye weil your hire;
Why pu' ye out the ground-wa' stane,
  To me lets in the fire?"

* "Wud:" furious, mad.

"Ye paid me weil my hire, lady;
　Ye paid me weil my fee:
But now I 'm Edom o' Gordon's man,
　Maun either do or die."

O, then outspake her little son,
　Sate on the nurse's knee:
Says, "Mither dear, gi' owre this house,
　For the reek it smither's me."

"I wad gie a' my gowd, my child,
　Sae wad I a' my fee,
For ane blast o' the western wind,
　To blaw the reek frae thee."

O, than outspake her dochter dear,
　She was baith jimp and sma':
"O, row me in a pair of sheets,
　And tow me owre the wa'."

They rowd her in a pair of sheets,
　And towd her owre the wa';
But on the point of Gordon's spear,
　She gat a deadly fa'.

O, bonnie, bonnie was her mouth,
　And cherry were her cheeks,
And clear, clear was her yellow hair,
　Whereon the red bluid dreips.

Then wi' his spear he turned her owre,
　O, gin her face was wan!
He said, "Ye are the first that ere
　I wished alive again."

He turned her owre and owre again,
  O, gin her skin was white!
"I might ha' spared that bonnie face
  To hae been some man's delight!

"Busk and boun, my merry men a',
  For ill dooms I do guess;
I canna luik in that bonnie face,
  As it lies on the grass."

"Who luiks to freits,* my master-dear,
  Then freits will follow them:
Let it ne'er be said brave Edom o' Gordon
  Was daunted by a dame."

But when the lady saw the fire
  Come flaming owre her head,
She wept and kist her children twain,
  Said, "Bairns, we been but dead."

The Gordon then his bugle blew,
  And said, "Awa', awa'!
This house o' the Rodes is a' in flame,
  I hauld it time to ga'."

O, then bespyed her ain dear lord,
  As he cam owre the lee;
He saw his castle all in a blaze,
  Sae far as he could see.

Then sair, O sair, his mind misgave,
  And all his heart was wae;
"Put on, put on, my wighty men,
  So fast as ye can gae.

* "Freits:" ill omens.

"Put on, put on, my wighty men,
　So fast as ye can drie;
For he that is hindmost of the throng
　Sall ne'er get guid o' me."

Then some they rode, and some they ran,
　Fu' fast out owre the bent;
But ere the foremost could get up,
　Baith lady and babes were brent.

He wrang his hands, he rent his hair,
　And wept in teenfu' mood:
"O traitors! for this cruel deed
　Ye sall weep tears o' bluid."

And after the Gordon he is gane,
　Sae fast as he might drie:
And soon i' the Gordon's foul heart's bluid
　He 's wroken his dear lady.

THE WIFE OF USHER'S WELL.

This ballad first appeared as a fragment in the "Minstrelsy of the Scottish Border." Mr Robert Chambers recovered two additional stanzas, from recitation, in Peeblesshire, which are here inserted within brackets.

There lived a wife at Usher's well,
　And a wealthy wife was she:
She had three stout and stalwart sons,
　And sent them o'er the sea.

They hadna been a week from her,
　A week but barely ane,
When word came to the carline wife
　That her three sons were gane.

They hadna been a week from her,
   A week but barely three,
When word came to the carline wife,
   That her sons she'd never see.

"I wish the wind may never cease,
   Nor fishes in the flood,
Till my three sons come hame to me
   In earthly flesh and blood!"

It fell about the Martinmas,
   When nights are lang and mirk,
The carline wife's three sons came hame,
   And their hats were o' the birk.

It neither grew in syke nor ditch,
   Nor yet in any sheugh;
But at the gates o' Paradise,
   That birk grew fair eneugh.*

*   *   *   *   *

"Blow up the fire, my maidens,
   Bring water from the well,
For a' my house shall feast this night,
   Since my three sons are well."

And she has made to them a bed,
   She's made it large and wide:
And she's ta'en her mantle her about,
   Set down at the bed-side.

*   *   *   *   *

* The notion that the souls of the blessed wear garlands
seems to be of Jewish origin.—SIR WALTER SCOTT.

Up then crew the red, red cock,
  And up and crew the gray;
The eldest to the youngest said,
  " 'Tis time we were away."

The cock he hadna crawed but once,
  And clapp'd his wings at a',
Whan the youngest to the eldest said,
  " Brother, we must awa'.

" The cock doth craw, the day doth daw,
  The channerin'* worm doth chide;
Gin we be mist out o' our place
  A sair pain we maun bide."

[" Lie still, lie still, but a little wee while,
  Lie still but if we may,
Gin our mother should miss us when she
    wakes,
  She will be mad ere day."

An' it 's they hae ta'en up their mother's
    mantle,
  And hung it on a pin,
" Oh, lang may ye hang, our mother's
    mantle,
  Ere ye hap us again.]

" Fare ye well, our mother dear !
  Fareweel to barn and byre !
And fare ye weel, the bonny lass,
  That kindles our mother's fire."

*   *   *   *   *

* "Channerin':" fretting.

SIR ROLAND.

This fragment, which some recent commentators without sufficient evidence have pronounced to be modern, was first printed in Motherwell's Collection. It was communicated to him, he says, " by an ingenious friend, who remembered having heard it sung in his youth. A good many verses at the beginning, some about the middle, and one or two at the end, seem to be wanting. More sanguine antiquaries than we are might, from the similarity of names, imagine they had in this ballad discovered the original romance whence Shakspeare had given this line—

'Child Rowland to the dark tower came.'
King Lear, Act III.

"The story is of a very gloomy and superstitious texture. A young lady, on the eve of her marriage, invited her lover to a banquet, where she murders him in revenge for some real or fancied neglect. Alarmed for her own safety, she betakes herself to flight; and in the course of her journey she sees a stranger knight riding slowly before her, whom she at first seeks to shun, by pursuing an opposite direction; but on finding that wheresoever she turned he still appeared between her and the moonlight, she resolves to overtake him. This, however, she finds in vain, till, of his own accord, he stays for her at the brink of a broad river. They agree to cross it; and when in the mid stream she implores his help to save her from drowning, to her horror she finds her fellow-traveller to be no other than the gaunt apparition of her dead lover."

*　　*　　*　　*　　*

WHAN he cam to his ain luve's bowir
  He tirl'd at the pin,
And sae ready was his fair fause luve
  To rise and let him in.

"O welcome, welcome, Sir Roland," she says,
  "Thrice welcome thou art to me,
For this night thou wilt feast in my secret bowir,
  And to-morrow we'll wedded be."

"This night is hallow-eve," he said,
　"And to-morrow is hallow-day;
And I dreamed a drearie dream yestreen,
　That has made my heart fu' wae.

"I dreamed a drearie dream yestreen,
　And I wish it may come to gude:
I dreamed that ye slew my best grew hound,
　And gied me his lappered blude."

*　　*　　*　　*　　*

"Unbuckle your belt, Sir Roland," she said,
　"And set you safely down."
"O your chamber is very dark, fair maid,
　And the night is wondrous lown."

"Yes, dark, dark is my secret bowir,
　And lown the midnight may be,
For there is none waking in a' this tower,
　But thou, my true-love, and me."

*　　*　　*　　*　　*

She has mounted on her true love's steed,
　By the ae light o' the moon;
She has whipped him and spurred him,
　And roundly she rade frae the toun.

She hadna ridden a mile o' gate,
　Never a mile but ane,
Whan she was aware of a tall young man,
　Slow riding o'er the plain.

She turned her to the right about,
　Then to the left turned she,
But aye, 'tween her and the wan moonlight,
　That tall knight did she see.

And he was riding burd alane,
  On a horse as black as jet,
But tho' she followed him fast and fell,
  No nearer could she get.

"O stop! O stop! young man," she said,
  "For I in dule am dight;
O stop, and win a fair lady's luve,
  If you be a leal true knight."

But nothing did the tall knight say,
  And nothing did he blin;
Still slowly rode he on before,
  And fast she rade behind.

She whipped her steed, she spurred her steed,
  Till his breast was all a foam,
But nearer unto that tall young knight,
  By our ladye, she could not come.

"O if you be a gay young knight,
  As well I trow you be,
Pull tight your bridle reins, and stay
  Till I come up to thee."

But nothing did that tall knight say,
  And no whit did he blin,
Until he reached a broad river's side,
  And there he drew his rein.

"O, is this water deep," he said,
  "As it is wondrous dun?
Or is it sic as a saikless maid
  And a leal true knight may swim?"

"The water it is deep," she said,
    "As it is wondrous dun;
But it is sic as a saikless maid
    And a leal true knight may swim."

The knight spurred on his tall black steed,
    The lady spurred on her brown;
And fast they rade unto the flood,
    And fast they baith swam down.

"The water weets my tae," she said,
    "The water weets my knee,
And hold up my bridle reins, 'sir knight,
    For the sake of Our Ladye."

"If I would help thee now," he said,
    "It were a deadly sin,
For I've sworn neir to trust a fair may's word,
    Till the water weets her chin."

"O, the water weets my waist," she said,
    "Sae does it weet my skin,
And my aching heart rins round about,
    The burn maks sic a din.

"The water is waxing deeper still,
    Sae does it wax mair wide,
And aye the farther that we ride on
    Farther off is the other side.

"O help me now, thou false, false knight,
    Have pity on my youth,
For now the water jawes owre my head,
    And it gurgles in my mouth."

The knight turned right and round about,
   All in the middle stream,
And he stretched out his head to that lady,
   But loudly she did scream.

"O, this is hallow-morn," he said,
   " And it is your bridle day,
But sad would be that gay wedding
   If bridegroom and bride were away.

"And ride on, ride on, proud Margaret !
   Till the water comes o'er your bree,
For the bride maun ride deep, and deeper yet,
   Wha rides this ford wi' me.

"Turn round, turn round, proud Margaret !
   Turn ye round and look on me,
Thou hast killed a true knight under trust
   And his ghost now links on with thee."

*   *   *   *   *

FAUSE FOODRAGE

Was first published in the " Minstrelsy of the Scottish Border," where it is stated to be given chiefly from Mrs Brown of Falkland's MSS. The ballad is popular in Scotland, and there can be no reasonable doubt of its authenticity. Like others, however, it has lost none of its beauties by being distilled through the alembic established at Abbotsford for the purification of ancient song. —MOTHERWELL.

KING Easter has courted her for her lands,
   King Wester for her fee ;
King Honour for her comely face,
   And for her fair bodie.

They had not been four months married,
  As I have heard them tell,
Until the nobles of the land
  Against them did rebel.

And they cast kevils * them amang,
  And kevils them between ;
And they cast kevils them amang,
  Wha suld gae kill the king.

O, some said yea, and some said nay,
  Their words did not agree ;
Till up and got him Fause Foodrage,
  And swore it suld be he.

When bells were rung, and mass was sung,
  And a' men bound to bed,
King Honour and his gay ladye
  In a hie chamber were laid.

Then up and raise him, Fause Foodrage,
  When a' were fast asleep,
And slew the porter in his lodge,
  That watch and ward did keep.

O, four and twenty silver keys
  Hung hie upon a pin ;
And aye, as ae door he did unlock,
  He has fastened it him behind.

Then up and raise him king Honour,
  Says—"What means a' this din ?
Or what's the matter, Fause Foodrage,
  Or wha has loot you in ?"

* "Kevils :" lots.

"O ye my errand weel sall learn,
    Before that I depart."
Then drew a knife, baith lang and sharp,
    And pierced him to the heart.

Then up and got the queen hersell,
    And fell low down on her knee:
"O spare my life, now, Fause Foodrage!
    For I never injured thee.

"O spare my life, now, Fause Foodrage!
    Until I lighter be!
And see gin it be lad or lass,
    King Honour has left wi' me."

"O gin it be a lass," he says,
    "Weel nursed it sall be;
But gin it be a lad bairn,
    He sall be hanged hie.

"I winna spare for his tender age,
    Nor yet for his hie, hie kin;
But soon as e'er he born is,
    He sall mount the gallows pin."

O four and twenty valiant knights
    Were set the queen to guard!
And four stood aye at her bowir door,
    To keep both watch and ward.

But when the time drew near an end,
    That she suld lighter be,
She cast about to find a wile,
    To set her body free.

K

O she has birled these merry young men,
  With the ale but and the wine,
Until they were as deadly drunk
  As any wild-wood swine.

"O narrow, narrow, is this window,
  And big, big am I grown!"
Yet through the might of Our Ladye,
  Out at it she has gone.

She wandered up, she wandered down,
  She wandered out and in ;
And, at last, into the swine's stythe,
  The queen brought forth a son.

Then they cast kevils them amang,
  Which suld gae seek the queen ;
And the kevil fell upon Wise William,
  And he sent his wife for him.

O when she saw Wise William's wife,
  The queen fell on her knee ;
"Win up, win up, madam !" she says,
  "What needs this courtesie?

"O out o' this I winna rise,
  Till a boon ye grant to me ;
To change your lass for this lad bairn,
  King Honour left me wi'.

"And ye maun learn my gay goss hawk
  Right weel to breast a steed ;
And I sall learn your turtle dow
  As weel to write and read.

"And ye maun learn my gay goss hawk
  To wield baith bow and brand;
And I sall learn your turtle dow
  To lay gowd with her hand.

"At kirk and market when we meet,
  We'll dare mak nae avowe,
But—'Dame, how does my gay goss hawk?'
  'Madame, how does my dow?'"

When days were gane, and years come on,
  Wise William he thought lang;
And he's ta'en king Honour's son
  A hunting for to gang.

It sae fell out, at this hunting,
  Upon a simmer's day,
That they came by a fair castell,
  Stood on a sunny brae.

"O dinna ye see that bonny castell,
  Wi' halls and towers sae fair?
Gin ilka man had back his ain,
  Of it you suld be heir."

"How I suld be heir of that castell,
  In sooth I canna see:
For it belongs to Fause Foodrage,
  And he is na kin to me."

"O gin ye suld kill him, Fause Foodrage,
  You would do but what was right;
For, I wot, he killed your father dear,
  Or ever ye saw the light.

"And gin ye suld kill him, Fause Foodrage,
  There is no man durst you blame;
For he keeps your mother a prisoner,
  And she daurna take ye hame."

The boy stared wild, like a gray goss hawk:
  Says—"What may a' this mean?"
"My boy, ye are king Honour's son,
  And your mother's our lawful queen."

"O gin I be king Honour's son,
  By Our Ladye, I swear,
This night I will that traitor slay,
  And relieve my mother dear!"

He has set his bent bow to his breast,
  And leaped the castell wa';
And soon he has seized Fause Foodrage,
  Wha loud for help 'gan ca'.

"O haud your tongue now, Fause Foodrage,
  Frae me ye shanna flee."
Syne pierced him through the fause, fause heart,
  And set his mother free.

And he has rewarded Wise William
  Wi' the best half of his land;
And sae has he the turtle dow
  Wi' the troth o' his right hand.

THE TWA CORBIES.

This poem was communicated to Sir Walter Scott by Mr Kirkpatrick Sharpe, as written down, from tradition, by a lady. "It is a singular circumstance," says Sir Walter, "that it should coincide so very nearly with the ancient dirge, called *The Three Ravens*, published by Mr Ritson in his 'Ancient Songs;' and that, at the same time, there should exist such a difference as to make the one appear rather a counterpart than copy of the other. In order to enable the curious reader to contrast these two singular poems, and to form a judgment which may be the original, I take the liberty of copying the English ballad from Mr Ritson's Collection. The learned Editor states it to be given from 'Ravenscroft's Melismata. Musical Phansies, fitting the Cittie and Country Humours, to 3, 4, and 5 Voyces, London, 1611, 4to.'"

In this version, the chorus of—

"Down, down—hey derry down,"

after every line, is omitted.

There were three ravens sat on a tre,
They were as blacke as they might be :

The one of them said to his mate,
"Where shall we our breakfast take?"

"Downe in yonder grene field,
There lies a knight slain under his shield ;

"His hounds they lie down at his feete,
So well do they their master keepe ;

"His haukes they flie so eagerly,
There's no fowle dare come him nie.

"Down there comes a fallow doe,
As great with young as she might goe.

"She lift up his bloudy hed,
And kist his wounds that were so red.

"She got him up upon her backe,
And carried him to earthen lake.

"She buried him before the prime,
She was dead her selfe ere euen song time.

"God send euery gentleman,
Such haukes, such houndes, and such a leman."

As I was walking all alane,
I heard twa corbies making a mane;
The tane unto the other 'gan say,
"Where sall we gang and dine to-day?"

"In behint yon auld fail* dyke,
I wot there lies a new-slain knight;
And naebody kens that he lies there,
But his hawk, his hound, and his lady fair.

"His hound is to the hunting gane,
His hawk to fetch the wild-fowl hame,
His lady's ta'en another mate,
So we may make our dinner sweet.

"Ye sall sit on his white hause bane,
And I'll pike out his bonny blue een:
Wi' ae lock o' his gowden hair,
We'll theek† our nest when it grows bare.

"Mony a ane for him makes mane,
But nane sall ken whare he is gane:
O'er his white banes, when they are bare,
The wind sall blaw for evermair."

* "Fail:" turf.   † "Theek:" thatch.

THE TWA CORBIES.

SECOND VERSION.

From Motherwell's Collection, but evidently much modernised.

THERE were twa corbies sat on a tree,
Large and black as black might be,
And one until the other 'gan say,
"Where shall we go and dine to-day?
Shall we dine by the wild salt sea?
Shall we dine 'neath the greenwood tree?"

"As I sat on the deep sea sand,
I saw a fair ship nigh at land;
I waved my wings, I bent my beak,
The ship sunk, and I heard a shriek:
There they lie, one, two, and three—
I shall dine by the wild salt sea."

"Come, I will shew ye a sweeter sight,
A lonesome glen, and a new-slain knight;
His blood yet on the grass is hot,
His sword half drawn, his shafts unshot,—
And no one knows that he lies there,
But his hawk, his hound, and his lady fair.

"His hound is to the hunting gane,
His hawk to fetch the wild-fowl hame,
His lady's away with another mate,
So we shall make our dinner sweet;
Our dinner's sure, our feasting free,
Come, and dine by the greenwood tree.

" Ye shall sit on his white hause-bane,
I will pick out his bonny blue een ;
Ye 'll take a tress of his yellow hair,
To theak your nest when it grows bare ;
The gowden down on his young chin
Will do to rowe my young ones in.

" O, cauld and bare his bed will be,
When winter storms sing in the tree ;
At his head a turf, at his feet a stone,
He will sleep, nor hear the maiden's moan ;
O'er his white bones the birds shall fly,
The wild deer bound, and foxes cry."

———

MAY COLVIN; OR, FALSE SIR JOHN.

This ballad was published by Motherwell, from a copy
obtained from recitation, collated from another copy to be
found in Herd's collection, 1776.   It is sometimes called
May Collean.

FALSE Sir John a-wooing came,
  To a maid of beauty rare ;
May Colvin was the lady's name,
  Her father's only heir.

He's courted her butt, and he's courted her ben,
  And he's courted her into the ha',
Till once he got this lady's consent
  To mount and ride awa'.

She 's gane to her father's coffers,
  Where all his money lay ;
And she 's taken the red, and she 's left the white,
  And lightly she tripped away.

She's gane down to her father's stable,
   Where all his steeds did stand ;
And she's taken the best, and left the warst,
   That was in her father's land.

He rode on, and she rode on,
   They rode a lang simmer's day,
Until they came to a broad river,
   An arm of a lonesome sea.

"Loup off the steed," says false Sir John ;
   "Your bridal bed you see ;
For its seven king's daughters I have drowned here,
   And the eighth I'll out make with thee.

"Cast off, cast off your silks so fine,
   And lay them on a stone,
For they are o'er good and o'er costly
   To rot in the salt sea foam.

"Cast off, cast off your holland smock,
   And lay it on this stone,
For its too fine and o'er costly
   To rot in the salt sea foam."

"O turn you about, thou false Sir John,
   And look to the leaf o' the tree ;
For it never became a gentleman
   A naked woman to see."

He's turned himself straight round about,
   To look to the leaf o' the tree ;
She's twined her arms about his waist,
   And thrown him into the sea.

"O hold a grip of me, May Colvin,
    For fear that I should drown;
I 'll take you hame to your father's gates,
    And safely I 'll set you down."

"O lie you there, thou false Sir John,
    O lie you there," said she,
"For you lie not in a caulder bed
    Then the ane you intended for me."

So she went on her father's steed,
    As swift as she could flee;
And she came hame to her father's gates
    At the breaking of the day.

Up then spake the pretty parrot:
    "May Colvin, where have you been?
What has become of false Sir John,
    That wooed you so late yestreen?"

Up then spake the pretty parrot,
    In the bonnie cage where it lay:
"O what hae ye done with the false Sir John,
    That he behind you does stay?

"He wooed you butt, he wooed you ben,
    He wooed you into the ha',
Until he got your own consent
    For to mount and gang awa'."

"O hold your tongue, my pretty parrot,
    Lay not the blame upon me;
Your cage will be made of the beaten gold
    And the spakes of ivorie."

Up then spake the king himself,
  In the chamber where he lay:
"Oh! what ails the pretty parrot,
  That prattles so long ere day?"

"It was a cat cam to my cage door;
  I thought 'twould have worried me;
And I was calling on May Colvin
  To take the cat from me."

LADY MAISRY.

This excellent old ballad, which is very popular in many parts of Scotland, is given from Mr Jamieson's Collection. —MOTHERWELL.

THE young lords o' the north country
  Have all a-wooing gane,
To win the love o' Lady Maisry;
  But o' them she wou'd hae nane.

O, thae hae sought her, Lady Maisry,
  Wi' broaches and wi' rings;
And they hae courted her, Lady Maisry,
  Wi' a' kin kind of things;

And they hae sought her, Lady Maisry,
  Frae father and frae mither;
And they hae sought her, Lady Maisry,
  Frae sister and frae brither.

And they hae followed her, Lady Maisry,
  Through chamber and through ha';
But a' that they could say to her,
  Her answer still was "Na."

"O haud your tongues, young men," she said,
　"And think nae mair on me ;
For I 've gi'en my love to an English lord,
　Sae think nae mair on me."

Her father's kitchen boy heard that
　(An ill death mot he die !)
And he is in to her brother,
　As fast as gang cou'd he.

"O, is my father and my mother weel,
　Bot and my brothers three ?
Gin my sister Lady Maisry be weel,
　There 's naething can ail me."

"Your father and your mother is weel,
　Bot and your brothers three ;
Your sister, Lady Maisry 's weel ;
　Sae big wi' bairn is she."

"A malison light on the tongue,
　Sic tidings tells to me !
But gin it be a lie you tell,
　You shall be hanged hie."

He 's doen him to his sister's bower,
　Wi' mickle dool and care ;
And there he saw her, Lady Maisry,
　Combing her yellow hair.

"O, wha is aucht that bairn," he says,
　"That ye sae big are wi ?
And gin ye winna own the truth,
　This moment ye shall die."

She's turned her richt and round about,
   And the kembe fell frae her han';
A trembling seized her fair bodie,
   And her rosy cheek grew wan.

"O pardon me, my brother dear,
   And the truth I 'll tell to thee;
My bairn is to Lord William,
   And he is betrothed to me."

"O cou'dna ye gotten dukes, or lords,
   Intil your ain countrie,
That ye drew up wi' an English dog,
   To bring this shame on me?

"But ye maun gi'e up your English lord,
   Whan your young babe is born;
For, gin ye keep by him an hour langer,
   Your life shall be forlorn."

"I will gi'e up this English lord,
   Till my young babe is born;
But the never a day nor hour langer,
   Though my life should be forlorn."

"O where is a' my merry young men
   Wham I gi'e meat and fee,
To pu' the bracken and the thorn,
   To burn this vile whore wi'."

"O whare will I get a bonny boy
   To help me in my need,
To rin wi' haste to Lord William,
   And bid him come wi' speed?"

O out it spak a bonny boy,
  Stood by her brother's side;
"It's I wad rin your errand, lady,
  O'er a' the warld wide.

"Aft ha'e I run your errands, lady,
  When blawin baith wind and weet;
But now I 'll rin your errand, lady,
  Wi' saut tears on my cheek."

O whan he came to broken briggs,
  He bent his bow and swam;
And whan he came to grass growin',
  He slack'd his shoon and ran.

And whan he came to Lord William's yetts,
  He badena to chap or ca';
But set his bent bow to his breast,
  And lightly lap the wa';
And, or the porter was at the yett,
  The boy was in the ha'.

"O is my biggins broken, boy?
  Or is my towers won?
Or is my lady lighter yet,
  O' a dear daughter or son?"

"Your biggin isna broken, sir,
  Nor is your towers won;
But the fairest lady in a' the land
  This day for you maun burn."

"O saddle to me the black, the black,
  Or saddle to me the brown;
Or saddle to me the swiftest steed
  That ever rade frae a town."

Or he was near a mile awa',
   She heard his weir-horse sneeze ;
"Mend up the fire, my fause brother,
   It 's nae come to my knees."

O, whan he lighted at the yett,
   She heard his bridle ring :
"Mend up the fire, my fause brother ;
   It 's far yet frae my chin.

"Mend up the fire to me, brother,
   Mend up the fire to me ;
For I see him comin' hard and fast
   Will soon men't up for thee.

"O gin my hands had been loose, Willy,
   Sae hard as they are boun',
I wad hae turned me frae the gleed,
   And casten out your young son."

"O, I 'll gar burn for you, Maisry,
   Your father and your mother ;
And I 'll gar burn for you, Maisry,
   Your sister and your brother ;

"And I 'll gar burn for you, Maisry,
   The chief o' a' your kin ;
And the last bonfire that I come to,
   Mysel' I will cast in."

THE BONNIE EARL OF MURRAY.

"The 7 of Februarij this zeire, 1592, the Earle of Murray was cruelly murthered by the Earle of Huntly, at his house in Dunibrissell, in Fyffeshyre, and with him Dumbar, Shriffe of Murray; it [was] given out, and publickly talked that the Earle of Huntly was only the instrument of perpetratting this facte, to satisffie the Kinges jelosie of Murray, quhom the Queine, more rashlie than wyslie, some few dayes before had commendit in the Kinges heiringe, with too many epithetts of a proper and gallant man. The ressons of these surmisses proceidit from proclamatione of the Kinges the 18 of Marche following, inhibitting the younge Earle of Murray to persew the Earle of Huntly for his father's slaughter, in respecte he being, wardit in the castell of Blacknesse for the same murther, was willing to abyde his tryell; averring that he had done nothing, bot by the King's ma^{ties} commissione : and so was neither airt nor pairt of the murther."—*Annales of Scotland by Sir James Balfour*, vol. i., Edin. 1824. For other accounts of this transaction, see Spottiswood, Moyse's Memoires, Calderwood's History of the Church, and Gordon's Genealogical History of the Earldom of Sutherland.
—MOTHERWELL.

> Ye Highlands, and ye Lawlands,
>   Oh ! where hae ye been ?
> They hae slaine the Earl of Murray,
>   And hae lain him on the green.
>
> Now wae be to thee, Huntly !
>   And wherefore did you say ?
> I bade you bring him wi' you,
>   But forbade you him to slay.
>
> He was a braw gallant,
>   And he rid at the ring ;
> And the bonnie Earl of Murray,
>   Oh ! he might hae been a king.

He was a braw gallant,
   And he play'd at the ba';
And the bonnie Earl of Murray
   Was the flower amang them a'.

He was a braw gallant,
   And he play'd at the gluve;
And the bonnie Earl of Murray,
   Oh! he was the Queenes luve.

Oh! lang will his lady
   Look owre the castle Downe,
Ere she see the Earl of Murray,
   Come sounding thro' the towne.

THE EARL O' MURRAY.

This ballad, on the same subject as the preceding, resembles in its structure of verse the fragment of *Bonnie George Campbell.* Several of the phrases employed are all but identical.

OPEN the gates,
   And let him come in;
He is my brother Huntly,
   He'll do him nae harm.

He's ben and ben,
   And ben to his bed;
And with a sharp rapier
   He stabbed him dead.

The lady came down the stair,
   Wringing her hands:
"He has slain the Earl o' Murray,
   The flower o' Scotland."

But Huntly lap on his horse ;
  Rade to the king,
" Ye 're welcome hame, Huntly ;
  And whare hae ye been ?

" Whare hae ye been ?
  And how hae ye sped ? "
" I 've killed the Earl o' Murray,
  Dead in his bed."

" Foul fa' you, Huntly ;
  And why did ye so ?
You might hae taen the Earl of Murray,
  And saved his life too."

" Her bread it 's to bake,
  Her yill is to brew ;
My sister 's a widow,
  And sair do I rue."

" Her corn grows ripe,
  Her meadows grow green ;
But in bonnie Dinnibristle
  I darena be seen."

YOUNG WATERS.

This ballad, like the two former, has been supposed to refer to the fate of the unfortunate Earl of Murray; but this is a mere guess. The allusion to the "Round Table" would seem to throw it back to the fabulous antiquity of the days of King Arthur. There is a longer, and in some respects better version in Buchan's Ancient Ballads; but the version here given is the one commonly accepted.

ABOUT Yule, when the wind blew cool,
    And the round table began;
Ah! there is come to our king's court
    Mony a well-favor'd man.

The queen luikit owre the castle wa',
    Beheld baith dale and down,
And there she saw young Waters,
    Come riding to the town.

His footmen they did rin before,
    His horsemen rode behind,
And his mantle of the burning gowd
    Did keep him frae the wind.

Gowden graith'd his horse before,
    And siller shod behind;
The horse young Waters rade upon
    Was fleeter than the wind.

Out then spak a wylie lord,
    And to the queen said he:
"O tell me wha's the fairest face
    Rides in the company?"

"I've seen lords, and I've seen lairds,
    And knights of high degree,
But a fairer face than young Waters',
    Mine eyne did never see."

Out then spak the jealous king,
　(And an angry man was he):
"An', if he had been twice as fair,
　You might have excepted me."

"You 're neither laird nor lord," she says,
　"But the king that wears the crown;
There 's not a knight in fair Scotland,
　But to thee maun bow down."

For a' that she could do or say,
　Appeased he wadna be;
But for the words which she had said,
　Young Waters he maun die.

Syne they hae ta'en young Waters,
　Put fetters to his feet;
Syne they hae ta'en young Waters,
　An' thrown in dungeon deep.

"Aft I have ridden thro' Stirling town,
　In the wind bot and the weit;
But I ne'er rade through Stirling town
　Wi' fetters at my feet.

"Aft I have ridden thro' Stirling town,
　In the wind bot and the rain;
But I ne'er rode thro' Stirling town
　Ne'er to return again."

They hae ta'en him to the headin' hill,
　That knight sae fair to see;
And for the words the queen had spak,
　Young Waters he did die.

THE BONNIE BANKS O' FORDIE

Is given from two copies obtained from recitation, which differ but little from each other. Indeed, the only variation is in the verse where the outlawed brother unweetingly slays his sister. One reading is—

> "He's taken out his wee penknife,
>   Hey how bonnie;
> And he 's twined her o' her ain sweet life,
>   On the bonnie banks o' Fordie."

The other reading is that adopted in the text. This ballad is popular in the southern parishes of Perthshire, where it is called *The Duke of Perth's Three Daughters;* but where the scene is laid the Editor has not ascertained.— MOTHERWELL.

Professor Aytoun suggests that Baby Lon, which Motherwell calls the "fantastic name" of the hero, is a misprint for "Burd-alane," or a solitary person; and lays the scene at the Burn of Fordie, six miles to the east of Dunkeld. A similar legend is currnt in Denmark.

THERE were three ladies lived in a bower,
  Eh vow bonnie,
And they went out to pull a flower,
  On the bonnie banks o' Fordie.

They hadna pu'ed a flower but ane,
When up started to them a banisht man.

He's ta'en the first sister by her hand,
And he 's turned her round and made her stand.

"Its whether will ye be a rank robber's wife,
Or will ye die by my wee penknife?"

"Its I 'll not be a rank robber's wife,
But I 'll rather die by your wee penknife."

He's killed this May and he 's laid her by,
For to bear the red rose company.

He's taken the second ane by the hand,
And he's turned her round and made her stand.

"Its whether will ye be a rank robber's wife,
Or will ye die by my wee penknife?"

"I 'll not be a rank robber's wife,
But I 'll rather die by your wee penknife."

He's killed this May and he's laid her by,
For to bear the red rose company.

He's taken the youngest ane by the hand,
And he's turned her round and made her stand.

Says, "Will ye be a rank robber's wife,
Or will ye die by my wee penknife?"

"I 'll not be a rank robber's wife,
Nor will I die by your wee penknife;

"For I hae a brother in this wood,
And gin ye kill me, it's he 'll kill thee."

"What's thy brother's name, come tell to me?"
"My brother's name is Baby Lon."*

"O sister, sister, what have I done,
O have I done this ill to thee?

"O since I've done this evil deed,
Good sall never be seen o' me."

He's taken out his wee penknife,
And he's twyned himsel o' his ain sweet life.

* "Baby Lon :" Burd-alane.

THE DÆMON LOVER.

"This ballad, which contains some verses of merit, was taken down from recitation by Mr William Laidlaw, tenant in Traquair-knowe. It contains a legend, which, in various shapes, is current in Scotland. I remember to have heard a ballad in which a fiend is introduced paying his addresses to a beautiful maiden; but, disconcerted by the holy herbs which she wore in her bosom, makes the following lines the burden of his courtship :—

> 'Gin ye wish to be leman mine,
>   Lay aside the St John's wort and the vervain.'

"The heroine of the following tale was unfortunately without any similar protection."—SIR WALTER SCOTT.

Mr Motherwell was of opinion that Mr Laidlaw had "improved" the original ballad to its detriment.

"O WHERE have you been my long, long love,
  This long seven years and mair?"
"O I 'm come to seek my former vows,
  Ye granted me before."

"O hold your tongue of your former vows,
  For they will breed sad strife;
O hold your tongue of your former vows,
  For I am become a wife."

He turned him right and round about,
  And the tear blinded his ee;
"I wad never hae trodden on Irish ground,
  If it had not been for thee.

"I might have had a king's daughter,
  Far, far beyond the sea;
I might have had a king's daughter,
  Had it not been for love o' thee."

"If ye might have had a king's daughter,
  Yersel ye had to blame;
Ye might have taken the king's daughter,
  For ye kend that I was nane."

"O false are the vows o' womankind,
  But fair is their false bodie;
I never wad hae trodden on Irish ground,
  Had it not been for love o' thee."

"If I was to leave my husband dear,
  And my two babes also,
O what have you to take me to,
  If with you I should go?"

"I have seven ships upon the sea,
  The eighth brought me to land;
With four-and-twenty bold mariners,
  And music on every hand."

She has taken up her two little babes,
  Kissed them baith cheek and chin:
"O fare ye weel, my ain twa babes,
  For I'll never see you again."

She set her foot upon the ship,
  No mariners could she behold;
But the sails were o' the taffetie,
  And the masts o' the beaten gold.

She had not sailed a league, a league,
  A league, but barely three,
When dismal grew his countenance,
  And drumlie grew his ee.

The masts that were like the beaten gold,
  Bent not on the heaving seas ;
But the sails, that were o' the taffetie,
  Filled not in the eastland breeze.

They had not sailed a league, a league,
  A league, but barely three,
Until she espied his cloven foot,
  And she wept right bitterlie.

"O hold your tongue of your weeping," says he,
  "Of your weeping now let me be ;
I will shew you how the lilies grow
  On the banks of Italy."

"O what hills are yon, yon pleasant hills,
  That the sun shines sweetly on ?"
"O yon are the hills of heaven," he said,
  "Where you will never win."

"O whaten a mountain is yon," she said,
  "All so dreary wi' frost and snow ?"
"O yon is the mountain of hell," he cried,
  "Where you and I will go."

And aye when she turned her round about,
  Aye taller he seemed to be ;
Until that the tops o' the gallant ship
  Nae taller were than he.

[The clouds grew dark and the wind grew
    loud,
  And the levin filled her ee ;
And waesome wailed the snow-white sprites,
  Upon the gurlie sea.]*

* Professor Aytoun believes this stanza to be an interpolation.

He strack the tapmast wi' his hand,
  The foremast wi' his knee;
And he brake that gallant ship in twain,
  And sank her in the sea.

FAIR JANET.

This is by far the most complete, and apparently
genuine, copy that we have yet met with, of the ballad
which is usually printed under the title of *Willie and
Annet*, or of that improved version of the same ballad,
published by Mr Finlay, under the title of *Sweet Willie*.
It is taken from the "Ballad Book" of Mr Charles Kirkpatrick Sharpe.

To *Fair Janet* Mr Sharpe has prefixed the following
notice :—"This ballad, the subject of which appears to
have been very popular, is printed as it was sung by an
old woman in Perthshire. The air is extremely beautiful."
From the ballads of *Willie and Annet* and *Sweet Willie* we
have taken three stanzas, and inserted them in this copy;
but these are enclosed by brackets, so as to preserve the
purity and integrity of Mr Sharpe's text undisturbed.—
MOTHERWELL.

"YE maun gang to your father, Janet,
  Ye maun gang to him soon;
Ye maun gang to your father, Janet,
  In case that his days are dune!"

Janet's awa' to her father,
  As fast as she could hie;
"O, what's your will wi' me, father?
  O, what's your will wi' me?"

"My will wi' you, Fair Janet," he said,
  "It is both bed and board;
Some say that ye lo'e Sweet Willie,
  But ye maun wed a French Lord."

"A French Lord maun I wed, father?
  A French Lord maun I wed?
Then, by my sooth," quo' Fair Janet,
  "He's ne'er enter my bed."

Janet's awa' to her chamber,
  As fast as she could go;
Wha's the first ane that tapped there,
  But Sweet Willie, her jo!

"O, we maun part this love, Willie,
  That has been lang between;
There's a French Lord coming o'er the sea
  To wed me wi' a ring;
There's a French Lord coming o'er the sea
  To wed and tak me hame."

"If we maun part this love, Janet,
  It causeth mickle woe;
If we maun part this love, Janet,
  It makes me into mourning go."

"But ye maun gang to your three sisters,
  Meg, Marion, and Jean:
Tell them to come to Fair Janet,
  In case that her days are dune."

Willie's awa' to his three sisters,
  Meg, Marion, and Jean:
"O, haste, and gang to Fair Janet;
  I fear that her days are dune."

They drew to them their silken hose,
  They drew to them their shoon,
They drew to them their silk manteils,
  Their coverings to put on;
And they're awa' to Fair Janet,
  By the ae light o' the moon.

*   *   *   *   *

"O, I have born this babe, Willie,
    Wi' mickle toil and pain :
Take hame, take hame, your babe, Willie,
    For nurse I dare be nane."

He's tane his young son in his arms,
    And kist him cheek and chin—
And he's awa' to his mother's bower,
    By the ae light o' the moon.

"O, open, open, mother," he says,
    "O, open, and let me in ;
The rain rains on my yellow hair,
    And the dew drops o'er my chin—
And I hae my young son in my arms,
    I fear that his days are dune."

With her fingers lang and sma'
    She lifted up the pin ;
And with her arms lang and sma'
    Received the baby in.

"Gae back, gae back, now Sweet Willie,
    And comfort your fair lady ;
For where ye had but ae nourice
    Your young son shall hae three."

Willie he was scarce awa',
    And the lady put to bed,
When in and came her father dear,
    "Make haste, and busk the bride."

"There's a sair pain in my head, father,
　There's a sair pain in my side;
And ill, O ill, am I, father,
　This day for to be a bride."

"O ye maun busk this bonnie bride,
　And put a gay mantle on;
For she shall wed this auld French Lord,
　Gin she should die the morn."

Some put on the gay green robes,
　And some put on the brown,
But Janet put on the scarlet robes,
　To shine foremost through the town.

And some they mounted the black steed,
　And some mounted the brown,
But Janet mounted the milk-white steed,
　To ride foremost through the town.

"O, wha will guide your horse, Janet?
　O, wha will guide him best?"
"O, wha but Willie, my true love?
　He kens I lo'e him best!"

And when they cam to Marie's kirk,
　To speak the holy name,
Fair Janet's cheek looked pale and wan,
　And her colour gaed and came.

When dinner it was past and done,
　And dancing to begin;
"O, we'll go take the bride's maidens,
　And we'll go fill the ring."

O ben then cam the auld French Lord,
   Saying, "Bride, will ye dance with me?"
"Awa', awa', ye auld French Lord,
   Your face I downa see."

O ben then came now Sweet Willie,
   He came with ane advance;
"O, I'll go tak the bride's maidens,
   And we'll go tak a dance."

"I've seen ither days wi' you, Willie,
   And so has mony mae;
Ye would hae danced wi' me mysel,
   Let a' my maidens gae."

O ben then came now Sweet Willie,
   Saying, "Bride, will ye dance wi' me?"
"Ay, by my sooth, and that I will,
   Gin my back should break in three."

[And she's ta'en Willie by the hand;
   The tear blinded her ee;
"O, I wad dance wi' my true love,
   Tho' burst my heart in three!"]

She hadna turned her through the dance,
   Through the dance but thrice,
When she fell down at Willie's feet,
   And up did never rise!

[She's ta'en her bracelet frae her arm,
   Her garter frae her knee;
"Gie that, gie that to my young son,
   He'll ne'er his mother see."]

Willie's ta'en the key of his coffer,
    And gi'en it to his man,
"Gae hame and tell my mother dear,
    My horse he has me slain.;
Bid her be kind to my young son,
    For father he has nane."

["Gar deal, gar deal the bread," he cried,
    "Gar deal, gar deal the wine,
This day has seen my true love's death,
    This night shall witness mine."]

The tane was buried in Marie's kirk,
    And the tither in Marie's quier.
Out of the tane there grew a birk,
    And the tither a bonnie brier.*

BARBARA ALLAN.

From Allan Ramsay's "Tea-Table Miscellany."   A
longer though inferior version appeared in Percy's Reliques.

It was in and about the Martinmas time,
    When the green leaves they were fallen,
That Sir John Graem, in the west country,
    Fell in love with Barbara Allan.

He sent his man down through the town,
    To the place where she was dwelling;
"O haste and come to my master dear,
    Gin you be Barbara Allan."

* This verse is the common property of all the ballad-
makers—a despised stage-decoration that does duty whenever and wherever it is wanted.

O hooly, hooly rose she up,
    To the place where he was lying,
And when she drew the curtain, said,
    "Young man, I think you 're dying."

"O I am sick and very sick,
    And it 's all for Barbara Allan."
"O the better for me ye 's never be,
    Tho' your heart's blood were a-spillin'.

"O dinna ye mind, young man," said she,
    "When the red wine ye were fillin',
That ye made the healths gae round and round,
    And slighted Barbara Allan ?"

He turned his face unto the wall,
    And death was with him dealing ;
"Adieu, adieu, my dear friends all,
    Be kind to Barbara Allan."

Slowly, slowly rose she up,
    And slowly, slowly left him,
And sighing, said, she could not stay,
    Since death of life had left him.

She had not gone a mile but twa,
    When she heard the dead-bell knellin',
And every jow that the dead-bell gied,
    Cried, "Woe to Barbara Allan !"

"O mother, mother, make my bed,
    O make it fast and narrow ;
Since my love died for me to-day,
    I 'll die for him to-morrow."

FAIR HELEN OF KIRCONNEL.

The following very popular ballad has been handed down by tradition in its present imperfect state. The affecting incident on which it is founded is well known. A lady, of the name of Helen Irving, or Bell, (for this is disputed by the two clans,) daughter of the laird of Kirconnel, in Dumfriesshire, and celebrated for her beauty, was beloved by two gentlemen in the neighbourhood. The name of the favoured suitor was Adam Fleming, of Kirkpatrick; that of the other has escaped tradition, though it has been alleged that he was a Bell, of Blacket House. The addresses of the latter were, however, favoured by the friends of the lady, and the lovers were therefore obliged to meet in secret, and by night, in the churchyard of Kirconnel, a romantic spot, surrounded by the river Kirtle. During one of these private interviews, the jealous and despised lover suddenly appeared on the opposite bank of the stream, and levelled his carbine at the breast of his rival. Helen threw herself before her lover, received in her bosom the bullet, and died in his arms. A desperate and mortal combat ensued between Fleming and the murderer, in which the latter was cut to pieces. Other accounts say that Fleming pursued his enemy to Spain, and slew him in the streets of Madrid.—SIR W. SCOTT.

I WISH I were where Helen lies!
Night and day on me she cries;
O that I were where Helen lies,
    On fair Kirconnel Lee!

Curst be the heart that thought the thought,
And curst the hand that fired the shot,
When in my arms burd* Helen dropt,
    And died to succour me!

O think na ye my heart was sair,
When my love dropt down and spak nae mair!
There did she swoon wi' meikle care,
    On fair Kirconnel Lee.

* "Burd:" maid.

As I went down the water side,
None but my foe to be my guide,
None but my foe to be my guide
    On fair Kirconnel Lee ;

I lighted down, my sword did draw,
I hacked him in pieces sma',
I hacked him in pieces sma',
    For her sake that died for me.

O Helen fair, beyond compare !
I 'll make a garland of thy hair,
Shall bind my heart for evermair,
    Until the day I die.

O that I were where Helen lies !
Night and day on me she cries ;
Out of my bed she bids me rise,
    Says, " Haste, and come to me !"

O Helen fair ! O Helen chaste !
If I were with thee, I were blest,
Where thou lies low, and takes thy rest,
    On fair Kirconnel Lee.

I wish my grave were growing green,
A winding sheet drawn ower my een,
And I in Helen's arms lying.
    On fair Kirconnel Lee.

I wish I were where Helen lies !
Night and day on me she cries ;
And I am weary of the skies,
    For her sake that died for me.

This ballad has often been imitated, but never improved. The reader who remembers Tennyson's *Oriana*
may see at what fire the modern poet lighted his torch in
that beautiful composition.

CLERK SAUNDERS.

"This ballad is taken from Mr Herd's MSS., with several corrections from a shorter and more imperfect copy, in the same volume, and one or two conjectural emendations in the arrangement of the stanzas. The resemblance of the conclusion to the ballad beginning, 'There came a ghost to Margaret's door,' will strike every reader. The tale is uncommonly wild and beautiful, and apparently very correct. The custom of the passing bell is still kept up in many villages in Scotland. The sexton goes through the town ringing a small bell, and announcing the death of the departed, and the time of the funeral. The three concluding verses have been recovered since the first edition of this work; and I am informed by the reciter, that it was usual to separate from the rest that part of the ballad which follows the death of the lovers, as belonging to another story. For this, however, there seems no necessity, as other authorities give the whole as a complete tale."—SIR WALTER SCOTT.

Two different copies of this ballad have been published; the one by Sir Walter Scott, in "The Minstrelsy of the Scottish Border," which is followed here, and the other by Mr Jamieson, which, though of inferior beauty, is not the less valuable, as illustrating the transmutations to which traditionary song is inevitably subjected. To the copy we have adopted, we were almost inclined to prefix the following verses, which begin the copy preserved by Mr Jamieson :—

> "Clerk Saunders was an earl's son,
> He lived upon sea sand;
> May Margaret was a king's daughter,
> She lived in upper land.
>
> "Clerk Saunders was an earl's son,
> Weel learned at the scheel;
> May Margaret was a king's daughter,
> They baith lo'ed ither weel."

Because they supply information as to the rank in society respectively held by these ill-fated lovers, and by hinting at the scholastic acquirements of Clerk Saunders, they prepare us for the casuistry by which he seeks to reconcile May Margaret's conscience to a most jesuitical oath. —MOTHERWELL.

Clerk Saunders and May Margaret,
    Walked over yon garden green ;
And sad and heavy was the love
    That fell thir twa between.

" A bed, a bed," Clerk Saunders said,
    " A bed for you and me !"
" Fye, na, fye, na," said May Margaret,
    " Till anes we married be.

" For in may come my seven bauld brothers,
    Wi' torches burning bright ;
They 'll say—' We hae but ae sister,
    And behold she 's wi' a knight !'"

" Then take the sword frae my scabbard,
    And slowly lift the pin ;
And you may swear, and save your aith,
    Ye ne'er let Clerk Saunders in.

" And take a napkin in your hand,
    And tie up baith your een ;
And ye may swear, and safe your aith,
    Ye saw me na since late yestreen."

It was about the midnight hour,
    When they asleep were laid,
When in and cam her seven brothers,
    Wi' torches burning red.

When in and cam her seven brothers,
    Wi' torches shining bright ;
They said—" We hae but ae sister,
    And behold her wi' a knight !"

Then out and spake the first o' them,
  "My sword shall gar him die!"
And out and spake the second o' them,
  "His father has nae mair than he!"

And out and spake the third o' them,
  "I wot they're lovers dear!"
And out and spake the fourth o' them,
  "They hae been in love this mony a year!"

Then out and spake the fifth o' them,
  "'Twere sin true love to twain!"
And out and spake the sixth o' them,
  "It were shame to slay a sleeping man!"

Then up and gat the seventh o' them,
  And never a word spake he;
But he has striped his bright brown brand,
  Out through Clerk Saunders' fair bodye.

Clerk Saunders he started, and Margaret she
      turned
  Into his arms as asleep she lay;
And sad and silent was the night
  That was atween thir twae.

And they lay still and sleeped sound,
  'Till the day began to daw,
And kindly to him she did say,
  "Its time, true love, you were awa."

But he lay still and sleeped sound,
  Though the sun began to sheen;
She looked atween her and the wa',
  And dull and drowsie were his een.

Then in and came her father dear,
　　Said—"Let a' your mourning be ;
I 'll carry the dead corpse to the clay,
　　And I 'll come back and comfort thee."

"Comfort weel your seven sons,
　　For comforted will I never be ;
I ween 'twas neither knave nor lown
　　Was in the bower last night wi' me."

The clinking bell gaed through the town,
　　To carry the dead corpse to the clay ;
And Clerk Saunders stood at May Margaret's
　　　window,
　　I wot, an hour before the day.

"Are ye sleeping, Margaret ?" he says,
　　"Or are ye wauking presently ?
Give me my faith and troth again,
　　I wot, true love, I gave to thee."

"Your faith and troth ye sall never get,
　　Nor our true love sall never twin,
Until ye come within my bower,
　　And kiss me cheek and chin."

"My mouth it is full cold, Margaret,
　　It has the smell now of the ground ;
And if I kiss thy comely mouth,
　　Thy days of life will not be lang.

"O cocks are crowing a merry midnight,
　　I wot, the wild-fowls are boding day ;
Give me my faith and troth again,
　　And let me fare upon my way."

"Thy faith and troth thou sall na get,
   And our true love sall never twin,
Until ye tell what comes of women,
   I wat, who die in strong traivelling."

"Their beds are made in the heavens high,
   Down at the feet of our good Lord's knee,
Weel set about wi' gillyflowers,
   I wot, sweet company for to see.

"O cocks are crowing a merry midnight,
   I wot, the wild-fowls are boding day;
The psalms of heaven will soon be sung,
   And I ere now will be missed away."

Then she has ta'en a crystal wand,
   And she has stroken her troth thereon;
She has given it him out at the shot window,
   Wi' mony a sigh and heavy groan.

"I thank ye, Marg'ret; I thank ye, Marg'ret;
   And aye I thank ye heartilie;
Gin ever the dead come for the quick,
   Be sure, Marg'ret, I 'll come for thee."

It 's hosen and shoon, and gown alone,
   She climbed the wall and followed him,
Until she came to the green forest,
   And there she lost the sight o' him.

"Is there ony room at your head, Saunders?
   Is there ony room at your feet?
Or ony room at your side, Saunders,
   Where fain, fain I would sleep?"

"There's nae room at my head, Marg'ret,
   There's nae room at my feet;
My bed it is full lowly now:
   Amang the hungry worms I sleep.

"Cauld mould is my covering now,
   But and my winding sheet:
The dew it falls nae sooner down,
   Than my resting place is weet.

"But plait a wand o' bonnie birk,
   And lay it on my breast;
And shed a tear upon my grave,
   And wish my saul gude rest.

"And fair Marg'ret, and rare Marg'ret,
   And Marg'ret o' veritie,
Gin ere ye love another man,
   Ne'er love him as ye did me."

Then up and crew the milk-white cock,
   And up and crew the gray;
Her lover vanished in the air,
   And she gaed weeping away.

WILLIE AND MAY MARGARET;

OR, THE TWO CRUEL MOTHERS.

Published in a complete state by Motherwell, as procured by Mr Jamieson from Mrs Brown of Falkland,—a lady to whom much of the traditionary poetry of Scotland is indebted for preservation. Motherwell added several stanzas in the appendix to his volume, and completed the story; which has since been adopted by Mr R. Chambers, Mr P. Buchan, and Professor Aytoun. The additions, with the exception of the opening stanza, have been pre-

served in the following ; though, as a work of art, the
fragment was more beautiful than the entire ballad.

    "Gie corn to my horse, mither,
        Gie meat unto my man ;
    For I maun gang to Margaret's bower
        Before the nicht comes on."

    "O, stay at hame, my son Willie !
        The wind blaws cald and dour ;
    The nicht will be baith mirk and late
        Before ye reach her bower."

    "O, though the night were never sae dark,
        Or the wind blew never sae cauld,
    I will be in May Margaret's bower
        Before twa hours be tauld."

    "O, gin ye gang to May Margaret,
        Without the leave of me,
    Clyde's water's wide and deep enough ;—
        My malison drown thee !"

    He mounted on his coal-black steed,
        And fast he rade awa' ;
    But, ere he came to Clyde water,
        Fu' loud the wind did blaw.

    As he rode o'er yon high, high hill,
        And down yon dowie den,
    There was a roar in Clyde's water
        Wad fear'd a hunder men.

    His heart was warm, his pride was up ;
        Sweet Willie kentna fear ;
    But yet his mother's malison
        Aye sounded in his ear.

O, he has swam through Clyde water
　Though it was wide and deep;
And he came to May Margaret's door
　When a' were fast asleep.

O, he 's gane round and round about,
　And tirled at the pin;
But doors were steek'd, and windows barr'd,
　And nane wad let him in.

"O, open the door to me, Margaret—
　O, open and let me in!
For my boots are full o' Clyde's water,
　And frozen to the brim."

"I darena open the door to you,
　Nor darena let you in;
For my mither she is fast asleep,
　And I darena mak a din."

"O, gin ye winna open the door,
　Nor yet be kind to me,
Now tell me o' some out-chamber
　Where I this nicht may be."

"Ye canna win in this nicht, Willie,
　Nor here ye canna be;
For I 've nae chambers out nor in,
　Nae ane but barely three:

"The ta'en o' them is fu' o' corn,
　The tither is fu' o' hay—
The tither is fu' o' merry young men;
　They winna remove till day."

"O, fare ye weel, then, May Margaret,
  Sin' better maunna be;
I 've won my mother's malison,
  Coming this nicht to thee."

He 's mounted on his coal-black steed—
  O, but his heart was wae!
But ere he came to Clyde water,
  'Twas half up o'er the brae.

When he came to Clyde's water,
  'Twas flowing ower the brim;
The rushing that was in Clyde's water
  Took Willie's cane frae him.

He leaned him ower his saddle bow,
  To catch his cane again;
The rushing that was in Clyde's water
  Took Willie's hat frae him.

He leaned him ower his saddle bow,
  To catch his hat by force;
The rushing that was in Clyde's water
  Took Willie frae his horse.

His brother stood upon the bank,
  Says, "Fye, man, will ye drown?
Ye 'll turn ye to your high horse head,
  And learn ye how to soom."

"How can I turn to my high horse head,
  And learn me how to soom?
I 've gotten my mother's malison,
  It 's here that I maun droon."

The very hour the young man sank
  Into the pot sae deep,
Up it waken'd her, May Marg'ret,
  Out of her drowsy sleep.

"Come here, come hear, my mother dear,
  And read this dreary dream ;
I dreamed my love was at our yetts,
  And nane wuld let him in."

"Lye still, lye still now, May Marg'ret,
  Lye still, and tak your rest,
Syn your true love was at your yetts,
  Its but twa quarters past."

Nimbly, nimbly raise she up,
  And nimbly put she on ;
And the higher that the lady cried,
  The louder blew the win'.

The firsten step that she stepped,
  She stepped to the cuit—*
"Ohon! alas!" said that ladie,
  "This water's wondrous deep."

The neister step that she wade in
  She waded till the knee,
Says she, "I would wade further in,
  Gin I my love could see."

The neister step that she wade in
  She waded to the chin ;
The deepest pot† in Clyde water
  She got Sweet Willie in.

* "Cuit :" ankle.   † "Pot :" hole.

"You 've had a cruel mother, Willie,
And I have had another;
But we shall sleep in Clyde water,
Like sister and like brother."

THE MARCHIONESS OF DOUGLAS.

This ballad, evidently very imperfect and corrupt, was inserted in the Appendix to Motherwell's volume, under the title of *Lord James Douglas*. Mr Robert Chambers calls it more appropriately *The Marchioness of Douglas;* but his version differs considerably from that preserved by Motherwell. Professor Aytoun has published a third reading, from collation with ballads supplied to him in the MS. collection of Mr Kinloch. Several of the stanzas, it will be observed, are identical, or nearly so, with the beautiful ballad of *Waly! Waly!* published in Allan Ramsay's "Tea-Table Miscellany,"—a ballad considered the very flower and gem of Scottish traditionary and popular poetry. It is extremely difficult to decide which of the two is the original, and whether *Waly! Waly!* is an abbreviation of *The Marchioness of Douglas*, or *The Marchioness of Douglas* an expansion of *Waly! Waly!* The story narrated in all these poems is that of Lady Barbara Erskine, daughter of John, the ninth Earl of Mar, and wife of James, second Marquis of Douglas. "This lady," says Mr Robert Chambers, " was divorced, or at least expelled from the society of her husband, in consequence of some malignant scandals which a former and disappointed lover, Lowrie of Blackwood, was so base as to insinuate into the ear of her husband. What added greatly to the distress of the case was, that she was confined in childbed at the time when the plot took effect against her. Her father, on hearing what had taken place, came and conveyed her away. . . . It must be allowed to add greatly to the pathetic interest of the ballad that it refers, not, as hitherto supposed, to an unfortunate amour, but to the more meritorious distresses

of wedded love."   It is not recorded in history or bio-
graphy that the marquis and marchioness ever met again
after their separation; and there is no warrant whatever
for the fate of the traitor Blackwood, recorded in the
ballad.

O WALY, waly up the bank,
  And waly, waly down the brae
And waly, waly by yon burn side,
  Where me and my lord wont to gae.
Hey nonny, nonnie! but love is bonnie,
  A little while when it is new;
But when it's auld it grows mair cauld,
  And fades away like the morning dew.

I lean'd my back against an aik,
  And thocht it was a trustie tree,
But first it bowed and syne it break,
  And sae did my fause luve to me.
My mother tauld me when I was young,
  That young man's love was ill to trow,
But until her I would give nae ear,
  And alas! my ain wand dings me now!

O wherefore need I busk my head?
  Or wherefore should I kaim my hair?
For my good lord has me forsook,
  And says he'll never love me mair.
Gin I had wist or I had kist,
  That love had been sae ill to win,
I would hae lockt my heart wi' a key o' gowd,
  And pinn'd it wi' a siller pin.

An I had kent what I ken now,
  I'd never crost the water o' Tay,
But stayèd still at Athole's gates,
  He would have made me his lady gay.

When lords and lairds cam to this toun,
  And gentlemen o' high degree,
I took my young son in my arms,
  And went to my chamber pleasantlie.

But when lords and lairds come through this
    toun,
  And gentlemen o' high degree,
I must sit alane intil the dark,
  And the babie on the nurse's knee.
Awa, awa, thou fause Blackwood,
  Aye, and an ill death may thou die;
Thou wert the first and occasion last
  Of parting my gude lord and me.

When I lay sick, and very sick,
  Sick I was and like to die,
A gentleman, a friend of mine,
  He came on purpose to visit me;
But Blackwood whispered in my lord's ear
  He was ower lang in chamber with me,
When I was sick and very sick,
  Sick I was and like to die.

I drew me near to my stairhead,
  And I heard my ain lord lichtly me;
Come down, come down, O Jamie Douglas,
  And drink the orange wine with me,
I 'll set thee on a chair of gold,
  And daut thee kindly on my knee.

When sea and sand turn far inland,
  And mussels grow on ilka tree;
When cockle shells turn siller bells,
  I 'll drink the orange wine wi' thee.

What ails you at our youngest son,
      That sits upon the nurse's knee?
I 'm sure he 's never done any harm,
      An it 's not to his ain nurse and me.

When my father came to hear
      That my gay lord had forsaken me,
He sent five score of his soldiers bright
      To take me safe to my ain countrie.
Up in the mornin' when I arose,
      My bonnie palace for to lea',
I whispered in at my lord's window,
      But the never a word he would answer me.

Fare ye weel, then, Jamie Douglas,
      I need care as little as ye for me;
The Earl of Mar is my father dear,
      And I soon will see my ain countrie.
Ye thought that I was like yoursel,
      And loving ilk ane I did see;
But here I swear by the heavens clear,
      I never loved a man but thee.

Slowly, slowly rose I up,
      And slowly, slowly I cam down;
And when he saw me sit in my coach,
      He made his drums and trumpets sound.
When I into my coach was set,
      My tenants all were with me tane;
They set them down upon their knees,
      And begg'd me to come back again.

It 's fare ye weel, my bonnie palace,
      And fare ye weel, my children three;
God grant your father may get mair grace,
      And love thee better than he has done me.

It 's fare ye weel, my servants all,
   And you, my bonnie children three,
God grant your father grace to be kind
   Till I see you safe in my ain countrie.
But wae be to you, fause Blackwood,
   Aye, and ill death may you die ;
Ye are the first, and I hope the last,
   That put strife between my good lord and
     me.

When I came in through Edinburgh town,
   My loving father came to meet me,
With trumpets sounding on every side ;
   But it was no comfort at all to me,
For no mirth nor music sounds in my ear,
   Since the Earl of Mar has forsaken me.

" Hold your tongue, my daughter dear,
   And of your weeping, pray let be ;
For I 'll send to him a bill of divorce,
   And I 'll get as good a lord to thee."
" Hold your tongue, my father dear,
   And of your scoffing, pray let be ;
I would rather hae a kiss o' my ain lord's
     mouth
   Than all the lords in the north countrie."

When she came to her father's land,
   The tenants a' cam out to see ;
Never a word she could speak to them,
   But the buttons aff her clothes did flee.
" The linnet is a bonnie bird,
   And aften flees far frae its nest ;
So all the world may plainly see
   They 're far awa that I love best !"

N

She looked out at her father's window,
   To take a view of the countrie;
Wha did she see but Jamie Douglas,
   And along with him her children
      three.
There came a soldier to the gate,
   And he did knock right hastilie:
"If Lady Douglas be within,
   Bid her come down and speak to me.

"O come away, my lady fair,
   Come away, now, alang with me;
For I have hanged fause Blackwood
   At the very place where he told the
      lie."

WALY, WALY, UP THE BANK.

This ballad is founded upon, and mainly extracted from
the preceding. It bears upon it the marks of a master-
hand in popular poetry, and first appeared in Allan Ramsay's "Tea-Table Miscellany" with the signature of "Z,"
shewing that it was of an antiquity unknown to the
Editor.

O, WALY, waly up the bank,
   And waly, waly down the brae,
And waly, waly yon burnside,
   Where I and my love wont to gae.
I leaned my back unto an aik,
   An' thocht it was a trusty tree,
But first it bowed, and syne it brak,
   Sae my true love did lichtly me.

O waly, waly, but love is bonnie
    A little time while it is new,
But when it's auld it waxes cauld,
    And fades away like morning dew.
O wherefore should I busk my head,
    Or wherefore should I kame my hair,
For my true love has me forsook,
    And says he 'll never love me mair.

Now Arthur's Seat * shall be my bed,
    The sheets shall ne'er be pressed† by
      me,
St Anton's well shall be my drink,
    Since my true love has forsaken me.
Martinmas wind, when wilt thou blaw,
    And shake the green leaves off the tree!
O gentle Death, when wilt thou come,
    For of my life I am wearie!

'Tis not the frost that freezes fell,
    Nor blawing snaw's inclemencie,
'Tis not sic cauld that makes me cry,
    But my love's heart's grown cauld to
      me.
When we came in by Glasgow toun
    We were a comely sicht to see;
My love was clad in the black velvet,
    And I mysel in cramasie.

* Arthur's Seat, the picturesque and romantic hill
that overlooks Edinburgh, and forms part of the chase or
park which surrounds the ancient palace of Holyrood.
St Anthony's well is a small spring on the side of the hill,
which takes its name from a hermitage that it formerly
supplied with water.
† "Pressed:" filed or defiled in the original.

But had I wist before I kist
  That love had been sae ill to win,
I 'd locked my heart in a case of gold,
  And pinned it wi' a siller pin.
Oh, oh ! if my young babe were born,
  And set upon the nurse's knee,
And I myself were dead and gane,
  And the green grass growing over me !*

LADY MARY ANN.

"I have extracted these beautiful stanzas from Johnson's 'Poetical Museum.' They are worthy of being better known—a circumstance which may lead to a discovery of the persons whom they celebrate."—*Scottish Historical and Romantic Ballads*, vol. i. Edin. 1808. The stanza are certainly beautiful, and it is probable they may refer to some of the Dundonald family. The thrifty habits of one lady of that noble house, at least, have already been commemorated in some wretched stuff, still preserved by tradition in Paisley :—

> " My lady Dundonald sits singing and spinning,
>   Drawing a thread frae her tow rock ;
>   And it weel sets me for to wear a gude cloak,
>   And I span ilka thread o't mysel, so 1 did."

—MOTHERWELL.

O LADY MARY ANN looks o'er the castle wa',
She saw three bonnie boys playing at the ba',
The youngest he was the flower among them a';
  My bonnie laddie 's young, but he 's growin' yet.

* "For a maid again I'll never be : "
is the reading in Allan Ramsay's version; but one less pathetic, less beautiful, and less delicate than the line as amended from the recitation of an " old nurse," and which is now most commonly, and very properly, adopted.

O father, O father, an' ye think it fit,
We 'll send him a year to the college yet;
We 'll sew a green ribbon round about his hat,
And that will let them ken he 's to marry yet.

Lady Mary Ann was a flower in the dew,
Sweet was its smell, and bonnie was its hue,
And the langer it blossomed, the sweeter it grew;
For the lily in the bud will be bonnier yet.

Young Charlie Cochran was the sprout of an aik,
Bonnie and blooming and straight was its make,
The sun took delight to shine for its sake;
And it will be the brag o' the forest yet.

The summer is gane when the leaves they were
 green,
And the days are awa' that we hae seen,
But far better days I trust will come again;
For my bonnie laddie 's young, but he 's growin'
 yet.

JOHN THOMSON AND THE TURK.

This curious ballad is of respectable antiquity. Dunbar
has written a piece, entitled, *Prayer that the King war
John Thomsoun's man*, the fourth line of each stanza
being, "God gif ye war John Thomsoun, man!" In his
note on this poem, Mr Pinkerton says: "This is a proverbial expression, meaning a henpecked husband. I
have little doubt but the original proverb was *Joan* Thomson's man; *man*, in Scotland, signifies either *husband* or
servant." Pinkerton was ignorant of the existence of the
ballad: had he been acquainted with it, he would have
saved himself the trouble of writing a foolish conjecture.
Colville, in his *Whigs' Supplication, or the Scotch Hudibras*,
alludes twice to John Thomson :—

> "We read in greatest warriors' lives,
> They oft were ruled by their wives, &c.
> And so the imperious Roxalan
> Made the great Turk Johne Thomson's man."

Again—

> " —— And these we ken,
> Have ever been John Thomson's men,
> That is still ruled by their wives."

Pennicuik, in his *Linton Address to the Prince of Orange*,
also alludes to the proverbial expression—

> "Our *Lintoun* wives shall blaw the coal,
> And women here, as weel we ken,
> Would have us all *John Thomson's* men."

Two or three stanzas of the ballad were known to Dr
Leyden when he published his edition of the *Complaynt of
Scotland*. These he has given in the glossary appended
to that work.

In Kelly's Proverbs, London, 1721, there is this notice
of the proverb: "Better be John Thomson's man than
Ringan Dinn's or John Knox's;" and Kelly gives this
gloss: "John Thomson's man is he that is complaisant
to his wife's humours; Ringan Dinn's is he whom his
wife scolds; John Knox's is he whom his wife beats." In
the West Country, my friend, Mr A. Crawford, informs

me that when a company are sitting together sociably, and a neighbour drops in, it is usual to welcome him thus—"Come awa, we're a' John Tamson's bairns."—MOTHER-WELL.

JOHN THOMSON fought against the Turks
    Three years, intil a far countrie;
And all that time, and something mair,
    Was absent from his gay ladie.

But it fell ance upon a time,
    As this young chieftain sat alane,
He spied his lady in rich array,
    As she walk'd ower a rural plain.

"What brought ye here, my lady gay,
    So far awa from your ain countrie?
I've thought lang, and very lang,
    And all for your fair face to see."

For some days she did with him bide,
    Till it fell ance upon a day,
"Fareweel, for a time," she said,
    "For now I must boun hame away."

He's gi'en to her a jewel fine,
    Was set with pearl and precious stane;
Says, "My love, beware of these savages bold
    That's in your way as ye gang hame.

"Ye'll tak the road, my lady fair,
    That leads you fair across the lea:
That keeps you from wild Hind Soldan,
    And likewise from base Violentrie."

Wi' heavy heart thir twa did pairt,
   She mintet as she wuld gae hame;
Hind Soldan by the Greeks was slain,
   But to base Violentrie she's gane.

When a twelvemonth had expired,
   John Thomson he thought wondrous lang,
And he has written a braid letter,
   And sealed it weel wi' his ain hand.

He sent it with a small vessel
   That there was quickly gaun to sea;
And sent it on to fair Scotland,
   To see about his gay ladie.

But the answer he received again—
   The lines did grieve his heart right sair:
Nane of her friends there had her seen,
   For a twelvemonth and something mair.

Then he put on a Palmer's weed,
   And took a pike-staff in his hand;
To Violentrie's castel he hied,
   But slowly, slowly he did gang.

When within the hall he came,
   He jooked and couch'd out ower his tree;
"If ye be lady of this hall,
   Some of your good bountith gie me."

"What news, what news, Palmer?" she said,
   "And from what far countrie cam ye?"
"I'm lately come from Grecian plains,
   Where lies some of the Scots armie."

" If ye be come from Grecian plains,
    Some mair news I will ask of thee—
Of one of the chieftains that lies there,
    If he has lately seen his gay ladie."

" It is twa months and something mair,
    Since we did pairt on yonder plain ;
And now this knight has began to fear
    One of his foes he has her ta'en."

" He has not ta'en me by force nor slight,
    It was a' by my ain free will ;
He may tarry into the fight,
    For here I mean to tarry still.

" And if John Thomson ye do see,
    Tell him I wish him silent sleep ;
His head was not so coziely,
    Nor yet sa weel as lies at my feet."

With that he threw aff his disguise,
    Laid by the mask that he had on ;
Said, " Hide me now, my lady fair,
    For Violentrie will soon be hame."

" For the love I bore thee ance,
    I 'll strive to hide thee if I can."
Then she put him down in a dark cellar
    Where there lay many a new-slain man.

But he hadna in the cellar been,
    Not an hour but barely three,
Than hideous was the noise he heard,
    When in at the gate cam Violentrie.

Says, "I wish you well, my lady fair,
    It's time for us to sit to dine;
Come, serve me with the good white bread,
    And likewise with the claret wine.

"That Scots chieftain, our mortal fae,
    Sae aft frae field has made us flee,
Ten thousand zechins this day I'll give
    That I his face could only see."

"Of that same gift wuld ye give me—
    I fairly hold you at your word—
If I wuld bring him unto thee?
    Come ben, John Thomson, to my lord."

Then from the vault John Thomson came,
    Wringing his hands most piteouslie,
"What would ye do," the Turk he cried,
    "If ye had me as I hae thee?"

"If I had you as ye have me,
    I'll tell you what I'd do to thee;
I'd hang you up in good green wood,
    And cause your ain hand wale the tree.

"I meant to stick you with my knife
    For kissing my beloved ladie."
"But that same weed ye've shaped for me,
    It quickly shall be sewed for thee."

Then to the wood they baith are gane;
    John Thomson clamb frae tree to tree;
And aye he sighed and said, "Och hone,
    Here comes the day that I must die."

He tied a ribbon on every branch,
    Put up a flag his men might see;
But little did his false faes ken
    He meant them any injurie.

He set his horn unto his mouth,
    And he has blawn baith loud and shrill:
And then three thousand armed men
    Cam tripping all out ower the hill.

"Deliver us our chief," they all did cry;
    "It's by our hand that ye must die."
"Here is your chief," the Turk replied,
    With that fell on his bended knee.

"O mercy, mercy, good fellows all,
    Mercy, I pray you'll grant to me;"
"Such mercy as ye meant to give,
    Such mercy we shall give to thee."

This Turk they in his castel burnt,
    That stood upon yon hill so hie;
John Thomson's gay ladie they took
    And hanged her on the greenwood tree!

THE CRUEL MOTHER.

A small fragment of this ballad appeared in the introductory note to the ballad of *Lady Anne*, printed in "The Border Minstrelsy," vol. ii. Through the kindness of a friend we are now enabled to give the ballad in a complete state. Like many other ancient pieces of a similar description, it has a burden of no meaning and much childishness, the repetition of which, at the end of the first and third lines of every stanza, has been omitted. The reader, however, has a right to have the ballad as we received it, and therefore he may, in the first of the places pointed out, insert—

> "Three, three, and three by three;"

and in the second—

> "Three, three, and thirty-three;"

which will give him it entire and unmutilated.—MOTHERWELL.

SHE leaned her back unto a thorn,
And there she has her two babes born.

She took frae 'bout her ribbon-belt,
And there she bound them hand and foot.

She has ta'en out her wee penknife,
And there she ended baith their life.

She has howked a hole baith deep and wide,
She has put them in baith side by side.

She has covered them o'er wi' a marble stane,
Thinking she would gang maiden hame.

As she was walking by her father's castle wa',
She saw twa pretty babes playing at the ba'.

"O bonnie babes, gin ye were mine,
I would dress you up in satin fine!

"O, I would dress you in the silk,
And wash you aye in morning milk!"

"O cruel mother, we were thine,
And thou made us to wear the twine.

"O cursed mother! heaven 's high,
And that 's where thou will ne'er win nigh.

"O cursed mother! hell is deep,
And there thou 'll enter step by step."

THE FIRE OF FRENDRAUGHT.

For the recovery of this interesting ballad, hitherto supposed to have been lost, the public is indebted to the industrious research of Charles Kirkpatrick Sharpe, Esq., of Edinburgh. It has already appeared in a small volume of exceeding rarity, privately printed at Edinburgh, in the beginning of 1824, under the title of *A North Countrie Garland*; but with the disadvantage of containing a very considerable number of slight verbal and literal inaccuracies, which in the present copy are carefully corrected by collation with Mr Sharpe's MS. The ballad itself has a high degree of poetic merit, and probably was written at the time by an eye-witness of the event which it records; for there is a horrid vivacity of colouring and circumstantial minuteness in the description of the agonies of the unhappy sufferers which none but a spectator could have given.

The guilt or innocence of Frendraught and his Lady has been, and, perhaps, will always be, problematical; it were but a fruitless waste of words now to seek to prove the one or to establish the other.

Spalding, whom Gordon, in his "History of the Illustrious Family of Gordon," says, "lived not far from the place, and had his account from eye-witnesses," minutely details the circumstances on which the ballad is founded.

THE eighteenth of October,
  A dismal tale to hear,
How good Lord John and Rothiemay
  Were both burnt in the fire.

When steeds was saddled and well bridled,
  And ready for to ride,
Then out came her and false Frendraught,
  Inviting them to bide.

Said—"Stay this night until we sup,
  The morn until we dine;
'Twill be a token of good 'greement
  'Twixt your good Lord and mine."

"We'll turn again," said good Lord John—
  "But no," said Rothiemay—
"My steed's trapann'd, my bridle's broke,
  I fear the day I'm fey."

When mass was sung, and bells was rung,
  And all men bound for bed,
Then good Lord John and Rothiemay
  In one chamber were laid.

They had not long cast off their cloaths,
  And were but now asleep—
When the weary smoke began to rise,
  Likewise the scorching heat.

"O waken, waken, Rothiemay,
  O waken, brother dear,
And turn you to our Saviour—
  There is strong treason here."

When they were dressed in their cloaths,
    And ready for to boun ;
The doors and windows was all secured
    The roof-tree burning down.

He did him to the wire-window
    As fast as he could gang—
Says—"Wae to the hands put in the stancheons,
    For out we'll never win."

When he stood at the wire-window,
    Most doleful to be seen,
He did espy her, Lady Frendraught,
    Who stood upon the green.

Cried—"Mercy, mercy, Lady Frendraught,
    Will ye not sink with sin ?
For first your husband killed my father,
    And now you burn his son."

O then out spoke her, Lady Frendraught,
    And loudly did she cry—
"It were great pity for good Lord John,
    But none for Rothiemay.
But the keys are casten in the deep draw-well,
    Ye cannot get away."*

* Mr Finlay, after regretting that all his attempts to recover this ballad have proved unsuccessful, gives, in the words of a correspondent, the following particulars regarding it, which we subjoin as illustrative of the lines above cited :—"A lady, a near relation of mine, lived near the spot in her youth for some time, and remembers having heard the old song mentioned by Ritson, but cannot repeat it. She says there was a verse which stated, that the lord and lady locked the door of the tower, and flung the keys into the draw-well, and that, many years ago, when the well was cleared out, this tradition was

While he stood in this dreadful plight,
  Most piteous to be seen,
There called out his servant Gordon,
  As he had frantic been.

"O loup, O loup, my dear master,
  O loup and come to me;
I 'll catch you in my arms two,
  One foot I will not flee.

"O loup, O loup, my dear master,
  O loup and come away,
I 'll catch you in my arms two,
  But Rothiemay may lie.

"The fish shall never swim in the flood,
  Nor corn grow through the clay,
Nor the fiercest fire that was ever kindled
  Twin me and Rothiemay."

"But I cannot loup, I cannot come,
  I cannot win to thee;
My head 's fast in the wire window,
  My feet burning from me.

"My eyes are seething in my head,
  My flesh roasting also,
My bowels are boiling with my blood.
  Is not that a woeful woe?

"Take here the rings from my white fingers,
  That are so long and small,
And give them to my Lady fair,
  Where she sits in her hall.

corroborated by their finding the keys—at least such was
the report of the country."—*Preface to Scottish Historical and Romantic Ballads*, p. xxi.

"So I cannot loup, I cannot come,
  I cannot loup to thee—
My earthly part is all consumed,
  My spirit but speaks to thee."

Wringing her hands, tearing her hair,
  His Lady she was seen,
And thus addressed his servant Gordon,
  Where he stood on the green:

"O wae be to you, George Gordon,
  An ill death may you die,
So safe and sound as you stand there,
  And my Lord bereaved from me."

"I bade him loup, I bade him come,
  I bade him loup to me,
I 'd catch him in my arms two,
  A foot I should not flee.

"He threw me the rings from his white fingers,
  Which were so long and small,
To give to you his Lady fair,
  Where you sat in your hall."

Sophia Hay, Sophia Hay,
  O bonnie Sophia was her name—
Her waiting maids put on her clothes,
  But I wat she tore them off again.

And aft she cried, "Ohon! alas!
  A sair heart 's ill to win;
I wan a sair heart when I married him,
  And the day it 's well return'd again."
O

LORD INGRAM AND CHIEL WYET.

This beautiful ballad, which appeared in the "North Countrie Garland" before referred to, was kindly communicated to us by the same gentleman, who, from the circumstance of its retaining the word "bonheur," conjectures that it may probably have had a French original. A ballad on a similar subject, and indeed nothing else than a different copy of the present, has been published by Mr Jamieson, in the second volume of his ballads, from Mr Herd's MSS. Mr Jamieson's copy, however, wants the catastrophe,—a deficiency supplied by the present copy. —MOTHERWELL.

Lord Ingram and Chiel Wyet
  Were baith born in one bower ;
Laid baith their hearts on one Lady,
  The less was their bonheur.

Chiel Wyet and Lord Ingram
  Were baith born in one hall ;
Laid baith their hearts on one Lady,
  The worse did them befall.

Lord Ingram woo'd her, Lady Maisry,
  From father and from mother ;
Lord Ingram woo'd her, Lady Maisry,
  From sister and from brother.

Lord Ingram woo'd her, Lady Maisry,
  With leave of a' her kin ;
And every one gave full consent,
  But she said No to him.

Lord Ingram woo'd her, Lady Maisry,
  Into her father's ha' ;
Chiel Wyet woo'd her, Lady Maisry,
  Amang the sheets so sma'.

Now it fell out upon a day,
  She was dressing her head,
That ben did come her father dear,
  Wearing the gold so red.

He said—"Get up now, Lady Maisry,
  Put on your wedding gown—
For Lord Ingram he will be here,
  Your wedding must be done."

"I'd rather be Chiel Wyet's wife,
  The white fish for to kill,
Before I were Lord Ingram's wife,
  To wear the silk so well.

"I'd rather be Chiel Wyet's wife,
  With him to beg my bread,
Before I were Lord Ingram's wife,
  To wear the gold so red.

"Where will I get a bonnie boy,
  Will win gold to his fee,
And will run unto Chiel Wyet's
  With this letter from me?"

"O here I am," the boy says,
  "And will win gold to my fee,
And carry away any letter
  To Chiel Wyet from thee."

And when he found the bridges broke,
  He bent his bow and swam;
And when he found the grass growing,
  He hastened and he ran.

And when he came to Chiel Wyet's castle,
  He did not knock nor call,

But set his bent bow to his breast,
   And lightly leaped the wall ;
And ere the porter open'd the gate,
   The boy was in the hall.

The first line that he looked on,
   A grieved man was he—
The next line that he looked on,
   The tear blinded his ee—
Says—"I wonder what ails my one brother,
   He 'll not let my love be !

" But I 'll send to my brother's bridal,
   The reckon shall be mine,
Full four and twenty buck and roe,
   And ten tun of the wine,
And bid my love be blythe and glad,
   And I will follow syne."

There was not a groom about that castle,
   But got a coat of green,
And all was blythe, and all was glad,
   But Lady Maisry she was neen.

There was no cook about that kitchen,
   But got a gown of gray ;
And all was blythe and all was glad,
   But Lady Maisry was wae.

Between Mary kirk and that castle
   Was all spread ower with garl,*
To keep Lady Maisry and her maidens
   From tramping on the marl.

* "Garl :" so written in Mr Sharpe's MS., and probably
an abbreviated mode of pronouncing the word "gravel."

Between Mary kirk and that castle
   Was spread a cloth of gold,
To keep Lady Maisry and her maidens
   From treading on the mould.

When mass was sung and bells were rung,
   And all men bound for bed;
Then Lord Ingram and Lady Maisry
   In one bed they were laid.

When they were laid into their bed,
   It was baith saft and warm;
He laid his hand over her side,
   Says—"I think you are with bairn!"

"I told you once, so did I twice,
   When ye came me to be my wooer,
That Chiel Wyet, your only brother,
   One night lay in my bower.

"I told you twice, I told you thrice,
   Ere ye came me to wed,
That Chiel Wyet, your one brother,
   One night lay in my bed."

"O will you father your bairn on me,
   And on no other man?
And I 'll give him to his dowry
   Full fifty ploughs of land."

"I will not father my bairn on you,
   Nor on no wrongous man,
Though ye would give him to his dowry
   Five thousand ploughs of land."

Then up did stand him Chiel Wyet,
  Shed by his yellow hair,
And gave Lord Ingram to the heart
  A deep wound and a sair.

Then up did start him Lord Ingram,
  Shed up his yellow hair,
And gave Chiel Wyet to the heart,
  A deep wound and a sair.

There was no pity for thae twa lords,
  Where they were lying slain ;
But all was for her, Lady Maisry,
  In that bower she gaed brain.*

There was no pity for thae twa lords,
  When they were lying dead ;
But all was for her, Lady Maisry,
  In that bower she went mad.

Said—"Get to me a cloak of cloth,
  A staff of good hard tree ;
If I have been an evil woman,
  I shall beg till I dee.

"For a bit I 'll beg for Chiel Wyet,
  For Lord Ingram I 'll beg three ;
All for the good and honourable marriage
  At Mary kirk he gave me."

* " Brain :" frantic.

THE DOUGLAS TRAGEDY.

"The ballad of *The Douglas Tragedy* is one of the few
to which popular tradition has ascribed complete locality.
The farm of Blackhouse, in Selkirkshire, is said to have
been the scene of this melancholy event. There are the
remains of a very ancient tower, adjacent to the farm-
house, in a wild solitary glen, upon a torrent named
Douglas Burn, which joins the Yarrow after passing a
craggy rock called the Douglas Craig. From this ancient
tower Lady Margaret is said to have been carried by her
lover. Seven large stones, erected upon the neighbouring
heights of Blackhouse, are shewn as marking the spot
where the seven brothers were slain; and the Douglas
Burn is averred to have been the stream at which the
lovers stopped to drink: so minute is tradition in ascertaining the scene of a tragical tale, which, considering the
rude state of former times, had probably foundation in
some real event."—*Border Minstrelsy*, vol. ii.

The copy here followed is that given in the work from
which the above extract has been taken. Any recited
copy that we have heard has been incomplete, wanting
not only the circumstance of the lovers halting at the
stream, but likewise that of their death and burial. Our
copy supplies these unimportant variations.

> He has lookit over his left shoulder,
>   And through his bonnie bridle rein,
> And he spy'd her father and her seven bold brethren,
>   Come riding down the glen.
>
> "O hold my horse, Lady Marg'ret," he said,
>   "O hold my horse by the bonnie bridle rein,
> Till I fight your father and seven bold brethren,
>   As they come riding down the glen."
>
> Some time she rade, and some time she gaed,
>   Till she that place did near;
> And there she spy'd her seven bold brethren slain,
>   And her father who loved her so dear.
>
> "O hold your hand, sweet William," she said,
>   "Your bull baits are wondrous sair;
> Sweethearts I may get many a one,
>   But a father I will never get mair."

She has taken a napkin from off her neck,
  That was of the cambrick so fine,
And aye as she wiped her father's bloody wounds,
  The blood ran red as the wine.

Two stanzas are here omitted, in which Lord William
offers her the choice of returning to her mother, or of
accompanying him; and the ballad concludes with this
stanza, which is twice repeated in singing :—

He set her upon the milk-white steed,
  Himself upon the brown;
He took a horn out of his pocket,
  And they both went weeping along.
—MOTHERWELL.

"RISE up, rise up, now, Lord Douglas," she says,
  "And put on your armour so bright;
Let it never be said that a daughter of thine
  Was married to a lord under night.

"Rise up, rise up, my seven bold sons,
  And put on your armour so bright;
And take better care of your youngest sister,
  For your eldest's awa' the last night."

He's mounted her on a milk-white steed,
  And himself on a dapple gray,
With a buglet horn hung down by his side,
  And lightly they rode away.

Lord William lookit o'er his left shoulder,
  To see what he could see;
And there he spy'd her seven brethren bold,
  Come riding over the lee.

"Light down, light down, Lady Marg'ret," he said,
  "And hold my steed in your hand,
Until that against your seven brethren bold
  And your father I make a stand."

She held his steed in her milk-white hand,
    And never shed one tear,
Until that she saw her seven brethren fa',
    And her father hard fighting, who loved her so
      dear.

"O hold your hand, Lord William!" she said,
    "For your strokes they are wondrous sair;
True lovers I can get many a ane,
    But a father I can never get mair."

O she's ta'en out her handkerchief,
    It was o' the holland sae fine,
And aye she dighted her father's bloody wounds,
    That were redder than the wine.

"O chuse, O chuse, Lady Marg'ret," he said,
    "O whether will ye gang or bide?"
"I'll gang, I'll gang, Lord William," she said,
    "For ye have left me no other guide."

He's lifted her on a milk-white steed,
    And himself on a dapple gray,
With a bugelet horn hung down by his side,
    And slowly they baith rade away.

O they rade on, and on they rade,
    And a' by the light of the moon,
Until they came to yon wan water,
    And there they lighted down.

They lighted down to tak a drink
    Of the spring that ran so clear;
And down the stream ran his gude heart's blood,
    And sair she 'gan to fear.

"Hold up, hold up, Lord William," she says,
  "For I fear that you are slain!"
"'Tis naething but the shadow of my scarlet cloak,
  That shines in the water sae plain."

O they rade on, and on they rade,
  And a' by the light of the moon,
Until they came to his mother's ha' door,
  And there they lighted down.

"Get up, get up, Lady Mother," he says,
  "Get up and let me in!—
Get up, get up, Lady Mother," he says,
  "For this night my fair Lady I've win.

"O mak my bed, Lady Mother," he says,
  "O mak it braid and deep!
And lay Lady Marg'ret close at my back,
  And the sounder I will sleep."

Lord William was dead lang ere midnight,
  Lady Marg'ret lang ere day—
And all true lovers that go thegither,
  May they have mair luck than they!

Lord William was buried in St Marie's kirk,*
  Lady Marg'ret in Marie's quire;
Out o' the Lady's grave grew a bonnie red rose,
  And out o' the Knight's a brier.

* This passage has been imitated in the well-known
English ballad of *Lord Lovel*:—

  "Lady Nancy was laid in St Pancras' church,
    Lord Lovel was laid in the choir;
  And out of her bosom there grew a red rose,
    And out of her lover's a brier, brier,
    And out of her lover's a brier.

  "They grew, and they grew, to the church steeple, too,
    And then they could grow no higher;
  So there they entwined in a true lover's knot,
    For all lovers true to admire-mire,
    For all lovers true to admire."

And they twa met, and they twa plat,
  And fain they wad be near;
And a' the warld might ken right weel
  They were twa lovers dear.

But by and rade the Black Douglas,
  And wow but he was rough!
For he pulled up the bonnie brier,
  And flang 't in St Marie's Loch.

WILLIAM AND MARJORIE.

This ballad appears in Motherwell's Collection, without note or comment; and is quoted, but not annotated, by more recent editors.

LADY MARJORIE, Lady Marjorie
  Sat sewing her silken seam,
And by her came a pale, pale ghost
  Wi' mony a sigh and mane.

"Are ye my father the king?" she says,
  "Or ye my brither John?
Or are ye my true love, sweet William,
  From England newly come?"

"I 'm not your father the king," he says,
  "No, no, nor your brither John;
But I 'm your true love, sweet William,
  From England that 's newly come."

"Have ye brought me any scarlets sae red?
  Or any of the silks sae fine?
Or have ye brought me any precious things
  That merchants have to tine?"

"I have not brought you any scarlets sae red,
  No, no, nor the silks sae fine;
But I have brought you my winding-sheet
  Ower many a rock and hill.

"Lady Marjorie, Lady Marjorie!
  For faith and charitie,
Will ye gie to me my faith and troth
  That I gave once to thee?"

"O your faith and troth I'll not gie to thee,
  No, no, that will not I,
Until I get ae kiss of your ruby lips,
  And in my arms you lye."

"My lips they are sae bitter," he says—
  "My breath it is sae strang;
If you get ae kiss of my ruby lips,
  Your days will not be lang.

"The cocks are crawing, Marjorie," he says—
  "The cocks are crawing again;
It's time the Dead should part the Quick—
  Marjorie, I must be gane."

She followed him high,—she followed him low,
  Till she came to yon churchyard green;
And there the deep grave opened up,
  And young William he lay down.

"What three things are these, sweet William,"
      she says,
  "That stand here at your head?"
"O it's three maidens, Marjorie," he says,
  "That I promised once to wed."

"What three things are these, sweet William,"
   she says,
 "That stand close at your side?"
"O it's three babes, Marjorie," he says,
 "That these three maidens had."

"What three things are these, sweet William,"
   she says,
 "That lye close at your feet?"
"O it's three hell-hounds, Marjorie," he says,
 "That's waiting my soul to keep."

O she took up her white, white hand,
 And she struck him on the breast;
Saying—"Have there again your faith and troth,
 And I wish your saul gude rest."

THE WATER O' WEARIE'S WELL.

A similar story is narrated in the English ballad of *The
Outlandish Knight*, in *May Colvin, or False Sir John;* and
in several Danish and German ballads, with variations of
the catastrophe. Carlton Castle, on the coast of Carrick,
in Ayrshire, is pointed out as the residence of the false
knight, and Gamesloup, a high rock overlooking the sea,
"as the place where he was in the habit of drowning his
wives." The heroine of the ballad is said to have been a
member of the family of Kennedy, Earls of Cassilis. Mr
Dixon, in his Scottish Ballads, published for the Percy Society, transfers the scene to Balwearie Castle, in Fifeshire.

   THERE cam' a bird out o' a bush,
     On water for to dine;
   An' siching sair, says the king's dochter,
     "O wae's this heart o' mine."

He 's ta'en a harp into his hand,
  He 's harpit them a' asleep ;
Except it was the king's dochter,
  Wha ae wink couldna get.

He 's loupen on his berry-brown steed,
  Ta'en her behin' himsel ;
Then baith rade doun to that water
  That they ca' Wearie's Well.

"Wade in, wade in, my ladye fair,
  No harm shall thee befall ;
Oft times hae I watered my steed
  Wi' the water o' Wearie's Well."

The first step that she steppit in,
  She steppit to the knee ;
And, sichin', says this ladye fair,
  "This water 's nae for me."

"Wade in, wade in, my ladye fair,
  No harm shall thee befall ;
Oft times hae I watered my steed
  Wi' the water o' Wearie's Well."

The next step that she steppit in,
  She steppit to the middle ;
O, sichin', says this ladye fair,
  "I 've wat my gowden girdle."

"Wade in, wade in, my ladye fair,
  No harm shall thee befall ;
Oft times hae I watered my steed
  Wi' the water o' Wearie's Well."

The next step that she steppit in,
    She steppit to the chin;
O, sichin', says this ladye fair,
    "They sud gar twa luves twin."

"Seven king's dochters I 've drounèd there,
    I' the water o' Wearie's Well;
An' I 'll mak ye the eighth o' them,
    An' ring the common bell."

"Sin' I am standin' here," she says,
    "This dowie death to dee;
One kiss o' your comelie mouth
    I'm sure would comfort me."

He louted him o'er his saddle bow,
    To kiss her cheek an' chin;
She's ta'en him in her arms twa,
    An' thrown him headlong in.

"Sin' seven king's daughters ye 've drounèd
      there,
    I' the water o' Wearie's Well,
I 'll mak ye the bridegroom to them a',
    An' ring the bell mysel."

An' aye she warsled, and aye she swam,
    An' she swam to dry lan';
An' thankit God most cheerfullie,
    For the dangers she o'ercam.

THE BROOM BLOOMS BONNIE AND SAYS IT IS FAIR.

The revolting nature of the subject of this ballad might, in the opinion of many readers, have been a sufficient reason for withholding its publication; but as tales of this kind abound in the traditionary poetry of Scotland, a collection like the present would have been incomplete without at least one solitary specimen. In its details, too, the Editor conceives it to be less abhorrent than either the ballad of *Lizie Wan*,[*] or that of *The Bonny Hynd*;[†] he also preferred it to the fragment of another ballad, on a similar subject, which, like the present, he obtained from recitation. The fragment begins thus :—

> "Lady Margaret sits in her bow window,
>   Sewing her silken seam;
> She dropt her thimble at her toe,
>   Her scissars at her heel,
> And she's awa to the merry green wood,
>   To see the leaves grow green;"

and in its principal features bear a strong resemblance to *The Bonny Hynd.*

With the exception of three verses, which appeared in Johnson's "Musical Museum," vol. v. p. 474, under the title of *The broom blooms bonny, the broom blooms fair,* the present ballad is for the first time printed. It is evidently a composition of considerable antiquity; and, in poetical merit, it may stand a comparison with either of the ballads above referred to. The alternate lines—

> *The broom blooms bonnie and says it is fair,*
> *And we'll never gang down to the broom onie mair.*

are repeated in each stanza.—MOTHERWELL.

It is talked, it is talked, the warld all over,
    The broom blooms bonnie and says it is fair,
That the king's dochter gaes wi' child to her
        brother,
    And we'll never gang down to the broom onie
        mair.

[*] Ancient and Modern Scottish Songs, Heroic Ballads, &c., Edin. 1776, vol. i. p. 98.

[†] Border Minstrelsy, fifth edition, vol. iii. p. 102.

He 's ta'en his sister down to her father's deer
    park,
Wi' his yew tree bow and arrows fast slung at
    his back.

"O when that ye hear me gie a loud, loud cry,
Shoot an arrow frae thy bow, and there let me lye.

"And when that ye see I am lying cauld and
    dead,
Then ye 'll put me in a grave wi' a turf at my
    head."

Now when he heard her gie a loud, loud cry,
His silver arrow frae his bow he suddenly let fly.

He has houkit a grave that was lang and was
    deep,
And he has buried his sister wi' her baby at her
    feet.

And when he came hame to his father's court ha',
There was music and minstrels and dancing
    'mang them a'.

"O Willie! O Willie! what makes thee in pain?"
"I have lost a sheath and knife that I 'll never
    see again."

"There are ships o' your father's sailing on the sea,
That will bring as good a sheath and a knife unto
    thee."

"There are ships o' my father's sailing on the sea,
But sic a sheath and knife they can never bring
    to me!"

P

YOUNG JOHNSTONE.

For the first complete copy of this ballad the public is indebted to Mr Finlay of Glasgow, in whose collection it appeared, prefaced with the following notice :—" A fragment of this fine old ballad has been repeatedly published, under the title of *The Cruel Knight*. The present edition has been completed from two recited copies. Young Johnstone's reason for being 'sae late a coming in' has been suppressed, as well as a concluding stanza of inferior merit, in which the catastrophe is described in a manner quite satisfactory, but not very poetical."

The present copy of this excellent ballad was obtained from recitation ; for a few verbal emendations recourse has been had to Mr Finlay's copy ; but those parts which that gentleman's taste led him to reject, the Editor of this compilation did not conceive himself warranted to suppress. Refinement in matters of taste may be carried to a pernicious extreme ; and, in an editor of ancient poetry, too much delicacy in this respect may oftentimes be a very questionable virtue.

The reciters of old ballads frequently supply the best commentaries upon them, when any obscurity or want of connexion appears in the poetical narrative. This ballad, as it stands, throws no light on young Johnstone's motive for stabbing his lady ; but the person from whose lips it was taken down alleged that the barbarous act was committed unwittingly, through young Johnstone's suddenly waking from sleep, and in that moment of confusion and alarm unhappily mistaking his mistress for one of his pursuers. It is not improbable but the ballad may have had at one time a stanza to the above effect, the substance of which is still remembered, though the words in which it was couched have been forgotten. At all events, it is a more likely inference than that which Mr Gilchrist has chosen to draw from the premises. See a "Collection of Ancient and Modern Scottish Ballads, Tales, and Songs, with Explanatory Notes and Observations, by John Gilchrist," vol. i. p. 185, Edin. 1815.—MOTHERWELL.

Young Johnstone and the young Col'nel
   Sat drinking at the wine;
"O gin ye wad marry my sister,
   It's I wad marry thine."

"I wadna marry your sister,
   For a' your houses and land;
But I'll keep her for my leman,
   When I come o'er the strand.

"I wadna marry your sister,
   For a' your gowd and fee;
But I'll keep her for my leman,
   When I come o'er the sea."

Young Johnstone had a nut-brown sword,
   Hung low down by his gair,
And he ritted* it through the young Col'nel,
   That word he ne'er spak mair.

But he's awa' to his sister's bower,
   He's tirled at the pin;
"Whare hae ye been, my dear brither,
   Sae late a coming in?

"I've dreamed a dream this night," she says,
   "I wish it may be for good;
They were seeking you with hawks and hounds,
   And the young Col'nel was dead."

* "Ritted:" thrust violently. In *Sir Tristrem* it is used simply to cut. *Vide* Fytte I. Stanza xliv. In the copy obtained by the Editor, the word "ritted" did not occur; instead of which the word "stabbed" was used. The "nut-brown sword" was also changed into "a little small sword."

"Hawks and hounds they may seek me,
　　As I trow well they be ;
For I have killed the young Col'nel,
　　And thy true love was he."

"If ye hae killed the young Col'nel,
　　O dule and wae is me ;
But I wish ye may be hanged on a hie
　　　　gallows,
　　And hae nae power to flee."

And he's awa' to his true love's bower,
　　He's tirled at the pin ;
"Whar hae ye been, my dear Johnstone,
　　Sae late a coming in ?

"I have dreamed a dreary dream," she says,
　　"I wish it may be for good ;
They were seeking you with hawks and hounds,
　　And the young Col'nel was dead."

"Hawks and hounds they may seek me,
　　As I trow well they be ;
For I hae killed the young Col'nel,
　　And thy ae brother was he."

"If ye hae killed the young Col'nel,
　　O dule and wae is me ;
But I care the less for the young Col'nel,
　　If thy ain body be free.

"Come in, come in, my dear Johnstone,
　　Come in and take a sleep ;
And I will go to my casement,
　　And carefully I 'll thee keep."

He hadna weel got up the stair,
    And entered in her bower,
When four and twenty belted knights
    Came riding to the door.

"O did you see a bloody squire,
    A bloody squire was he;
O did you see a bloody squire
    Come riding o'er the lea?"

"What colour were his hawks?" she says,
    "What colour were his hounds?
What colour was the gallant steed
    That bore him from the bounds?"

"Bloody, bloody were his hawks,
    And bloody were his hounds;
And milk-white was the gallant steed
    That bore him from the bounds."

"Yes, bloody, bloody were his hawks,
    And bloody were his hounds;
And milk-white was the gallant steed
    That bore him from the bounds.

"But light ye down now, gentlemen,
    And take some bread and wine;
An the steed be good he rides upon,
    He's past the brig o' Lyne."

"We thank you for your bread, Lady,
    We thank you for your wine;
But I wad gie thrice three thousand pound,
    That bloody knight was ta'en."

"Lie still, lie still, my dear Johnstone,
  Lie still and take a sleep;
For thy enemies are past and gone,
  And carefully I will thee keep." *

But young Johnstone had a little wee sword,
  Hung low down by his gair,
And he stabbed it in fair Annet's breast,
  A deep wound and a sair.

"What aileth thee now, dear Johnstone?
  What aileth thee at me?
Hast thou not got my father's gold
  Bot and my mither's fee?"

"Now live, now live, my dear Ladye,
  Now live but half an hour;
And there's no a leech in a' Scotland
  But shall be in thy bower."

"How can I live, how shall I live?
  Young Johnstone, do not you see
The red, red drops o' my bonnie heart's blood
  Rin trickling down my knee?

"But take thy harp into thy hand,
  And harp out owre yon plain,
And ne'er think mair on thy true love,
  Than if she had never been."

He hadna weel been out o' the stable,
  And on his saddle set,
Till four and twenty broad arrows
  Were thrilling in his heart.

* One version ends here. The concluding stanzas seem
to have been added by another hand.

JOHNNIE SCOT.

In preparing this ballad for the press, three recited
copies, all obtained from people considerably advanced in
years, have been used. The ballad itself is popular in the
shires of Renfrew, Dumbarton, and Stirling; and though
the Editor has obtained no copy of it from the south of
Scotland, yet he has been assured that it is also well
known there; a fact of which there can be no doubt, as
the Border names of Scot and Percy sufficiently identify
it with that part of the country.

Whether the glory of the high achievement recorded in
the ballad should of right belong to the name of Scot or
to that of M'Nauchton, is a question very hard of solution.
Scot, of Satchels, in that strangest of all literary curiosi-
ties, his metrical " History of the Right Honourable Name
of Scot," is dumb on the subject; and Buchanan, in his
account of Scottish Surnames, is as profoundly silent
regarding any one belonging to the ancient family of
M'Nauchton, to whom the honour of this notable duel
can with any degree of likelihood be attributed.   For his
own part, the Editor has been somewhat gravelled to
make up his mind on this momentous point; but at length
he has been inclined to concede the adventure perilous,
even to Johnnie Scot, whoever he was, not only on the
account that two copies of the ballad, and these by far the
most perfect in their narrative, are quite unanimous on this
head, but that these likewise retain the word "Tailliant,"
which, in the corresponding part of the third copy, is
changed into "Champion."   This word Tailliant he has
never before met with in any ballad; but it is an evident
derivative from the French verb Taillader.*—MOTHER-
WELL.

O JOHNNIE SCOT's to the hunting gane,
   Unto the woods sae wild;
And Earl Percy's ae daughter
   To him goes big wi' child.

* Quere—Is it not a misprint for Valiant or Valiant
Man—i. e., Champion?

O word is to the kitchen gane,
    And word is to the ha';
And word is to the highest towers,
    Among the nobles a'.

"If she be wi' child," her father said,
    "As woe forbid it be !
I 'll put her into a prison strang,
    And try the veritie."

"But if she be wi' child," her mother said,
    "As woe forbid it be !
I 'll put her intil a dungeon dark,
    And hunger her till she die."

O Johnnie 's called his waiting man,
    His name was Germanie ;*
"It 's thou must to fair England gae,
    Bring me that gay ladie.

"And here it is a silken sark ;
    Her ain hand sewed the sleeve ;
Bid her come to the merry green wood,
    To Johnnie her true love."

He rode till he came to Earl Percy's gate,
    He tirled at the pin ;
"O wha is there ?" said the proud porter,
    "But I daurna let thee in."

* All the copies which mention Johnnie's waiting-man
concur in giving this name, which is probably descriptive
of his country. In one copy, he, in place of Johnnie's
uncle, is the person who heroically offers wager of battle.
But in another copy the whole words and actions ascribed
to Johnnie's uncle, who "spak so bitterlie," are transferred to "Guid King James."

It 's he rode up, and he rode down,
  He rode the castle about,
Until he spied a fair ladie,
  At the window looking out.

"Here is a silken sark," he said,
  "Thine ain hand sewed the sleeve;
And ye must gae to the merry green wood,
  To Johnnie Scot, thy love."

"The castle it is high, my boy,
  And walled round about;
My feet are in the fetters strong,
  And how can I win out?

"My garters are o' the gude black iron,
  And oh! but they be cold;
My breastplate 's o' the sturdy steel,
  Instead of beaten gold.

"But had I paper, pen, and ink,
  Wi' candle at my command,
It 's I would write a long letter
  To Johnnie in fair Scotland."

Then she has written a braid letter,
  And sealed it wi' her hand;
And sent it to the merry green wood,
  Wi' her ain boy at command.

The first line o' the letter Johnnie read,
  A loud, loud laueh leuch he;
But he had not read ae line but twa,
  Till the saut tears did blind his ee.

"Oh, I must up to England go,
  Whatever me betide;
For to relieve mine own fair ladie,
  That lay last by my side."

Then up and spak Johnnie's auld mither,
  A weel spoken woman was she:
"If you do go to England, Johnnie,
  I may take farewcel o' thee."

And out and spak his father then,
  And he spak well in time:
"If thou unto fair England go,
  I fear ye 'll ne'er come hame."

But out and spak his uncle then,
  And he spak bitterlie:
"Five hundred of my good life-guards
  Shall bear him companie."

When they were all on saddle set,
  They were comely to behold;
The hair that hung owre Johnnie's neck shined
  Like the links o' yellow gold.

When they were all marching away,
  Most pleasant for to see,
There was not so much as a married man,
  In Johnnie's companie.

Johnnie Scott himsel was the foremast man,
  In the company that did ride;
His uncle was the second man,
  Wi' his rapier by his side.

The first gude town that Johnnie came to,
    He made the bells be rung;
And when he rode the town all owre,
    He made the psalms be sung.

The next gude town that Johnnie came to,
    He made the drums beat round;
And the third gude town that he came to,
    He made the trumpets sound,
Till King Henry and all his merry men
    A-marvelled at the sound.

And when they came to Earl Percy's yetts,
    They rode them round about;
And who saw he but his own true love,
    At a window looking out!

"Oh! the doors are bolted with iron and steel,
    So are the windows about;
And my feet they are in fetters strong;
    And how can I win out?

"My garters they are of the lead,
    And oh! but they be cold;
My breastplate 's of the hard, hard steel,
    Instead of beaten gold."

But when they came to Earl Percy's yett,
    They tirled at the pin;
None was so ready as Earl Percy himsel
    To open and let them in.

"Art thou the King of Aulsberry?*
    Or art thou the King of Spain?
Or art thou one of our gay Scots lords,
    M'Nachton to thy name?"

* It may puzzle the historian to give any account of

> "I'm not the King of Aulsberry,
> 　Nor yet the King of Spain;
> But I am one of our gay Scots lords,
> 　Johnnie Scot I am called by name."

this king's reign, or to fix the limits of his dominions; being associated, however, with the King of Spain, this circumstance may afford some cue for obtaining information on these important points. One copy of the ballad has, "Art thou the Duke of Mulberry," another, "Art thou the Duke of York;" but, for the sake of heraldic justice, the present reading was preferred. This stanza, and that which precedes it, we give now as they occur in the three different copies of the ballad recovered by the Editor, so that the reader may have it in his power to choose the reading which hits his fancy.

JOHNNIE SCOT.

> "Are you the Duke of York?" he said,
> 　"Or James our Scottish King?
> Or are you one of our Scottish Lords,
> 　From hunting now come home?"

> "I'm not the Duke of York," he said,
> 　"Nor James your Scottish King;
> But I'm one of the Scottish Lords,
> 　Earl Hector is my name."

JOHNNIE SCOT.

> "Art thou the King of Aulsberry?
> 　Or art thou the King of Spain?
> Or art thou one of our gay Scots Lords?
> 　M'Nachton to thy name?"

> "I'm not the King of Aulsberry,
> 　Nor yet the King of Spain;
> But I am one of our gay Scots Lords,
> 　Johnnie Scot I am called by name."

JOHNNIE M'NACHTON.

> "Are you the Duke of Mulberry?
> 　Or James our Scottish King?
> Are you the Duke of Mulberry,
> 　From Scotland new come home?"

> "I'm not the Duke of Mulberry,
> 　Nor James our Scottish King;
> But I am a true Scottishman,
> 　M'Nachton is my name."

—MOTHERWELL.

When Johnnie came before the king,
  He fell low down on his knee :
"If Johnnie Scot be thy name," he said,
  "As I trow weel it be ;
Then the brawest lady in a' my court,
  Gaes big wi' child to thee."

"If she be with child," fair Johnnie said,
  "As I trow weel she be ;
I 'll make it heir owre a' my land,
  And her my gay ladie."

"But if she be wi' child," her father said,
  "As I trow weel she be ;
To morrow again eight o'clock,
  High hanged thou shalt be."

Out and spoke Johnnie's uncle then,
  And he spak bitterlie :
"Before that we see fair Johnnie hanged,
  We 'll a' fight till we die."

"But is there ever a Tailliant about your court
  That will fight duels three ?
For before that I be hanged," Johnnie said,
  "On the Tailliant's sword I 'll die."

"Say on, say on," said then the king,
  "It is weel spoken of thee ;
For there is a Tailliant in my court
  Shall fight you three by three."

O some is to the good green wood,
  And some is to the plain ;
The Queen with all her ladies fair,
  The King with his merry men,
Either to see fair Johnnie flee,
  Or else to see him slain.

They fought on, and Johnnie fought on,
   Wi' swords o' temper'd steel,
Until the draps o' red, red blood
   Ran trinkling down the field.

They fought on, and Johnnie fought on,
   They fought right manfullie,
Till they left not alive in a' the King's court
   A man only but three.

And they begoud at eight of the morn,
   And they fought on till three;
When the Tailliant, like the swallow swift,
   Owre Johnnie's head did flee:

But Johnnie being a clever young boy,
   He wheeled him round about;
And on the point of Johnnie's broadsword,
   The Tailliant he slew out.

"A priest, a priest," fair Johnnie cried,
   "To wed my love and me!"
"A clerk, a clerk," her father cried,
   "To sum her tocher free."

"I 'll hae none of your gold," fair Johnnie
    cried,
   "Nor none of your other gear;
But I will have my own fair bride,
   For this day I 've won her dear."

He 's ta'en his true love by the hand,
   He led her up the plain:
"Have you any more of your English dogs,
   You want for to have slain?"

He put a little horn to his mouth,
    He blew 't baith loud and shrill ;
And Honour is into Scotland gone,
    In spite of England's Skill.

He put his little horn to his mouth,
    He blew it owre again ;
And aye the sound the good horn cryed,
    Was "Johnnie and his men !"

CATHERINE JOHNSTONE.

Of this ballad two versions have already been published, one in the Border Minstrelsy, the other in "A North Countrie Garland." The present copy was obtained from recitation, in the West of Scotland, and is now given as exhibiting the state in which this popular ballad is there preserved. The tenth stanza seems to contain an allusion to the Knights of the Round Table.—MOTHERWELL.

THERE was a lass, as I heard say,
    Lived low doun in a glen ;
Her name was Catherine Johnstone,
    Weel known to many men.

Doun came the Laird o' Lamington,
    Doun from the south countrie ;
And he is for this bonnie lass,
    Her bridegroom for to be.

He 's ask'd her father and mother,
    The chief of a' her kin ;
And then he ask'd the bonnie lass,
    And did her favour win.

Doun came an English gentleman,
  Doun from the English border;
He is for this bonnie lass,
  To keep his house in order.

He ask'd her father and mother,
  As I do hear them say;
But he never asked the lass hersel,
  Till on her wedding-day.

But she has wrote a long letter,
  And sealed it with her hand;
And sent it to Lord Lamington,
  To let him understand.

The first line o' the letter he read,
  He was baith glad and fain,
But ere he read the letter o'er,
  He was baith pale and wan.

Then he has sent a messenger,
  And out through all his land;
And four-and-twenty armed men
  Were all at his command.

But he has left his merry men all;
  He's left them on the lee;
And he's awa to the wedding-house,
  To see what he could see.

But when he came to the wedding-house,
  As I do understand;
There were four-and-twenty belted knights
  Sat at a table round.

They rose all to honour him,
    For he was of high renown ;
They rose all for to welcome him,
    And bade him to sit down.

O meikle was the good red wine,
    In silver cups did flow ;
But aye she drank to Lamington,
    For with him would she go.

O meikle was the good red wine,
    In silver cups gaed round ;
At length they began to whisper words,
    None could them understand.

"O came ye here for sport, young man ?
    Or came ye here for play ?
Or came ye for our bonnie bride,
    On this her wedding-day ?"

"I came not here for sport," he said,
    "Neither did I for play ;
But for one word o' your bonnie bride,
    I 'll mount and go away."

They set her maids behind her,
    To hear what they would say ;
But the first question he ask'd at her
    Was always answered, Nay ;
The next question he ask'd at her
    Was, " Mount, and come away."

It 's up and to the Couden bank,
    And down the Couden brae ;
And aye she made the trumpet sound,
    " It 's a weel won play."

O meikle was the blood was shed,
    Upon the Couden brae;
And aye she made the trumpet sound,
    "It 's a' fair play.

"Come a' ye English gentlemen,
    That is of England born;
Come na doun to Scotland,
    For fear ye get the scorn.

"They 'll feed ye up wi' flattering words,
    And that 's foul play;
And they 'll dress you frogs instead of fish,
    Just on your wedding-day."

GILDEROY.

This very popular ballad appears to have been adapted
from a much older one by Sir Alexander Halket, brother
of Elizabeth Halket, Lady Wardlaw, authoress of " Hardyknute," and of many other imitations of ancient minstrelsy.
The hero was one Patrick MacGregor, a noted Highland
cateran, who was executed, with five of his gang, in Edinburgh, in 1638. He was usually called *Gillie Roy*—or the
Red Boy—from the colour of his hair. Hence the designation of Gilderoy, by which he is known to posterity
with almost as much romance thrown about his story as
that which has enveloped the exploits of Rob Roy, Claude
Duval, or Robin Hood. But almost every country has its
model thief; and Scottish romance possesses two in Rob
Roy and Gillie Roy.

GILDEROY was a bonnie boy,
    Had roses till his shoon;
His stockings were of silken soy,
    Wi' garters hanging doon.

It was, I ween, a comelie sight
  To see sae trim a boy;
He was my joy, and heart's delight,
  My handsome Gilderoy.

O twa sic charming een he had,
  Breath sweet as any rose;
He never wore a Highland plaid,
  But costly silken clothes.
He gain'd the luve of ladies gay,
  Nane e'er to him was coy;
Ah! wae is me, I mourn the day
  For my dear Gilderoy.

My Gilderoy and I were born
  Baith in a town together;
We scant were seven years beforn
  We 'gan to luve ilk ither.
Our daddies and our mammies they
  Were fill'd wi' mickle joy,
To think upon the bridal day
  Of me and Gilderoy.

For Gilderoy, that luve of mine,
  Gude faith, I freely bought
A wedding sark of Holland fine,
  Wi' dainty ruffles wrought;
And he gied me a wedding ring,
  Which I received wi' joy.
Nae lad nor lassie e'er could sing
  Like me and Gilderoy.

Wi' mickle joy we spent our prime,
  Till we were baith sixteen;
And aft we past the langsome time
  Amang the leaves sae green.

Aft on the banks we 'd sit us there
    And sweetly kiss and toy,
While he wi' garlands deck'd my hair,
    My handsome Gilderoy.

Oh, that he still had been content
    Wi' me to lead his life !
But, ah, his manfu' heart was bent
    To stir in deeds of strife !
And he in many a vent'rous deed
    His courage bauld wad try ;
And now this gars my heart to bleed
    For my dear Gilderoy.

And when of me his leave he tuik,
    The tears they wat mine ee ;
I gied him sic a parting luik ;—
    " My benison gang wi' thee.
God speed thee weil, mine ain dear heart,
    Far gane is all my joy ;
My heart is rent, sith we maun part,
    My handsome Gilderoy."

The Queen of Scots possessed nought
    That my love let me want ;
For cow and sow he to me brought,
    And e'en when they were strant,
All these did honestly possess ;
    He never did annoy
Who never failed to pay their less
    To my love, Gilderoy.

My Gilderoy, baith far and near,
    Was fear'd in every town ;
And bauldly bore away the gear
    Of mony a lowland loun.

For man to man durst meet him nane
    He was sae brave a boy;
At length wi' numbers he was ta'en,
    My winsome Gilderoy.

Wae worth the louns that made the laws,
    To hang a man for gear;
To reave of life for sic a cause
    As stealing horse or mare.
Had not their laws been made sae strict,
    I ne'er had lost my joy,
Wi' sorrow ne'er had wet my cheek
    For my dear Gilderoy.

Gif Gilderoy had done amiss,
    He maught hae banisht been;
Ah! what sair cruelty is this
    To hang such handsome men!
To hang the flower of Scottish land,
    Sae sweet and fair a boy!
Nae lady had sae white a hand
    As thee, my Gilderoy.

Of Gilderoy sae fear'd they were,
    Wi' irons his limbs they strung;
To Edinborow led him there,
    And on a gallows hung.
They hung him high aboon the rest,
    He was sae bauld a boy;
There died the youth whom I lued best,
    My handsome Gilderoy.

Sune as he yielded up his breath,
    I bore his corpse away;
Wi' tears that trickled for his death
    I wash'd his comelie clay.

And sicker in a grave right deep
I laid the dear-lued boy ;
And now for ever I maun weep
My winsome Gilderoy.

THE DOWIE DENS O' YARROW.

Of this ballad, "a collated edition," selected from various copies, professedly for the purpose of suiting the taste of "these more light and giddy-paced times," first appeared in "The Minstrelsy of the Scottish Border," under the title of *The Dowie Dens of Yarrow*. The present version, taken from the recitation of an old woman in Kilbarchan, though containing some additional incidents, not to be found in the copy published in the Border Minstrelsy, is chiefly valuable as shewing the state in which the song is preserved in the West of Scotland.—MOTHERWELL.

THERE were three lords birling at the wine,
   On the Dowie Dens o' Yarrow,
They made a compact them between
   They would go fecht to-morrow.

"Thou took our sister to be thy wife,
   And ne'er thocht her thy marrow,
Thou stealed her frae her daddy's back,
   When she was the Rose o' Yarrow."

"Yes, I took your sister to be my wife,
   And I made her my marrow ;
I stealed her frae her daddy's back,
   And she 's still the Rose o' Yarrow."

He is hame to his lady gane,
  As he had done before, O ;
Says, " Madam, I must go and fecht
  On the Dowie Dens o' Yarrow."

" Stay at hame, my lord," she said,
  " For that will breed much sorrow ;
For my three brethren will slay thee
  On the Dowie Dens o' Yarrow."

" Hold your tongue, my lady fair,
  For what needs a' this sorrow ?
For I 'll be hame gin the clock strikes nine,
  From the Dowie Dens o' Yarrow."

He wush his face, and she combed his hair,
  As she had done before, O ;
She dressed him up in his armour clear,
  Sent him forth to fecht on Yarrow.

" Come ye here to hawk or hound ?
  Or drink the wine that 's sae clear, O ?
Or come ye here to eat in your words,
  That you 're not the Rose o' Yarrow ?"

" I came not here to hawk or hound,
  Nor to drink the wine that 's sae clear, O ;
Nor cam' I here to eat in my words,
  For I 'm still the Rose o' Yarrow."

Then they all begoud to fecht,
  I wad they focht richt sore, O ;
Till a cowardly man cam' behind his back,
  And pierced his body thorough.

"Gae hame, gae hame, it's my man, John,
    As ye have done before, O;
And tell it to my gay ladye,
    That I soundly sleep on Yarrow."

His man, John, he has gane hame,
    As he had done before, O;
And told it to his gay ladye,
    That he soundly slept on Yarrow.

"I dream'd a dream now since yestreen,—
    God keep us a' frae sorrow,—
That my lord and I pu'd the heather green,
    From the Dowie Dens o' Yarrow."

Sometimes she rade, sometimes she gade,
    As she had done before, O;
And aye between she fell in a swoon,
    Lang or she cam' to Yarrow.

Her hair it was five quarters lang,
    'Twas like the gold for yellow;
She twisted it round his milk-white hand,
    And she's drawn him hame frae Yarrow.

Out and spak her father dear,
    Says, "What needs a' this sorrow?
For I'll get you a far better lord
    Than ever died on Yarrow."

"O hold your tongue, father," she said,
    "For you've bred a' my sorrow;
For that Rose 'll ne'er spring so sweet in May,
    As that Rose I lost on Yarrow!"

THE BRAES O' YARROW.

Though not strictly an ancient ballad, but only a comparatively modern imitation of the ancient manner, by William Hamilton of Bangour, the friend of Allan Ramsay, it has been thought inadvisable to exclude it from this collection. The ballad has consecrated the banks of Yarrow to all the lovers of poetry and song; and is the finest of many fine compositions which have made that stream as truly classic as Helicon or Meander.

A. Busk ye, busk ye, my bonnie, bonnie bride,
    Busk ye, busk ye, my winsome marrow;
Busk ye, busk ye, my bonnie, bonnie bride,
    And think nae mair on the braes o' Yarrow.

B. Where gat ye that bonnie, bonnie bride,
    Where gat ye that winsome marrow?
A. I gat her where I daurna weel be seen,
    Puin' the birks on the braes o' Yarrow.

Weep not! weep not! my bonnie, bonnie bride;
    Weep not! weep not, my winsome marrow,
Nor let thy heart lament to leave
    Puin' the birks on the braes o' Yarrow.

B. Why does she weep, thy bonnie, bonnie bride?
    Why does she weep, thy winsome marrow?
And why daur ye nae mair weel be seen
    Puin' the birks on the braes o' Yarrow?

A. Lang maun she weep, lang maun she weep,
    Lang maun she weep wi' dule and sorrow,
And lang maun I ne'er weel be seen
    Puin' the birks on the braes o' Yarrow.

For she has tint her lover, lover dear,
   Her lover dear, the cause of sorrow;
And I hae slain the comeliest swain
   That e'er pu'd birks on the braes o' Yarrow!

Why runs thy stream, O Yarrow, Yarrow, red?
   Why on thy braes is the voice of sorrow?
And why do ye, ye melancholy weeds,
   Hang on the bonnie birks o' Yarrow?

What yonder floats on the ruefu', ruefu' flude,
   What yonder floats? O dule and sorrow!
'Tis he the comely swain I slew
   Upo' the dulefu' braes o' Yarrow!

Wash, oh wash, his wounds, his wounds in
     tears,
   His wounds in tears o' dule and sorrow,
And wrap his limbs in mourning weeds,
   And lay him on the braes o' Yarrow.

Then build, then build ye sisters, sisters sad,
   Ye sisters sad, his tomb wi' sorrow,
And weep around in woeful wise
   His hapless fate on the braes o' Yarrow!

Curse ye, curse ye his useless, useless shield,
   My arm that wrought the deed of sorrow,
The fatal spear that pierced his breast,
   His comely breast, on the braes o' Yarrow!

Sweet smells the birk—green grows, green
     grows the grass,
   Yellow on Yarrow's banks the gowan,
Fair hangs the apple frae the rock;
   Sweet the wave o' Yarrow flowin'.

Flows Yarrow sweet? as sweet, as sweet flows
    Tweed!
As green its grass, its gowans as yellow,
As sweet smells on its braes the birk,
    The apple frae the rock as mellow.

Fair was thy love—fair, fair indeed thy love,
    In flowery bands thou didst him fetter;
Though he was fair and weel-beloved again,
    Than me he never loved thee better.

Then busk ye, busk ye, my bonnie, bonnie
    bride,
Busk ye, busk ye, my winsome marrow;
Come and love me on the banks o' Tweed,
    And think nae mair on the braes o' Yarrow.

She. How can I busk a bonnie, bonnie bride?
    How can I busk a winsome marrow?
And how love him on the banks o' Tweed
    That slew my love on the braes o' Yarrow?

O Yarrow fields! may never, never rain,
    Nor dew thy tender blossoms cover;
For there was basely slain my love,
    As though he hadna been a lover.

The boy put on his robes, his robes of green,
    His purple vest was my own sewin';
O wretched me, I little, little kenn'd
    He was in them to meet his ruin!

The boy took out his milk-white, milk-white
    steed,
    Unheedful of my dule and sorrow;
But e'er the to-fall of the night,
    He lay a corpse on the braes of Yarrow.

Much I rejoiced that waeful, waeful day,
    I sang—my voice the woods returning;
But lang e'er night the spear was flown
    That slew my love, and left me mournin'.

What can my barbarous, barbarous father do,
    But with his cruel rage pursue me?
My lover's blood is on thy spear,
    How canst thou, barbarous man, then
        woo me?

My happy sisters may be, may be proud;
    With cruel and ungentle scoffing,
May bid me seek on Yarrow braes
    My lover nailed in his coffin.

My brother Douglas may upbraid,
    And strive in threatening words to move me,
My lover's blood is on thy spear,
    How canst thou ever bid me love thee?

Yes! yes! prepare the bed, the bed of love,
    With bridal sheets my body cover;
Unbar, ye bridle maids, the door,
    Let in the expected husband-lover!

But who the expected husband, husband is?
    His hands methinks are bathed in slaughter;
Ah me! what ghastly spectre's yon,
    Comes in his pale shroud bleeding after?

Pale as he is, here lay him, lay him down,
    O lay his cold head on my pillow;
Take off, take off these bridal weeds,
    And crown my waefu' head wi' willow.

Pale tho' thou art, yet best, yet best beloved,
O could my warmth to life restore thee!
Yet lie all night between my breasts,
Nae youth lay ever there before ye!

Pale, pale indeed, O lovely, lovely youth,
Forgive, forgive so foul a slaughter;
And lie all night between my breasts,
No youth shall ever lie there after.

He. Return, return, O mournfu', mournfu' bride,
Return, and dry thy useless sorrow;
Thy lover heeds not of thy sighs,
He lies stone-dead on the braes of Yarrow.

THY BRAES WERE BONNIE, YARROW STREAM.

Another modern, but beautiful ballad, by John Logan
—lending a new grace to Yarrow.

THY braes were bonnie, Yarrow stream,
When first on them I met my lover;
Thy braes how dreary, Yarrow stream,
When now thy waves his body cover!

For ever now, O Yarrow stream,
Thou art to me a stream of sorrow;
For never on thy banks shall I
Behold my love—the flower o' Yarrow!

He promised me a milk-white horse,
    To bear me to his father's bowers;
He promised me a little page,
    To squire me to his father's towers.

He promised me a wedding-ring,
    The wedding-day was fix'd to-morrow;
Now he is wedded to his grave,
    Alas! a watery grave in Yarrow!

Sweet were his words when last we met,
    My passion as I freely told him;
Clasped in his arms, I little thought
    That I should never mair behold him.

Scarce was he gone, I saw his ghaist—
    It vanish'd wi' a shriek o' sorrow;
Thrice did the water-wraith ascend,
    And give a doleful groan thro' Yarrow!

His mother from the window look'd,
    With all the longing of a mother;
His little sister, weeping, walk'd
    The greenwood path to meet her brother.

They sought him east, they sought him west,
    They sought him all the forest thorough;
They only saw the clouds o' night—
    They only heard the roar o' Yarrow!

No longer from thy window look—
    Thou hast no son, thou tender mother!
No longer walk, thou lovely maid—
    Alas! thou hast no more a brother!

No longer seek him east or west,
  No longer search the forest thorough,
For, murder'd in the night so dark,
  He lies a lifeless corpse in Yarrow!

The tears shall never leave my cheek,
  No other youth shall be my marrow;
I 'll seek thy body in the stream,
  And then with thee I 'll sleep in Yarrow!

The tear did never leave her cheek,
  No other youth became her marrow;
She found his body in the stream,
  And wi' him now she sleeps in Yarrow!

ANNIE O' LOCHROYAN.

First published in Jamieson's collection, and strangely overlooked by Motherwell, who makes no mention of it. A version, possibly touched up by the hand of Sir Walter Scott, appeared in the Border Minstrelsy. *Willie and May Margaret* is a similar story, except that the treachery, as represented in Buchan's version, followed by that of Chambers, is represented as having been played off by the mother of the young woman, and not of the young man.

  "O, WHA will shoe my fair foot?
    And wha will glove my han'?
  And wha will lace my middle jimp
    Wi' a new-made London ban'? *

  "O, wha will comb my yellow hair
    Wi' a new-made silver kaim?
  Or wha 'll be father to my bairn,
    Till Love Gregòr comes hame?"

* Later versions read—
        " Wi' a lang, lang linen ban'."

"Your father 'll shoe your fair foot,
  Your mother glove your han',
Your sister lace your middle jimp,
  Wi' a new-made London ban'.

"Your brother 'll comb your yellow hair,
  Wi' a new-made silver kaim,
And God will father your poor bairn,
  Till Love Gregòr comes hame."

"O, gin I had a bonnie ship,
  And men to sail wi' me,
It's I wad gang to my true love,
  Sin' he winna come to me!"

Her father's gi'en her a bonnie ship,
  And sent her to the stran';
She's ta'en her bairnie in her arms,
  And turned her back to lan'.

She hadna been i' the sea sailin'
  About a month or more,
Till she landèd her bonnie ship
  Near her true lover's door.

The nicht was dark, the wind blew cauld,
  And her love was fast asleep,
And the wee, wee bairnie in her arms
  Fu' sair began to weep.

Lang stood she at her true love's door,
  And lang tirled at the pin,
At length up gat his fause mothèr,
  Sayin', "Wha's that wad be in?"

"O it is Annie o' Lochroyan,
    Your love, come o'er the sea,
I 've got your bairnie in my arms,
    So open the door to me."

" Awa', awa', ye ill woman,
    Ye 're nae come here for gude ;
Ye 're but a witch or vile warlòck,
    Or mermaid o' the flood."

" I 'm nae a witch, or vile warlòck,
    Or mermaiden," said she ;
" I 'm your Annie o' Lochroyan,
    So open the door to me."

" O gin ye 're Annie o' Lochroyan,
    As I trust not ye be,
What token can ye gie that e'er
    I kept your companie !"

"O dinna ye mind, Love Gregor," she says,
    " When we sat at the wine,
How we changed the napkins frae our
        necks ?—
    It 's nae sae lang sinsyne.

" And yours was gude and gude eneuch,
    But nae sae gude as mine,
For yours was o' the cambric clear,
    But mine o' silk sae fine.

" And dinna ye mind, Love Gregor," she says,
    " As we twa sat at dine,
How we changed the rings frae our fingers,
    And I can shew thee mine.

R

"And yours was gude and gude eneuch,
    But nae sae gude as mine,
For yours was o' the gude red gold,
    But mine o' diamond fine.

"So open the door now, Love Gregòr,
    And open it wi' speed,
Or your young son that's in my arms
    For cauld will soon be dead."

"Awa', awa', ye ill woman,
    Gae frae my door for shame,
For I hae gotten another love,
    Sae ye may hie ye hame."

"O hae ye gotten another love,
    For a' the oaths ye sware?
Then fare ye well now, fause Gregòr,
    Ye 'se never see me mair."

O hooly, hooly gaed she back,
    As the day began to peep,
She set her foot on good ship-board,
    And sair, sair did she weep.

"Tak doun, tak doun that mast o' goud,
    Set up the mast o' tree;
Ill sets it a forsaken ladie
    To sail so gallantlie.

"Tak down, tak down the sails o' silk,
    Set up the sails o' skin;
Ill sets the outside to be gay
    When there 's sic grief within."

Love Gregor started frae his sleep,
 And to his mother did say,
"I dreamt a dream this night, mither,
 That makes my heart right wae.

"I dreamt that Annie o' Lochroyan,
 The flower of a' her kin,
Was standing mournin' at my door,
 And nane wad let her in."

"There was a woman at the door,
 Wi' a bairnie in her arm,
But I wadna let her ben the house
 For fear she 'd do thee harm."

O quickly, quickly raise he up,
 And fast, fast ran to the stran',
And there he saw his fair Annie
 Fast sailin' from the lan'.

And "Heigh, Annie," and "Ho, Annie,
 O Annie, winna ye bide?"
But aye the louder he cried "Annie"
 The louder roared the tide.

And "Heigh, Annie," and "Ho, Annie,
 O Annie, speak to me;"
But aye the louder he cried "Annie,"
 The louder roared the sea.

The wind grew loud, the sea grew rough,
 The ship was rent in twain,
And soon he saw her, fair Annie,
 Come floating o'er the main.

He saw his young son in her arms,
  Baith tossed above the tide,
He wrung his hands, and fast he ran,
  And plunged in the sea sae wide.

He caught her by the yellow hair,
  And drew her to the strand,
But cauld and stiff was every limb
  Before he reached the land.

Oh! first he kissed her bonnie cheek,
  And syne he kissed her chin,
And sair he kissed her bonnie lips,
  But there was nae breath within.

Oh, he has mourned for fair Annie
  Till the sun again went down,
Syne wi' a sich his heart it brast,
  And his soul to heaven has flown.

BINNORIE.

Published in Jamieson's Collection, and in Scott's Border Minstrelsy. Scott seems to have touched without improving Jamieson's version. Such lines as—

> "A famous harper, passing by,
>   The sweet fair face chanced to espy,"

are not to be compared in vigour to the original minstrel's

> "By there cam' a harper fine,
>   That harped to the king at dine;"

and the phrase in which the first author says of the weird harp—

> "The harp untouched to the windes rang,
>   And sad and doleful was the sang,"

are infinitely preferable to such a bald modernism as—

> "The strings he formed of her yellow hair,
>   Whose notes made sad the listening ear."

THERE were twa sisters lived in a bower,
    Binnorie, O Binnorie!
There came a knicht to be their wooer
    By the bonnie mill-dams o' Binnorie.

He courted the eldest wi' glove and ring,
    Binnorie, O Binnorie!
But he loved the youngest aboon a' thing,
    By the bonnie mill-dams o' Binnorie.

He courted the eldest wi' broach and knife;
    Binnorie, O Binnorie!
But he loved the youngest as his life,
    By the bonnie mill-dams o' Binnorie.

The eldest she was vexèd sair,
    Binnorie, O Binnorie!
And sair envièd her sister fair,
    By the bonnie mill-dams o' Binnorie.

Intil her bower she couldna rest,
    Binnorie, O Binnorie!
Wi' grief and spite she maistly brast,
    By the bonnie mill-dams o' Binnorie.

Upon a mornin' fair and clear,
    Binnorie, O Binnorie!
She cried upon her sister dear
    By the bonnie mill-dams o' Binnorie.

O sister! come to the sea-strand,
    Binnorie, O Binnorie!
And see our father's ships come to land,
    By the bonnie mill-dams o' Binnorie.

She 's ta'en her by the milk-white hand,
 Binnorie, O Binnorie!
And led her down to yon sea-strand
 By the bonnie mill-dams o' Binnorie.

The youngest stood upon a stane,
 Binnorie, O Binnorie!
The eldest cam and threw her in,
 By the bonnie mill-dams o' Binnorie.

She took her by the middle sma',
 Binnorie, O Binnorie!
And dashed her bonnie back to ja'
 By the bonnie mill-dams o' Binnorie.

"O sister, sister, tak my hand,
 Binnorie, O Binnorie!
And I 'se mak ye heir to a' my land,
 By the bonnie mill-dams o' Binnorie.

"O sister, sister, save my life,
 Binnorie, O Binnorie!
And I 'll swear I 'se never be nae man's wife,
 By the bonnie mill-dams o' Binnorie."

"Foul fa' the hand that I should tak,
 Binnorie, O Binnorie!
It twined me o' my warld's mak,
 By the bonnie mill-dams o' Binnorie.

"Your cherry check and yellow hair,
 Binnorie, O Binnorie!
Gar me gang maiden for evermair,
 By the bonnie mill-dams o' Binnorie."

Sometimes she sank, sometimes she swam ;
   Binnorie, O Binnorie!
Till she cam to the mouth o' yon mill-dam,
   By the bonnie mill-dams o' Binnorie.

Oh, out it came the miller's son,
   Binnorie, O Binnorie!
And saw the fair maid soumin in,
   By the bonnie mill-dams o' Binnorie.

" O father, father, draw your dam,
   Binnorie, O Binnorie!
There 's either a mermaid or a swan
   In the bonnie mill-dams o' Binnorie."

The miller quickly drew the dam,
   Binnorie, O Binnorie!
And there he found a drowned woman
   By the bonnie mill-dams o' Binnorie.

" Sair will they be, whae'er they be,
   Binnorie, O Binnorie!
Thir hearts that live to weep for thee,
   By the bonnie mill-dams o' Binnorie.

" And sair and lang may their teen last,
   Binnorie, O Binnorie!
That wrought thee sic a dowie cast,"
   By the bonnie mill-dams o' Binnorie.

You couldna see her yellow hair,
   Binnorie, O Binnorie!
For goud and pearl that were so rare
   By the bonnie mill-dams o' Binnorie!

You couldna see her middle sma',
   Binnorie, O Binnorie!
For her gouden girdle sae braw,
   By the bonnie mill-dams o' Binnorie!

You couldna see her fingers white,
   Binnorie, O Binnorie!
For gouden rings that were sae bright,
   By the bonnie mill-dams o' Binnorie.

By there cam a harper fine,
   Binnorie, O Binnorie!
That harpèd to the king at dine,
   By the bonnie mill-dams o' Binnorie!

"O wha sall tell to thy father dear,
   Binnorie, O Binnorie!
The sad and waefu' sight that 's here,
   By the bonnie mill-dams o' Binnorie?

"And wha to thy mother sall tell,
   Binnorie, O Binnorie!
The weird her dearest bairn befell
   By the bonnie mill-dams o' Binnorie?

"And wha to thy lover sall speak,
   Binnorie, O Binnorie!
The news will gar his heart to break,
   By the bonnie mill-dams o' Binnorie."

He's ta'en three locks of her yellow hair,
   Binnorie, O Binnorie!
And wi' them strung his harp sae fair,
   By the bonnie mill-dams o' Binnorie.

And the harp untouched to the windis rang,
   Binnorie, O Binnorie!
An' sad an' dolefu' was the sang,
   By the bonnie mill-dams o' Binnorie.

The first tune it did play and sing,
   Binnorie, O Binnorie!
Was "Farewell to my father the king,"
   By the bonnie mill-dams o' Binnorie.

The nexten tune it playèd then
   Binnorie, O Binnorie!
Was "Farewell to my mither the queen,"
   By the bonnie mill-dams o' Binnorie.

The thirden tune it playèd then,
   Binnorie, O Binnorie!
Was "Wae to my sister fair Ellen!"
   By the bonnie mill-dams o' Binnorie.

But the lasten tune it played sae sma,
   Binnorie, O Binnorie!
Was saft and sadly sweet o'er a',
   By the bonnie mill-dams o' Binnorie.

The hardest heart would hae bled to hear,
   Binnorie, O Binnorie!
It moaned wi' sic a dowy cheer,
   By the bonnie mill-dams o' Binnorie.

And fareweel, O fareweel to thee
   Binnorie, O Binnorie!
The dearest youth o' life to me,
   By the bonnie mill-dams o' Binnorie.

LAMBERT LINKIN.

Of this very popular ballad various editions have been published.   The first, in point of time, we believe, is that which appeared in Mr Herd's Collection, Edinburgh, 1776, entitled *Lammikin;* the next, that which occurs in Mr Jamieson's Collection, Edinburgh, 1806, under the title of *Lamkin.*   Two different versions of it will also be found in Mr Finlay's Collection, Edinburgh, 1808, under the title of *Lammikin,* the first of which is a reprint of Mr Herd's copy, interlaced with a number of additional verses, while the latter professes to be given wholly from a manuscript, corrected from a recited copy.   Of all these copies, that given by Mr Jamieson is unquestionably the best, as well as apparently the most authentic ; the second copy, given by Mr Finlay, is also genuine, but an abridged form of the original ballad.   On the contrary, the copy in Mr Herd's work is out of all sight the worst, inasmuch as it contains sundry injudicious interpolations and rhetorical embellishments by a modern hand.

The present copy is given from recitation ; and though it could have received additions, and perhaps improvements, from another copy, obtained from a similar source, and of equal authenticity, in his possession, the Editor did not like to use a liberty which is liable to much abuse. To some, the present set of the ballad may be valuable, as handing down both name and nickname of the revengeful builder of Prime Castle ; for there can be little doubt that the epithet "Linkin," Mr Lambert acquired from the secrecy and address with which he insinuated himself into that notable strength.   Indeed, all the names of Lammer-linkin, Lammikin, Lamkin, Lankin, Linkin, Belinkin, can easily be traced out as abbreviations of Lambert Linkin.   In the present set of the ballad, Lambert Linkin and Belinkin are used indifferently, as the measure of the verse may require ; in the other recited copy, to which reference has been made, it is Lammerlinkin and Lamkin, and the nobleman for whom he "built a house" is stated to be "Lord Arran."   No allusion, however, is made here to the name of the owner of Prime Castle.   Antiquaries, peradventure, may find it as difficult to settle the precise

locality of this fortalice, as they have found it to fix the
topography of Troy.—MOTHERWELL.

Mr Whitelaw, in his Collection (Blackie & Son), prints
no less than five versions of this ballad; one version, first
published by Jamieson, and reproduced by Chambers and
Professor Aytoun, supplies many obvious gaps in the story.
Instead of Prime Castle—not a very Scottish designation—
the castle is called Lord Wearie's Castle; and Professor
Aytoun states that the bloodthirsty hero is known in
Scottish nurseries, of which he is the terror, under the
names of Lammikin, Belinkin, Lamkin, Linkin, Bold
Rankin, and Balcanqual. A few of the stanzas rejected
by Motherwell are inserted within brackets.

BELINKIN was as gude a mason
As e'er pickt a stane;
He built up Prime Castle,
But payment gat nane.

["O pay me now, Lord Wearie,
O pay me now my fee!"
" I canna pay you, Lammikin,
For I maun sail the sea."

" O pay me now, Lord Wearie,
O pay me out of hand!"
" I canna pay you, Lammikin,
Unless I sell my land."

" O gin ye winna pay me,
It's here I mak a vow,
Before that ye come hame again
Ye shall hae cause to rue."]

The lord said to his lady,
When he was going abroad,
"Oh, beware of Belinkin,
For he lies in the wood."

[But the nourrice was a fause limmer,
　As ever hung on tree,
She laid a plot wi' Lammikin,
　When her lord was o'er the sea.]

The gates they were bolted
　Baith outside and in ;
At the sma' peep of a window
　Belinkin crap in.

"Gude morrow, gude morrow,"
　Said Lambert Linkin ;
" Gude morrow to yoursell, sir,"
　Said the fause nurse to him.

" O whare is your gude lord ? "
　Said Lambert Linkin ;
" He 's awa to New England,
　To meet with his king."

" O where is his auld son ? "
　Said Lambert Linkin ;
" He 's awa to buy pearlings
　Gin our lady lie in."

" Then she 'll never wear them,"
　Said Lambert Linkin ;
" And that is nae pity,"
　Said the fause nurse to him.

" O where is your lady ? "
　Said Lambert Linkin ;
" She 's in her bouir sleepin',"
　Said the fause nurse to him.

"How can we get at her?"
  Said Lambert Linkin ;
"Stab the babe to the heart
  Wi' a silver bodkin."

"That wud be a pity,"
  Said Lambert Linkin ;
"Nae pity, nae pity,"
  Said the fause nurse to him.

Belinkin he rocked,
  And the fause nurse she sang,
Till a' the tores * o' the cradle
  Wi' the red blude down ran.

"O still my babe, nurice,
  O still him wi' the knife ;"
"He 'll no be still, lady,
  Tho' I lay down my life."

"O still my babe, nurice,
  O still him wi' the knife ;"
"He 'll no be still, lady,
  Tho' I lay down my life."

"O still my babe, nurice,
  O still him wi' the kame ;"
"He 'll no be still, lady,
  Till his daddy come hame."

* "Tores :" the projections or knobs at the corners of
old-fashioned cradles, and the ornamental balls commonly
found surmounting the backs of old chairs. Dr Jamieson
does not seem to have had a precise notion of this word.
Vide vol. iv. of his Dictionary, *voce Tore.*—MOTHERWELL.

"O still my babe, nurice,
　　O still him wi' the bell;"
"He 'll no be still, lady,
　　Till ye come down yoursell."

"It 's how can I come doun
　　This cauld, frosty nicht,
Without e'er a coal,
　　Or a clear candle-licht?"

"There 's twa smocks in your coffer,
　　As white as a swan,
Put ane o' them about you,
　　It will shew you licht doun."

She took ane o' them about her,
　　And came tripping doun;
But as soon as she viewed,
　　Belinkin was in.

"Gude morrow, gude morrow,"
　　Said Lambert Linkin;
"Gude morrow to yoursell, sir,"
　　Said the lady to him.

"Oh, save my life, Belinkin,
　　Till my husband come back,
And I 'll gie ye as much red gold
　　As ye 'll haud in your hat."

"I 'll not save your life, lady,
　　Till your husband come back,
Tho' you wud gie me as much red gold
　　As I could haud in a sack.

"Will I kill her?" quo Belinkin,
  "Will I kill her, or let her be?"
"You may kill her," said the fause nurse,
  "She was ne'er gude to me;
And ye'll be laird o' the Castle,
  And I'll be ladye."

Then he cut aff her head
  Fra her lily breast-bane,
And he hung't up in the kitchen,
  It made a' the ha' shine.

The lord sat in England
  A-drinking the wine:
"I wish a' may be weel
  Wi' my lady at hame;
For the rings o' my fingers
  They're now burst in twain!"

He saddled his horse,
  And he cam riding doun;
But as soon as he viewed,
  Belinkin was in.

He hadna well stepped
  Twa steps up the stair,
Till he saw his pretty young son
  Lying dead on the floor.

He hadna weel stepped
  Other twa up the stair,
Till he saw his pretty lady
  Lying dead in despair.

He hanged Belinkin
  Out over the gate;
And he burnt the fause nurice
  Being under the grate.

REEDISDALE AND WISE WILLIAM.

This excellent ballad is from the recitation of Mr
Nicol, Strichen, and was communicated by Mr P. Buchan
of Peterhead.—MOTHERWELL.

WHEN Reedisdale and Wise William
   Were drinking at the wine,
There fell a roosing them amang,
   On one unruly time.

For some of them hae roosed their hawks,
   And other some their hounds;
And other some their ladies fair,
   And their bow'rs where they walked in.

When out it spak him Reedisdale,
   And a rash word spak he:
Says, "There is not a lady fair,
   In bower wherever she be,
But I could aye her favour win
   With one blink of my ee."

Then out it spak him Wise William,
   And a rash word spak he:
Says, "I have a sister of my own,
   In bower wherever she be,
And ye will not her favour win,
   With three blinks of your ee."

"What will you wager, Wise William?
   My lands I'll wad with thee;"
"I'll wad my head against your land,
   Till I get more monie."

Then Reedisdale took Wise William—
  Laid him in prison strang ;
That he might neither gang nor ride,
  Nor no word to her send.

But he has written a braid letter,
  Between the night and day,
And sent it to his own sister,
  By dun feather and gray.

When she had read Wise William's letter,
  She smiled and she leuch ;
Said, " Very weel, my dear brother,
  Of this I have eneuch."

She looked out at her west window,
  To see what she could see,
And there she spied him Reedisdale
  Come riding o'er the lea.

Says, " Come to me, my maidens all,
  Come hitherward to me ;
For here it comes him Reedisdale,
  Who comes a-courting me."

" Come down, come down, my lady fair,
  A sight of you give me."
" Go from my yetts now, Reedisdale,
  For me you will not see."

" Come down, come down, my lady fair,
  A sight of you give me ;
And bonnie is the gowns of silk
  That I will give to thee."

"If you have bonnie gowns of silk,
    O mine is bonny tee ;
Go from my yetts now Reedisdale,
    For me you shall not see."

"Come down, come down, my lady fair,
    A sight of you I 'll see ;
And bonnie jewels, broaches, rings,
    I will give unto thee."

"If you have bonnie broaches, rings,
    O mine are bonny tee ;
Go from my yetts now, Reedisdale,
    For me you shall not see."

"Come down, come down, my lady fair,
    One sight of you I 'll see ;
And bonnie are the halls and bowers
    That I will give to thee."

"If you have bonny halls and bowers,
    O mine are bonny tee ;
Go from my yetts now, Reedisdale,
    For me you shall not see."

"Come down, come down, my lady fair,
    A sight of you I 'll see ;
And bonnie are my lands so broad
    That I will give to thee."

"If you have bonny lands so broad,
    O mine are bonny tee ;
Go from my yetts now, Reedisdale,
    For me you will not see."

"Come down, come down, my lady fair,
 A sight of you I'll see;
And bonnie are the bags of gold
 That I will give to thee."

"If you have bonnie bags of gold,
 I have bags of the same;
Go from my yetts now, Reedisdale,
 For down I will not come."

"Come down, come down, my lady fair,
 One sight of you I'll see,
Or else I'll set your house on fire,
 If better cannot be."

Then he has set the house on fire,
 And all the rest it took;
He turned his wight horse head about,
 Said, "Alas! they'll ne'er get out."

"Look out, look out, my maidens fair,
 And see what I do see;
How Reedisdale has fired our house,
 And now rides o'er the lea.

"Come hitherward, my maidens fair
 Come hither unto me;
For through this reek and through this smeek
 O through it we must be."

They took wet mantles them about,
 Their coffers by the band;
And through the reek and through the flame,
 Alive they all have wan.

When they had got out through the fire,
    And able all to stand,
She sent a maid to Wise William,
    To bruik Reedisdale's land.

"Your lands are mine, now, Reedisdale,
    For I have won them free."
"If there is a good woman in the world,
    Your one sister is she."

* * *

SIR JAMES THE ROSE.

This old north country ballad, which appears to be founded on fact, is well known in almost every corner of Scotland.   Pinkerton printed it in his *Tragic Ballads,* 1781, "from," as he says, "a modern edition in one sheet 12mo, after the old copy."   Notwithstanding this reference to authority, the ballad certainly received a few conjectural emendations from his own pen; at least, the present version, which is given as it occurs in early stall prints, and as it is to be obtained from the recitations of elderly people, does not exactly correspond with his.

Two modern ballads have sprung out of this old one, namely, *Sir James the Ross,* and *Elfrida and Sir James of Perth.*   The first of these is said to have been written by Michael Bruce; the latter is an anonymous production, and has found its way into Evans' Collection—*vide* vol. iv. Edin. 1810.   It might be curious to ascertain which of these mournful ditties is the senior, were it for nothing else than perfectly to enjoy the cool impudence with which the graceless youngster has appropriated to itself, without thanks or acknowledgment, all the best things which occur in the other.—MOTHERWELL.

O HEARD ye of Sir James the Rose,
    The young heir of Buleighan?
For he has killed a gallant squire,
    And his friends are out to take him.

Now he's gone to the house of Marr,
    Where the Nourice was his leman;
To seek his dear he did repair,
    Thinking she would befriend him.

"Where are you going, Sir James?" she says,
    "Or where now are you riding?"
"Oh, I am bound to a foreign land,
    For now I'm under hiding.

"Where shall I go? where shall I run?
    Where shall I go to hide me?
For I have killed a gallant squire,
    And they're seeking to slay me."

"O go ye down to yon ale-house,
    And I'll there pay your lawin';
And if I be a maiden true,
    I'll meet you in the dawin'."

"I'll no go down to yon ale-house,
    For you to pay my lawin';
There's forty shillings for one supper,
    I'll stay in't till the dawin'."

He's turned him richt and round about,
    And rowed him in his brechan;
And he has gone to take his sleep,
    In the lowlands of Buleighan.

He had not weel gone out o' sicht,
    Nor was he past Millstrethen,
Till four-and-twenty belted knights,
    Came riding owre the Lethan.

"O have ye seen Sir James the Rose,
  The young heir of Buleighan?
For he has killed a gallant squire,
  And we're sent out to take him."

"O I have seen Sir James," she says,
  "For he passed here on Monday;
If the steed be swift that he rides on,
  He's past the gates o' London."*

As they rode on man after man,
  Then she cried out behind them,
"If you do seek Sir James the Rose,
  I'll tell you where you'll find him."

"Seek ye the bank abune the mill,
  In the lowlands of Buleighan;
And there you'll find Sir James the Rose,
  Lying sleeping in his brechan.

"You must not wake him out of sleep,
  Nor yet must you affright him,
Till you drive a dart quite through his heart,
  And through his body pierce him."

They sought the bank abune the mill,
  In the lowlands of Buleighan,
And there they found Sir James the Rose,
  Lying sleeping in his brechan.

Up then spake Sir John the Graeme,
  Who had the charge a-keeping,
"It shall ne'er be said, dear gentlemen,
  We killed a man when sleeping."

* "He's past the hichts o' Lundie," (*Pinkerton*,) which
is probably the correct reading.

They seized his broad sword and his targe,
    And closely him surrounded ;
And when he waked out of his sleep,
    His senses were confounded.

"O pardon, pardon, gentlemen,
    Have mercy now upon me."
"Such as you gave, such you shall have,
    And so we fall upon thee."

"Donald, my man, wait me upon,
    And I 'll gie you my brechan ;
And if you stay here till I die,
    You 'll get my trews of tartan.

"There is fifty pounds in my pocket,
    Besides my trews and brechan,
Ye 'll get my watch and diamond ring,
    And take me to Loch-Largan."

Now they 've ta'en out his bleeding heart,
    And stuck it on a spear,
Then took it to the House of Marr,
    And gave it to his dear.

But when she saw his bleeding heart,
    She was like one distracted,
She wrung her hands and tore her hair,
    Crying—"Oh ! what have I acted.

"It 's for your sake, Sir James the Rose,
    That my poor heart 's a-breaking ;
Cursed be the day I did thee betray,
    Thou brave knight o' Buleighan."

Then up she rose, and forth she goes,
    And in that fatal hour
She bodily was borne away,
    And never was seen more.

But where she went was never kent;
    And so, to end the matter,
A traitor's end you may depend
    Can never be no better.

FAIR ANNIE.

A fragment of this beautiful ballad first appeared in the Collection of David Herd, 1781.* A complete copy of it, obtained from recitation, was afterwards given in "The Minstrelsy of the Scottish Border," under the title of *Lord Thomas and Fair Annie.* Two other copies, obtained from a similar source, appeared in the Appendix of Mr Jamieson's Collection, entitled *Lady Jane and Burd Helen,* from which he formed the ballad of *Lady Jane* received into the body of the work. The same gentleman has, in the work referred to, translated from the Kæmpe Viser a Danish ballad entitled *Skœn Annie,* the story of which is the same with the present. To this he has subjoined some valuable and curious remarks on the striking resemblance which exists between Scottish and Scandinavian traditionary songs. His views on this interesting subject are given much more extended in the second part of that very valuable volume, "Northern Antiquities." †

This ballad, Sir Walter Scott observes, is, in its subject, similar to the Breton Romance of *Lai le Frain, or the Lay of the Ash;* and, it is probable, as the same writer suggests, that many others of our popular ballads may be

* Mr Jamieson has fallen into a mistake in saying that the ballad first appeared in Pinkerton's Ballads, not reflecting that Mr P. deserves little credit for his industry in *collecting* unedited ballads, however much he may be entitled to for his pains in *inventing* some.—W. M.

† Illustrations of Northern Antiquities. Edin. 1814. 4to.

likewise traced to a romance original. In confirmation
of this opinion, it may be noticed here, that, in one of the
commonest of our stall ballads, namely, *The Factor's
Garland, in four parts*, (a deserved favourite with the
vulgar,) its principal, and certainly the most interesting,
incident will be found in the curious romance of Sir
Amadas.—MOTHERWELL.

" LEARN to mak your bed, Annie,
    And learn to lie your lane,
For I maun owre the salt seas gang,
    A brisk bride to bring hame.

"Bind up, bind up your yellow hair,
    And tie it in your neck ;
And see you look as maiden like
    As the day that we first met."

"O how can I look maiden-like,
    When maiden I 'll ne'er be ;
When seven brave sons I 've born to thee,
    And the eighth is in my bodie ?

"The eldest of your sons, my lord,
    Wi' red gold shines his weed ;
The second of your sons, my lord,
    Rides on a milk-white steed :

" And the third of your sons, my lord,
    He draws your beer and wine ;
And the fourth of your sons, my lord,
    Can serve you when you dine.

" And the fifth of your sons, my lord,
    He can both read and write ;
And the sixth of your sons, my lord,
    Can do it most perfyte :

" And the seventh of your sons, my lord,
   Sits on the nurse's knee ;
And how can I look maiden-like,
   When a maid I 'll never be ?

" But wha will bake your wedding bread,
   And brew your bridal ale ;
Or wha will welcome your brisk bride
   That you bring owre the dale ?"

" I 'll put cooks in my kitchen,
   And stewards in my hall,
And I 'll have bakers for my bread,
   And brewers for my ale ;
But you 're to welcome my brisk bride
   That I bring owre the dale."

He set his feet into his ship,
   And his cock-boat on the main ;
He swore it would be a year and day
   Or he returned again.

When a year and day was past and gane,
   Fair Annie she thocht lang,
And she is up to her bower head
   To behold both sea and land.

" Come up, come up, my eldest son,
   And see now what you see ;
Oh, yonder comes your father dear,
   And your stepmother to be."

" Cast off your gown of black, mother,
   Put on your gown of brown,
And I 'll put off my mourning weeds,
   And we 'll welcome him home."

She 's taken wine into her hand,
   And she has taken bread,
And she is down to the water side
   To welcome them indeed.

" You 're welcome, my lord, you 're welcome,
     my lord,
   Your welcome home to me,
So is every lord and gentleman
   That is in your companie.

" You 're welcome, my lady, you 're welcome,
     my lady,
   You 're welcome home to me,
So is every lady and gentleman
   That 's in your companie."

" I thank you, my girl, I thank you, my girl,
   I thank you heartily ;
If I live seven years about this house,
   Rewarded you shall be."

She served them up, she served them down,
   With the wheat bread and the wine,
But aye she drank the cauld water,
   To keep her colour fine.

She served them up, she served them down,
   With the wheat bread and the beer,
But aye she drank the cauld water
   To keep her colour clear.

When bells were rung, and mass was sung,
   And all were boune for rest,
Fair Annie laid her sons in bed,
   And a sorrowfu' woman she was.

“Will I go to the salt, salt seas,
　　And see the fishes swim?
Or will I go to the gay green wood,
　　And hear the small birds sing?”

Out an spoke an aged man,
　　That stood behind the door,
“Ye will not go to the salt, salt seas
　　To see the fishes swim,
Nor will ye go to the gay green wood
　　To hear the small birds sing;

“But ye’ll take a harp into your hand,
　　Go to their chamber door,
And aye ye’ll harp, and aye ye’ll mourn,
　　With the salt tears falling o’er.”

She’s ta’en a harp into her hand,
　　Went to their chamber door,
And aye she harped, and aye she mourned,
　　With the salt tears falling o’er.

Out and spak the brisk, young bride,
　　In bride-bed where she lay,
“I think I hear my sister Annie,
　　And I wish weel it may;
For a Scottish lord staw her awa’,
　　And an ill death may he die.”

“Wha was your father, my girl?” she says,
　　“Or wha was your mother?
Or had you ever a sister dear,
　　Or had you ever a brother?”

“King Henry was my father dear,
　　Queen Esther was my mother,
Prince Henry was my brother dear,
　　And Fanny Flower my sister.”

"If King Henry was your father dear,
 And Queen Esther was your mother,
If Prince Henry was your brother dear,
 Then surely I 'm your sister."

"Come to your bed, my sister dear,
 It ne'er was wranged for me,
Bot an ae kiss of his merry mouth,
 As we cam owre the sea."

"Awa, awa, ye forenoon bride,
 Awa, awa frae me ;
I wudna hear my Annie greet,
 For a' the gold I got wi' thee."

"There were five ships of gay red gold
 Cam owre the seas with me,
It's twa o' them will tak me hame,
 And three I 'll leave wi' thee.

"Seven ships o' white monie
 Came owre the seas wi' me,
Five o' them I 'll leave wi' thee,
 And twa will take me hame ;
And my mother will make my portion up
 When I return agian."

MARY HAMILTON.

Of this ballad two complete, but somewhat differing copies have already been published, one in the Border Min-strelsy, and the other in Mr Sharpe's Ballad Book ; the fragment of a third version is extant in "A North Coun-trie Garland," and this has subsequently appeared in "Gleanings of Old Ballads," by P. Buchan. The present copy differs from all these, and as it shews the state in

which it is frequently to be met with as preserved by
tradition in the west of Scotland, no apology is deemed
necessary for again presenting this interesting ballad to
the notice of those who are curious in matters of this
sort.

Sir Walter Scott inclines to ascribe the ballad to the
following incident mentioned by Knox. "In the very
time of the General Assembly there comes to public
notice a haynous murther committed in the Court; yea,
not far from the Queen's lap; for a Frenchwoman that
served in the Queen's chamber had played the whore with
the Queen's own apothecary. The woman conceived and
bare a childe, whom, with common consent, the father
and mother murthered; yet were the cries of a new-borne
childe hearde; searche was made, the childe and the
mother were both apprehended, and so were the man and
the woman condemned to be hanged in the publicke
street in Edinburgh. The punishment was suitable,
because the crime was haynous. But yet was not the
Court purged of whores and whoredoms, which was the
fountain of such enormities; for it was well knowne that
shame hasted marriage betwixt John Sempill, called the
Dancer,* and Mary Levingston, sirnamed the Lusty.
What bruit the Maries and the rest of the dancers of the
Court had, the ballads of that age do witness, which we,
for modestie's sake, omit."—*History of the Reformation*,
p. 373. For these modest scruples in omitting the ballads of the age, the historian, it is believed, will receive
but slender thanks at the hands of the poetic antiquary.
—MOTHERWELL.

THERE lives a knight into the north,
　And he had daughters three;
The ane of them was a barber's wife,
　The other a gay ladie;

And the youngest o' them to Scotland is gane,
　The Queen's Mary to be,
And for a' that they could say or do
　Forbidden she wouldna be.

* This was the ancestor of Sir James Sempill of Belltrees.

The prince's bed it was sae saft,
    The spices they were sae fine,
That out of it she could not lye
    While she was scarce fifteen.

She 's gane to the garden gay
    To pu' of the Savin tree,
But for a' that she could say or do
    The babie it would not die.

She 's rowed it in her handkerchief,
    She threw it in the sea,
Says—"Sink ye, swim ye, my bonnie babe,
    For ye 'll get nae mair of me."

Queen Mary came tripping down the stair,
    Wi' the gold strings in her hair;
"Oh, where 's the little babie," she says,
    "That I heard greet sae sair?"

"O hald your tongue, Queen Mary, my dame,
    Let all those words go free;
It was mysel wi' a fit o' the sair colic,
    I was sick just like to die."

"O hald your tongue, Mary Hamilton,
    Let all those words go free;
O where is the little babie
    That I heard weep by thee?"

"I rowed it in my handkerchief,
    And threw it in the sea;
I bade it sink, I bade it swim,
    It would get nae mair o' me."

“O wae be to thee, Mary Hamilton,
  And an ill death may you die,
For if you had saved the babie’s life,
  It might hae been an honour to thee.

“Busk ye, busk ye, Mary Hamilton,
  O busk ye to be a bride ;
For I am going to Edinburgh town
  Your gay wedding to bide.

“You must not put on your robes of black,
  Nor yet your robes of brown ;
But you must put on your yellow gold stuffs,
  To shine thro’ Edinburgh town.”

“I will not put on my robes of black,
  Nor yet my robes of brown,
But I will put on my yellow gold stuffs,
  To shine thro’ Edinburgh town.”

As she went up the Parliament Close,
  A-riding on her horse,
There she saw many a burgess’ lady
  Sit greeting at the cross.

“O what means a’ this greeting,
  I ’m sure it ’s nae for me,
For I ’m come this day to Edinburgh town
  Weel wedded for to be.”

When she gaed up the Parliament stair,
  She gied loud lauchters three ;
But ere that she had come down again,
  She was condemned to die.

"O little did my mother think,
　The day she prinned my gown,
That I was to come sae far frae hame
　To be hanged in Edinburgh town.

"O what 'll my poor father think,
　As he comes through the town,
To see the face of his Molly fair
　Hanging on the gallows pin.

"Here 's a health to the mariners
　That plough the raging main ;
Let neither my mother nor father ken
　But I 'm coming hame again.

"Here 's a health to the sailors
　That sail upon the sea ;
Let neither my mother nor father ken
　That I came here to die.

"Yestreen the Queen had four Maries,
　This night she 'll hae but three ;
There was Mary Beaton, and Mary Seaton,
　And Mary Carmichael, and me."

"O hald your tongue, Mary Hamilton,
　Let all those words go free ;
This night, ere ye be hanged,
　Ye shall gang hame wi' me."

"O hald your tongue, Queen Mary, my dame,
　Let all those words go free,
Since I have come to Edinburgh town,
　It 's hanged I shall be ;
For it shall ne'er be said that in your court
　I was condemned to die."

T

LORD RANDAL.

From Scott's Border Minstrelsy. The story narrated appears, with many variations, in the popular ballads of Scandinavia and Germany; and two, if not three versions are current in Scotland and England; in one of which a stepmother, and in another a rival, are the poisoners.

"Where hae ye been hunting,
   Lord Randal, my son?
Where hae ye been hunting,
   My handsome young man?"
"In yon wild-wood, O mither!
   So make my bed soon,
For I'm wae and I'm weary,
   And fain would lie down."

"Where got ye your dinner,
   Lord Randal, my son?
Where got ye your dinner,
   My handsome young man?"
"O! I dined wi' my true love
   So make my bed soon,
For I'm wae and I'm weary,
   And fain would lie down."

"O what was your dinner,
   Lord Randal, my son?
O what was your dinner,
   My handsome young man?"
"Eels boiled in broo, mither,
   So make my bed soon,
For I'm wae and I'm weary,
   And fain would lie down."

"O where did she find them,
 Lord Randal, my son,
O where did she catch them,
 My handsome young man?"
" 'Neath the bush of brown brechan,
 So make my bed soon,
For I'm wae and I'm weary,
 An' fain would lie doun."

"And where are your blood-hounds,
 Lord Randal, my son,
What came of your blood-hounds,
 My handsome young man?"
"They swelled and they died, mither,
 And sae maun I soon,
I am wae, I am weary,
 And fain would lie down."

"I fear you are poisoned,
 Lord Randal, my son,
I fear you are poisoned,
 My handsome young man!"
"O yes I am poisoned,
 So make my bed soon,
I am sick, sick at heart,
 An' I fain would lie doun."

WILLIE, DOO.

From "Ballads of the North of Scotland," collected by P.
Buchan. This appears to be an earlier, as well as a ruder
version of the story of *Lord Ronald* or *Lord Randal.*

"WHERE hae ye been a' the day?
 Willie, doo! Willie, doo!
Where hae ye been a' the day,
 Willie, my doo?"

"I've been to my stepmother,
   Mak my bed, lay me doun;
I've been to my stepmother,
   Die shall I soon."

"What got ye frae your stepmother?
   Willie, doo! Willie, doo!
What got ye frae your stepmother?
   Willie, my doo."

"She gae me a speckled trout,
   Mak my bed, lay me doun;
She gae me a speckled trout,
   Die shall I soon."

"Where got she the speckled trout,
   Willie, doo, Willie, doo?"
"She got it 'mong the heather hills,
   Die shall I now."

"What did she boil it in,
   Willie, doo, Willie, doo?"
"She boiled it in the billy-pot,
   Die shall I now."

"What gaed she you for to drink,
   Willie, doo! Willie, doo!
What gaed she you for to drink,
   Willie, my doo?"

"She gaed me hemlock stocks,
   Mak my bed, lay me doun;
Made in the brewing-pot,
   Die shall I soon."

They made his bed, laid him doun,
    Willie, doo! Willie, doo!
He turned his face to the wa',
    Dead is he now!

THE LAMENT OF THE BORDER WIDOW.

A well-known and beautiful fragment, said by Sir Walter Scott to have been obtained from recitation in the Forest of Ettrick, and to relate to the execution of Cockburne of Henderland, a Border freebooter, hanged over the gate of his own tower, by James V., in the course of that memorable expedition in 1529, which was fatal to Johnnie Armstrong, Adam Scott of Tushielaw, and many other marauders. Cockburne, says tradition, was surprised by the king while he was sitting at dinner. Some vestiges of the castle of Henderland still remain at the mouth of the river Meggat, which falls into the lake of St Mary in Selkirkshire. A mountain torrent rushes impetuously through a rocky chasm, called the Dow-glen, and passes near the site of the tower. The wife of Cockburne is said to have fled to the recesses of the glen during the execution of her husband, hoping to drown the cries of the soldiery in the roar of the cataract. The solitary spot is called the Lady's Seat. A large stone, broken in three parts, marks the place where both husband and wife were buried, in the old graveyard of the chapel. The following inscription is visible, on its surface: "Here lyes Perys of Cokburne and his wyfe Marjory." The ballad bears traces of a finer hand than that of any ancient minstrel; and Mr Motherwell was of opinion that it was an adaptation from the old English ballad of *The Lady turned Serving Man*, in Percy's Reliques. The first three stanzas shew evident signs of this origin. Perhaps the Ettrick Shepherd, or Sir Walter Scott himself, might have rightly claimed, had he chosen, the merit of the adaptation; but the story as it stands is both simple and beautiful, and has so entwined itself in the affections of the lovers of

Scottish poetry and romance, as to force its way into all collections of the legendary poetry of Scotland.

My love he built me a bonnie bower,
And clad it a' wi' lilye flower;
A brawer bower ye ne'er did see,
Than my true love he built for me.

There came a man, by middle day,
He spied his sport and went away,
And brought the king that very night,
Who brake my bower, and slew my knight.

He slew my knight, to me sae dear;
He slew my knight, and poined his gear;
My servants all for life did flee,
And left me in extremitie.

I sewed his sheet, making my mane;
I watched the corpse, myself alane;
I watched his body, night and day;
No living creature came that way.

I took his body on my back,
And whiles I gaed, and whiles I sat;
I digged a grave, and laid him in,
And happed him with the sod so green.

But think na ye my heart was sair,
When I laid the moul' on his yellow hair;
Think nae ye my heart was wae,
When I turned about, away to gae?

Nae living man I'll love again,
Since that my lovely knight is slain;
Wi' ae lock o' his yellow hair
I'll bind my heart for evermair.

THE MERMAID.

From Mr Finlay's Collection of Scottish Ballads, published in 1808. "This beautiful piece of poetry," says Mr Finlay, "was recovered from the recitation of a lady, who heard it sung by the servants in her father's family, above fifty years ago."

To yon fause stream that, near the sea,
   Hides mony an elf and plum,*
And rives wi' fearful din the stanes,
   A witless knicht did come.

The day shines clear—far in he's gane
   Whar shells are silver bright,
Fishes war loupin' a' aroun',
   And sparklin' to the light.

Whan, as he laved, sounds cam sae sweet
   Frae ilka rock an' tree ;
The brief was out, 'twas him it doomed
   The mermaid's face to see.

Frae 'neath a rock, sune, sune she rose,
   And stately on she swam,
Stopped i' the midst, and becked and sang
   To him to stretch his han'.

Gowden glist the yellow links
   That round her neck she'd twine ;
Her een war o' the skyie blue,
   Her lips did mock the wine ;

The smile upon her bonnie cheek
   Was sweeter than the bee ;
Her voice excelled the birdie's sang
   Upon the birchen tree.

* "Plum :" a deep hole in a river's bed.

Sae couthie, couthie did she look,
    And meikle had she fleeched ;*
Out shot his hand—alas! alas!
    Fast in the swirl he screeched.

The mermaid leuch, her brief was gane,
    And kelpie's blast was blawin',
Fu' low she dooked, ne'er raise again,
    For deep, deep was the fawin'.

Aboon the stream his wraith was seen,
    Warlocks tirled lang at gloamin';
That e'en was coarse, the blast blew hoarse,
    Ere lang the waves were foamin'.

GORDON OF BRACKLEY.

A version of this story appeared in Jamieson's Collection, 1806. Mr R. Chambers, in reproducing it, in 1829, in his Scottish Ballads, states that it records a real incident which took place, on the 16th of September 1666, between John Gordon of Brackley, in Aberdeenshire, and Farquharson of Invercauld, a noted freebooter on Deeside.

Down Deeside cam Inverayc
    Whistlin' and playing,
An' called loud at Brackley gate
    Ere the day dawing—
"Come, Gordon of Brackley,
    Proud Gordon, come down,
There's a sword at your threshold
    Mair sharp than your own."

* "Fleeched :" flattered, or beseeched.

"Arise now, gay Gordon,"
   His lady 'gan cry,
"Look, here is bold Inveraye
   Driving your kye."
"How can I go, lady,
   An' win them again,
When I have but ae sword,
   And Inveraye ten?"

"Arise up, my maidens,
   Wi' roke and wi' fan,
How blest had I been
   Had I married a man!
Arise up, my maidens,
   Tak' spear and tak' sword,
Go milk the ewes, Gordon,
   An' I will be lord."

The Gordon sprung up
   Wi' his helm on his head,
Laid his hand on his sword,
   An' his thigh on his steed.
An' he stooped low, and said,
   As he kissed his young dame,
"There's a Gordon rides out
   That will never ride hame."

There rode with fierce Inveraye
   Thirty and three,
But wi' Brackley were nane
   But his brother and he;
Twa gallanter Gordons
   Did never blade draw,
But against three and thirty,
   Wae's me! what are twa?

Wi' sword and wi' dagger
  They rushed on him rude;
The twa gallant Gordons
  Lie bathed in their blude.
Frae the springs o' the Dee
  To the mouth o' the Tay,
The Gordons mourn for him,
  And curse Inveraye.

"O were ye at Brackley?
  An' what saw ye there?
Was his young widow weeping,
  An' tearing her hair?"
"I looked in at Brackley,
  I looked in, and oh!
There was mirth, there was feasting,
  But naething o' woe.

"As a rose bloomed the lady,
  An' blithe as a bride,
As a bridegroom bold Inveraye
  Smiled by her side.
Oh! she feasted him there
  As she ne'er feasted lord,
While the blood of her husband
  Was moist on his sword.

"In her chamber she kept him
  Till morning grew gray,
Thro' the dark woods of Brackley
  She shewed him the way.
'Yon wild hill,' she said,
  'Where the sun's shining on,
Is the hill of Glentanner;—
  One kiss, and begone!'"

There 's grief in the cottage,
   There 's grief in the ha',
For the gude, gallant Gordon
   That 's dead an' awa'.
To the bush comes the bud,
   An' the flower to the plain,
But the gude and the brave
   They come never again.

ANNAN WATER.

First published in Scott's "Minstrelsy of the Scottish Border," and there said to be the original words of the tune of *Allan Water*, mentioned in "The Tea-Table Miscellany." "It is said," adds Sir Walter Scott, "that a bridge over the Annan was built in consequence of the melancholy catastrophe which it narrates." It is difficult to avoid a suspicion that either Scott or the Ettrick Shepherd had some hand in the composition of the ballad, which is alleged to have been taken from "tradition." Scott mentions another version of the ballad, but does not print it.

O! Annan water 's wide an' deep,
   An' my love Annie 's wondrous bonnie;
Shall I be loth to weet my feet
   For her whom I love best of ony?
Gar saddle me my bonnie black,
   Gar saddle soon an' mak him ready,
For I will down the Gatehope Slack,
   And a' to see my bonnie lady.

He 's loupen on his bonnie black,
   He 's stirred him wi' the spur fu' sairly,
An' e'er he won the Gatehope Slack,
   I wot the steed was wae and weary.

He 's loupen on his bonnie gray,
    He rode the right gate an' the ready;
O nought could make him stint or stay,
    For thinkin' o' his bonnie lady!

He 's ridden over field and fell,
    Thro' moss and stream, an' moor and mire,
His spurs of steel were sair to bide,
    An' frae her fore feet flew the fire.
"Now, bonnie gray! now play your part!
    An' gin ye bear me to my dearie,
On corn an' hay ye'se feed for aye,
    An' never spur shall make ye weary!"

She was a mare, a right good mare,
    But when she wan to Annan water,
She couldna hae ridden a furlong mair,
    Had a thousand merks been wadded at her!
"O boatman, haste! Put off your boat,
    Put off your boat for gouden money;
I cross the drumlie stream to-night,
    Or never more I meet my honey!"

"O! I was sworn late, late yestreen,
    An' not by ae oath but by many;
For a' the gowd in broad Scotland
    I maunna tak ye through to Annie."
The side was steep, the bottom deep,
    Frae bank to bank the water pouring,
An' the bonnie gray did shake for fear,
    She heard the water-kelpie roaring.

O! he 's pu'd aff his dapper coat,
    Wi' silver buttons glancin' bonnie;
The waistcoat bursted aff his breast,
    His heart leaped sae wi' melancholy.

He 's ta'en the ford at the stream tail,
   I wat he swam baith stout and steady ;
The stream was broad—his strength did fail—
   He never saw his bonnie lady.

O wae betide the fresh saugh wand,
   An' wae betide the bush o' brier,
They broke into my true love's hand,
   When strength did fail, and limbs did tire.
An' wae betide thee, Annan stream !
   Thou art a deep and deadly river;
But over thee I 'll build a bridge,
   That ye nae mair true love may sever!

THE WEE, WEE MAN.

The principal object in giving the present traditionary version of this well-known and singular ballad, is to restore to the mysterious little master whom it commemorates that marvellous breadth of shoulders which truly belongs to him, and of which, it will be seen, by comparison with the common printed copies, that he has been most unceremoniously and injudiciously deprived. The vast latitude of his chest, and formidable bigness of his head, contrasted with the tiny measurement of his limbs, add wondrously to the grotesqueness of his figure, and form too important a feature in the curious picture to be heedlessly omitted. There is an old poem in the Cotton MSS., which Ritson supposes to be of the time of Edward I. or II., which begins—

> "Als Y Yod on ay Mounday,"

and of which the present ballad appears to be a portion. This poem is printed in Mr Finlay's Collection, accompanied with some sensible remarks.—MOTHERWELL.

As I was walking mine alane,
  Betwixt the water and the wa';
There I espied a wee, wee man,
  He was the least ane that e'er I saw.

His leg was scarce a shaftmont * lang,
  Both thick and nimble was his knee; †
Between his een there was a span,
  Betwixt his shoulders there were ells three.

This wee, wee man pulled up a stane,
  He flang't as far as I could see;
Though I had been as Wallace strang,
  I wadna gotten it to my knee.

I said, "Wee man, oh! but you're strang,
  Where is your dwelling, an' where may't be?"
"My dwelling's at yon bonnie green,
  Fair lady, will ye go and see?"

On we lap and awa' we rade,
  Until we cam to yonder green;
We lighted down to rest our steed,
  And there came out a lady sheen,

Wi' four and twenty at her back,
  And they were a' weel clad in green;
Although he had been the king of Scotland,
  The warst o' them might hae been his queen.

* "Shaftmont:" This word, of which the derivation
has long been a puzzle, is supposed to mean, "As long as
the fist with the thumb turned out," or about six inches.
  † *Variation*—
      "His legs they were na a gude inch lang,
        And thick and nimble was his thie."

So on we lap and awa' we rade,
    Till we came to yon bonnie hall ;
The rafters were o' the beaten gold,
    And silver wire were the kebars all.

There were pipers playing in every neuk,
    And ladies dancing jimp and sma' ;
And aye the owreword o' their tune,
    Was—" Our wee, wee man has been lang awa' ! *

YOUNG BEARWELL

Is a fragment, and now printed in the hope that the
remainder of it may hereafter be recovered.   From circumstances, one would almost be inclined to trace it to a
Danish source ; or it may be an episode of some forgotten
metrical romance, but this cannot satisfactorily be ascertained from its catastrophe being unfortunately wanting.
—MOTHERWELL.

WHEN two lovers love each other weel,
    Great sin it were them to twinn ;
And this I speak from young Bearwell,
    He loved a lady ying,
The Mayor's daughter of Birktown-brae,
    That lovely liesome thing.

One day when she was looking out,
    Washing her milk-white hands,
Then she beheld him young Bearwell,
    As he came in the sands.

* The two last lines of the printed copies differ from
these ; but I never have found their reading sanctioned
by a recited copy of any antiquity :—
            " But in the twinkling of an ee
                My wee, wee man was clean awa' ! "
—MOTHERWELL.

Says—"Wae's me for you, young Bearwell,
  Such tales of you are tauld;
They'll cause you sail the salt sea so far,
  As beyond Yorkisfauld."

"Oh! shall I bide in good green wood,
  Or stay in bower with thee?"
"The leaves are thick in good green wood,
  Would hold you from the rain;
And if you stay in bower with me,
  You will be taken and slain.

"But I caused build a ship for you,
  Upon Saint Innocent's day;
I'll bid Saint Innocent be your guide,
  And our Lady that meikle may.
You are a lady's first true love,
  God carry you weel away!"

Then he sailed east and he sailed west,
  By many a comely strand;
At length a puff of northern wind
  Did blow him to the land.

When he did see the king and court,
  Were playing at the ba';
Gave him a harp into his hand,
  Says—"Stay, Bearwell, and play."

He had not been in the king's court
  A twelvemonth and a day,
Till there came lords and lairds enew,
  To court that lady gay.

They wooèd her with broach and ring,
  They nothing could keep back,
The very charters of their lands
  Into her hands they pat.

She's done her down to Heyvalin,
　With the light of the mune;
Says—"Will ye do this deed for me,
　And will ye do it sune?

"Will ye go seek him, young Bearwell,
　On seas wherever he be?
And if I live and bruik* my life,
　Rewarded ye shall be."

"Alas, I am too young a skipper,
　So far to sail the faem;
But if I live and bruik my life,
　I'll strive to bring him hame."

So he has sailed east and then sailed west,
　By many a comely strand;
Till there came a blast of northern wind,
　And blew him to the land.

And there the king and all his court,
　Were playing at the ba',
Gave him a harp into his hand,
　Says—"Stay, Heyvalin, and play."

He has tane up the harp in hand,
　And unto play went he;
And young Bearwell was the first man
　In all that companie.

＊　＊　＊　＊　＊　＊

* "Bruik:" endure or enjoy.

THE GAY GOSS-HAWK.

Sir Walter Scott first published in the Border Minstrelsy the ballad of the *Gay Goss-Hawk*, partly made
up, he informed the reader, from a version in Mrs Brown's
collection, and partly from "a MS. of some antiquity," in
his own. Mr Motherwell also published a shorter and
less complete version, under the title of the *Jolly Goss-
Hawk*, which Mr Peter Buchan sent to him; and, at a
later period, Mr Buchan published in his "Ancient Ballads of the North of Scotland," a version different from
both, entitled *The Scottish Squire*, which he took down
from recitation, and in which the messenger-bird is a
parrot instead of a goss-hawk. Mr Buchan was of opinion
that both Sir Walter Scott's version and Motherwell's
were inferior to his own "in delineation of character and
detail of incident." It has, no doubt, merits of its own,
and not only seems to have been less tampered with by
scholars than that of Sir Walter Scott, which is avowedly
composite, but to have the veritable smack of the street
ballad. Mr Buchan is further of opinion that the "parrot" is a better bird for the purposes of the story than
the goss-hawk;—an opinion with which few will, we
think, be found to coincide.

"O WALY, waly, my gay goss-hawk,
  Gin your feathering be sheen!"
"And waly, waly, my master dear,
  Gin ye look pale and lean!

"O have ye tint, at tournament,
  Your sword, or yet your spear!
Or mourn ye for the Southern lass,
  Whom you may not win near?"

"I have not tint at tournament,
  My sword, nor yet my spear;
But sair I mourn for my true love,
  Wi' mony a bitter tear.

"But weel's me on ye, my gay goss-hawk,
  Ye can baith speak and flee;
Ye sall carry a letter to my love,
  Bring an answer back to me."

"But how sall I your true love find,
  Or how suld I her know?
I bear a tongue ne'er wi' her spake,
  An eye that ne'er her saw."

"O weel sall ye my true love ken,
  Sae sune as ye her see;
For of a' the flowers of fair England,
  The fairest flower is she.

"The red that's on my true love's cheek
  Is like blood-drops on the snaw;
The white that is on her breast bare
  Like the down o' the white sea-maw.*

"And even at my love's bower door
  You'll find a bowing birk;
And ye maun sit and sing thereon
  As she gangs to the kirk.

"And four-and-twenty fair ladyes
  Will to the mass repair,
But weel may ye my ladye ken,
  The fairest lady there."

* Mr Buchan's version has these lines more pithily:—

  "O what is red of her is red
    As blude drapped on the snaw,
  And what is white of her is white
    As milk, or the wild sea-maw."

Lord William has written a love letter,
    Put it under his pinion gray;
And he is awa' to Southern land
    As fast as wings can gae.

And even at that lady's bower
    There grew a flowering birk;
And he sat down and sung thereon
    As she gaed to the kirk.

And weel he kent that ladye fair,
    Amang her maidens free,
For the flower that springs in May morning
    Was not sae sweet as she.

He lighted at the ladye's yate,
    And sat him on a pin,*
And sang fu' sweet the notes o' love,
    Till a' was cosh † within.

And first he sang a low, low note,
    And syne he sang a clear;
And aye the o'erword o' the sang
    Was—"Your love can no win here."

"Feast on, feast on, my maidens a',
    The wine flows you amang,
While I gang to my shot-window,
    And hear yon bonnie bird's sang.

"Sing on, sing on, my bonnie bird,
    The sang ye sung yestreen;
For weel I ken by your sweet singing
    Ye are frae my true love sen."

* "Pin:" Mr Motherwell's version reads "whin," or whin-bush, which seems a more appropriate resting-place for a bird than a pin; *i. e.*, a door-pin.
    † "Cosh:" quiet.

Oh, first he sang a merry sang,
    And syne he sang a grave;
And syne he peck'd his feathers gray,
    To her the letter gave.

"Have there a letter from Lord William;
    He says he's sent ye three;
He canna wait your love langer,
    But for your sake he'll die."

"Gae bid him bake his bridal bread,
    And brew his bridal ale,
And I shall meet him at Mary's kirk,
    Lang, lang ere it be stale."

The lady's gane to her chamber,
    And a moanfu' woman was she;
As gin she had ta'en a sudden brash,*
    And were about to die.

"A boon, a boon, my father dear,
    A boon I beg of thee!"
"Ask not that paughty Scottish lord,
    For him you ne'er shall see.

"But for your honest asking else,
    Weel granted it shall be."
"Then, gin I die in Southern land,
    In Scotland gar bury me.

"And the first kirk that ye come to
    Ye's gar the mass be sung,
And the next kirk that ye come to
    Ye's gar the bells be rung.

* "Brash:" sickness.

"And when ye come to St Mary's kirk,
    Ye's tarry there till night."
And so her father pledged his word,
    And so his promise plight.

She has ta'en her to her bigly bower
    As fast as she could fare;
And she has drank a sleepy draught
    That she had mix'd wi' care.

And pale, pale grew her rosy cheek,
    That was sae bright of blee,
And she seem'd to be as surely dead
    As any one could be.

Then spak her cruel step-minnie,
    "Tak ye the burning lead,
And drap a drap on her bosome,
    To try if she be dead."

They took a drap o' boiling lead,
    They drapp'd it on her breast;
"Alas! alas!" her father cried,
    "She's dead without the priest."

She neither chatter'd with her teeth,
    Nor shiver'd with her chin;
"Alas! alas!" her father cried,
    "There is nae breath within."

Then up arose her seven brethren,
    And hew'd to her a bier;
They hew'd it frae the solid aik,
    Laid it o'er wi' silver clear.

Then up and gat her seven sisters,
  And sewed to her a kell;
And every steek that they put in
  Sewed to a siller bell.

The first Scots kirk that they cam to,
  They garr'd the bells be rung;
The next Scots kirk that they cam to,
  They garr'd the mass be sung.

But when they cam to St Mary's kirk,
  There stude spearmen all on a raw;
And up and started Lord William,
  The chieftane amang them a'.

"Set down, set down the bier," he said;
  "Let me look her upon:"
But as soon as Lord William touched her
    hand,
  Her colour began to come.

She brighten'd like the lily flower,
  Till her pale colour was gone;
With rosy cheek, and ruby lip,
  She smiled her love upon.

"A morsel of your bread, my lord,
  And one glass of your wine:
For I hae fasted these three lang days,
  All for your sake and mine.

"Gae hame, gae hame, my seven bauld
    brothers!
  Gae hame and blaw your horn!
I trow ye wad hae gi'en me the skaith,
  But I 've gi'en you the scorn.

"Commend me to my gray father,
    That wish'd my saul gude rest;
But wae be to my cruel step-dame,
    Gar'd burn me on the breast."

"Ah! woe to you, you light woman!
    An ill death may you die!
For we left father and sisters at hame
    Breaking their hearts for thee."

THE JOLLY GOSS-HAWK.

MOTHERWELL'S VERSION.

"On, well is me, my jolly goss-hawk,
    That ye can speak and flee;
For ye can carry a love letter
    To my true love from me."

"Oh, how can I carry a letter to her,
    When her I do not know;
I bear the lips to her never spak,
    And the eyes that her never saw."

"The thing of my love's face that's white,
    Is that of dove or maw;
The thing of my love's face that's red,
    Is like blood shed on snaw.

"And when you come to the castel,
    Light on the bush of ash;
And sit you there and sing our loves,
    As she comes from the mass.

"And when she gaes into the house,
　　Sit ye upon the whin ;
And sit you there and sing our loves,
　　As she goes out and in."

And when he flew to that castel,
　　He lighted on the ash ;
And there he sat and sung their loves,
　　As she came from the mass.

And when she went into the house,
　　He flew unto the whin ;
And there he sat and sung their loves,
　　As she went out and in.

"Come hitherward, my maidens all,
　　And sip red wine anon ;
Till I go to my west window,
　　And hear a birdie's moan."

She 's gane unto her west window,
　　And fainly aye it drew ;
And soon into her white silk lap,
　　The bird the letter threw.

"Yere bidden send your love a send,
　　For he has sent you twa ;
And tell him where he can see you,
　　Or he cannot live ava."

"I send him the rings from my white fingers,
　　The garlands off my hair ;
I send him the heart that 's in my breast,
　　What would my love have mair ;
And at the fourth kirk in fair Scotland,
　　Ye 'll bid him meet me there."

She hied her to her father dear,
  As fast as gang could she;
"An asking, an asking, my father dear,
  An asking ye grant me,
That if I die in fair England,
  In Scotland gar bury me.*

"At the first kirk of fair Scotland,
  You cause the bells be rung;
At the second kirk of fair Scotland,
  You cause the mass be sung.

"At the third kirk of fair Scotland,
  You deal gold for my sake,
And at the fourth kirk of fair Scotland.
  Oh! there you'll bury me at.

"And now, my tender father dear,
  This asking grant you me;"
"Your asking is but small," he said,
  "Weel granted it shall be."

* Mr Buchan's version supplies an obvious gap in the
story at this passage :—

"Ask what you will, my dear daughter,
  And I will grant it thee;
Unless to marry yon Scottish squire,
  That's what shall never be."

"Oh that's the asking, father," she said,
  "That I'll ne'er ask of thee,
But if I die in South England,
  In Scotland ye'll bury me."

"The asking's nae sae great, daughter,
  But granted it shall be;
And though ye die in South England,
  In Scotland we ll bury thee."

[The lady asks the same boon, and receives a similar
answer, first from her mother, then from her sister, and
lastly from her seven brothers.]*

Then down as dead that lady drapp'd,
    Beside her mother's knee;
Then out it spak an auld witch wife,
    By the fire side sat she;

Says—"Drap the het lead on her cheek,
    And drap it on her chin;
And drap it on her rose-red lips,
    And she will speak again;
For much a lady young will do,
    To her true love to win."

They drapp'd the het lead on her cheek,
    So did they on her chin;
They drapp'd it on her red rose lips,
    But they breathed none again.

Her brothers they went to a room,
    To make to her a bier;
The boards of it were cedar wood,
    And the plates on it gold so clear.

* Buchan supplies a part of this hiatus :—

    And she has gane to her stepmother,
       Full low down on her knee;
    " An asking, an asking, mother dear,
       I pray you grant it me."

    " Ask what you please, my lily-white dove,
       And granted it shall be.'
    " If I do die in South England,
       In Scotland bury me."

    " O had these words been spoken again,
       I 'd not have granted thee;
    You hae a love in fair Scotland,
       Wi' him you fain would be."

    She scarce was to her chamber gane,
       Nor yet was well set doun,
    Till, on the sofa where she sat,
       She fell in deadly swoon.

Her sisters they went to a room,
  To make to her a sark ;
The cloth of it was satin fine,
  And the steeking silken wark.

"But well is me my jolly goss-hawk,
  That ye can speak and flee ;
Come shew to me any love tokens
  That you have brought to me."

"She sends you the rings from her fingers,
  The garlands from her hair ;
She sends you the heart within her breast,
  And what would you have mair ?
And at the fourth kirk of fair Scotland,
  She bids you meet her there."

"Come hither all my merry young men,
  And drink the good red wine ;
For we must on to fair England,
  To free my love from pine."

At the first kirk of fair Scotland,
  They gart the bells be rung ;
At the second kirk of fair Scotland,
  They gart the mass be sung.

At the third kirk of fair Scotland,
  They dealt gold for her sake ;
And the fourth kirk of fair Scotland,
  Her true love met them at.

"Set down, set down the corpse," he said,
  "Till I look on the dead ;
The last time that I saw her face,
  She ruddy was and red ;

But now alas, and woe is me,
    She's wallowed like a weed."

He rent the sheet upon her face,
    A little aboon her chin;
With lily white cheek and lemin' eyne,
    She lookt and laugh'd to him.

"Give me a chive of your bread, my love,
    A bottle of your wine;
For I have fasted for your love,
    These weary lang days nine;
There's not a steed in your stable,
    But would have been dead ere syne.

"Gae hame, gae hame my seven brothers,
    Gae hame and blaw the horn;
For you can say in the south of England,
    Your sister gave you the scorn.

"I came not here to fair Scotland,
    To lye amang the meal;
But I came here to fair Scotland,
    To wear the silks so weel.

"I came not here to fair Scotland,
    To lye amang the dead;
But I came here to fair Scotland,
    To wear the gold so red."

GYPSIE DAVY.

This copy of the popular ballad, which generally goes under the title of *Johnie Faa, or the Gypsie Laddie*, was obtained from the recitation of an old woman, and, as it contains some additional particulars not to be found in any copy hitherto printed, so far as known to the Editor, it has found a place in this collection. Mr Finlay has been at some pains in gathering the notices which tradition has preserved of this fair lady's delinquency, and of her dreary penance in the tower of Maybole.—MOTHERWELL.

THERE came singers to Earl Cassillis' gates,
   And oh but they sang bonnie;
They sang sae sweet and sae complete,
   Till down came the Earl's lady.

She came tripping down the stair,
   And all her maids before her;
As soon as they saw her weel-faur'd face
   They coost their glamourye ower her.

They gave her o' the gude sweet-meats,
   The nutmeg and the ginger;
And she gi'ed them a' far better things,
   Ten gowd rings aff her finger.

"Come with me, my bonnie Jeanie Faa,
   O come with me, my dearie;
For I do swear by the head o' my spear,
   Thy gude lord 'll nae mair come near thee."

"Tak from me my silken cloak,
   And bring me down my plaidie;
For it is good and good eneuch,
   To follow a Gypsie Davy.

"Yestreen I rode this water deep,
   And my gude lord beside me ;
But this night I maun set in my pretty fit and
    wade,
   A wheen blackguards wading wi' me.

"Yestreen I lay in a fine feather bed,
   And my gude lord beyond me,
But this night I maun lie in some cauld ten-
    ant's barn,
   A wheen blackguards waiting on me."

"Come to thy bed, my bonnie Jeanie Faa,
   Come to thy bed, my dearie ;
For I do swear by the head o' my spear,
   Thy gude lord 'll nae mair come near thee."

"I 'll go to bed," the lady she said,
   'I 'll go to bed to my dearie ;
For I do swear by the fan in my hand,
   That my lord shall nae mair come near me.

"I 'll mak a hap," the lady she said,
   "I 'll mak a hap to my dearie ;
And he 's get a' this petticoat gaes round,
   And my lord shall nae mair come near me."

When her gude lord came hame at night,
   He was asking for his lady;
One spake slow, and another whispered low,
   "She 's awa' wi' Gypsie Davy."

"Come saddle to me my horse," he said ;
   "Come saddle and make him ready ;
For I 'll neither sleep, eat, nor drink,
   Till I find out my lady."

They sought her up, they sought her down,
   They sought her through nations many;
Till at length they found her out in bonnie
     Abbaydale,
   Drinking wi' Gypsie Davy.

"Rise, oh, rise! my bonny Jeanie Faa;
   Oh, rise, and do not tarry:
Is this the thing that ye promised to me,
   When at first I did thee marry?"

They drunk her cloak, so did they her gown,
   They drunk her stockings and her shoon,
And they drunk the coat that was neist to her
     smock,
   And they pawned her pearled apron.

They were sixteen clever men,
   Suppose they were nae bonnie;
They are to be a' hanged on ae day,
   For the stealing o' Earl Cassillis lady.

"We are sixteen clever men,
   One woman was a' our mother;
We are a' to be hanged on ae day,
   For the stealing of a wanton lady."

WILLIE WALLACE.

This version of a popular ballad, which has been successively printed in Johnson's Museum, Jamieson's Old
Ballads, and Findlay's Ballads, is taken from Buchan's
"Gleanings of Scarce Old Ballads," Peterhead, 1825.
The Editor of that work states it to be given from the
recitation of an itinerant tinker and gypsy.   We prefer
it to the copy preserved in the Museum.   The reader will
find the subject of the ballad in the Fifth Book of Henry
the Minstrel's "Metrical Life of Walays."

WALLACE in the high highlans,
   Neither meat nor drink got he,
Said—" Fa' me life, or fa' me death,
   Now to some town I maun be."

He 's put on his short claiding,
   And on his short claiding put he,
Says—" Fa' me life, or fa' me death,
   Now to Perth-town I maun be."

He stepp'd o'er the river Tay,
   I wat he stepped on dry land ;
He wasna aware of a well-faured maid
   Was washing there her lilie hands.

" What news, what news, ye well-faured maid ?
   What news hae ye this day to me ?"
" No news, no news, ye gentle knight,
   No news hae I this day to thee,
But fifteen lords in the hostage-house
   Waiting Wallace for to see."

" If I had but in my pocket
   The worth of one single pennie,
I would go to the hostage-house,
   And there the gentlemen to see."

x

She put her hand in her pocket,
  And she has pull'd out half-a-crown,
Says—"Take ye that, ye belted knight,
  'Twill pay your way till ye come down."

As he went from the well-faured maid,
  A beggar bold I wat met he,
Was covered wi' a clouted cloak,
  And in his hand a trusty tree.

"What news, what news, ye silly auld man,
  What news hae ye this day to gie?"
"No news, no news, ye belted knight,
  No news hae I this day to thee,
But fifteen lords in the hostage-house
  Waiting Wallace for to see."

"You'll lend me your clouted cloak
  That covers you frae head to shie,
And I'll go to the hostage-house,
  Asking there for some supplie.

Now he's gone to the West-muir wood,
  And there he pull'd a trusty tree,
And then he's on to the hostage gone,
  Asking there for charitie.

Down the stair the captain comes,
  Aye the poor man for to see;
"If ye be a captain as good as ye look,
  Ye'll give a poor man some supplie;
If ye be a captain as good as ye look,
  A guinea, this day, ye'll gie to me."

"Where were ye born, ye crooked carle?
  Where were ye born, in what countrie?"
"In fair Scotland I was born,
  Crooked carle that I be."

"I would give you fifty pounds
  Of gold and white monie ;
I would give you fifty pounds,
  If the traitor Wallace ye 'd let me see."

"Tell down your money," said Willie Wallace,
  "Tell down your money, if it be good ;
I 'm sure I have it in my power,
  And never had a better bode.

"Tell down your money, if it be good,
  And let me see if it be fine,
I 'm sure I have it in my power
  To bring the traitor Wallace in."

The money was told on the table,
  Silver bright of pounds fiftie ;
"Now here I stand," said Willie Wallace,
  "And what hae ye to say to me ?"

He slew the captain where he stood,
  The rest they did quake an' roar ;
He slew the rest around the room,
  And ask'd if there were any more.

"Come, cover the table," said Willie Wallace,
  "Come, cover the table now, make haste,
For it will soon be three lang days
  Sin I a bit o' meat did taste."

The table was not well covered,
  Nor yet had he set down to dine,
Till fifteen more of the English lords
  Surrounded the house where he was in.

The guidwife she ran but the floor,
    And aye the guidman he ran ben;
From eight o'clock till four at noon,
    He has killed full thirty men.

He put the house in sic a swither,
    That five o' them he sticket dead;
Five o' them he drown'd in the river,
    And five hung in the West-muir wood.

Now he is on to the North-Inch gone,
    Where the maid was washing tenderlie;
"Now by my sooth," said Willie Wallace,
    "It's been a sair day's wark to me."

He 's put his hand in his pocket,
    And he has pulled out twenty pounds,
Says, "Tak ye that, ye weel-faured maid,
    For the gude luck of your half-crown."

SWEET WILLIE AND LADY MARGERIE.

This ballad was taken down by Mr Motherwell, in 1825, from the recitation of a lady then far advanced in years, with whose grandmother it was a favourite. It bears some resemblance to *Clerk Saunders*.

SWEET WILLIE was a widow's son,
    And he wore a milk-white weed O;
And weel could Willie read and write,
    Far better ride on steed O.

Lady Margerie was the first ladye
    That drank to him the wine O;
And aye as the healths gaed round and round,
    "Laddie, your love is mine O."

Lady Margerie was the first ladye
   That drank to him the beer O;
And aye as the healths gaed round and round,
   "Laddie, ye 're welcome here O.

"You must come intil my bower
   When the evening bells do ring O;
And you must come intil my bower
   When the evening mass doth sing O."

He 's taen four-and-twenty braid arrows,
   And laced them in a whang O;
And he 's awa' to Lady Margerie's bower,
   As fast as he can gang O.

He set his ae foot on the wa',
   And the other on a stane O;
And he 's kill'd a' the king's life-guards,
   He 's kill'd them every man O.

"Oh, open, open, Lady Margerie,
   Open and let me in O;
The weet weets a' my yellow hair,
   And the dew draps on my chin O."

With her feet as white as sleet
   She strode her bower within O;
And with her fingers lang and sma'
   She 's looten sweet Willie in O.

She 's louted down unto his foot,
   To louze sweet Willie's shoon O;
The buckles were sae stiff they wadna lowze,
   The blood had frozen in O.

" O Willie, O Willie, I fear that thou
　　Hast bred me dule and sorrow ;
The deed that thou hast done this nicht
　　Will kythe upon the morrow."

In then came her father dear,
　　And a braid sword by his gare O ;
And he 's gien Willie, the widow's son,
　　A deep wound and a sair O.

" Lye yont, lye yont, Willie," she says,
　　" Your sweat weets a' my side O ;
Lye yont, lye yont, Willie," she says,
　　" For your sweat I downa bide O."

She turned her back unto the wa',
　　Her face unto the room O ;
And there she saw her auld father
　　Fast walking up and doun O.

" Woe be to you, father," she said,
　　" And an ill death may you die O ;
For ye 've killed Willie, the widow's son,
　　And he would have married me O."

She turned her back unto the room,
　　Her face unto the wa' O ;
And with a deep and heavy sich,
　　Her heart it brak in twa O.

KEMPION.

The tale of *Kempion* seems, from the names of the
personages and the nature of the adventure, to have been
an old metrical romance, degraded into a ballad by the
lapse of time, and the corruption of reciters. The change
in the structure of the last verses from the common
ballad stanza to that which is proper to the metrical
romance, adds force to this conjecture.

Such transformations as the song narrates are common
in the annals of chivalry. In the 25th and 26th cantos
of the second book of the *Orlando Inamorato*, the paladin,
Brandimarte, after surmounting many obstacles, pene-
trates into the recesses of an enchanted palace. Here he
finds a fair damsel seated upon a tomb, who announces
to him that, in order to achieve her deliverance, he must
raise the lid of the sepulchre, and kiss whatever being
should issue forth. The knight, having pledged his faith,
proceeds to open the tomb, out of which a monstrous
snake issues forth with a tremendous hiss. *Brandimarte*,
with much reluctance, fulfils the *bizarre* conditions of the
adventure, and the monster is instantly changed into a
beautiful fairy, who loads her deliverer with benefits.

There is a ballad somewhat resembling *Kempion*, called
The Laidley Worm of Spindleston-heugh, which is very
popular upon the borders. The most common version
was either entirely composed, or re-written by the Reve-
rend Mr Lamb, of Norham.—Sir WALTER SCOTT.

"Cum heir, cum heir, ye freely feed,
   And lay your head low on my knee;
The heaviest weird I will you read
   That ever was read to gay ladye.

"O meikle dolour sall ye dree,
   And aye the salt seas o'er ye'se swim;
And far mair dolour sall ye dree,
   On Estmere crags, when ye them climb.

“ I weird ye to a fiery beast,
   And relieved sall ye never be,
Till Kempion, the kingis son,
   Cum to the crag, and thrice kiss thee.”

O meikle dolour did she dree,
   And aye the salt seas o’er she swam ;
And far mair dolour did she dree
   On Estmere crags, ere she them clamb.

And aye she cried for Kempion,
   Gin he would but come to her hand :
Now word has gane to Kempion,
   That sicken a beast was in his land.

“ Now, by my sooth,” said Kempion,
   “ This fiery beast I ’ll gang and see.”
“ And, by my sooth,” said Segramour,
   “ My ae brother, I ’ll gang wi’ thee.”

Then bigged hae they a bonnie boat,
   And they hae set her to the sea ;
But a mile before they reached the shore,
   Around them she gart the red fire flee.

“ O Segramour, keep the boat afloat,
   And lat her na the land owre near ;
For this wicked beast will sure gae wud,
   And set fire to a’ the land and mair.”

Syne has he bent an arblast bow,
   And aim’d an arrow at her head ;
And swore if she didna quit the land,
   Wi’ that same shaft to shoot her dead.

"O out of my stythe I winna rise,
    (And it is not for the awe o' thee,)
Till Kempion, the kingis son,
    Cum to the crag, and thrice kiss me."

He has louted him o'er the dizzy crag,
    And gi'en the monster kisses ane;
Awa she gaed, and again she cam,
    The fieriest beast that ever was seen.

"O out o' my stythe I winna rise,
    (And not for a' thy bow nor thee,)
Till Kempion, the kingis son,
    Cum to the crag, and thrice kiss me."

He's louted him o'er the Estmere crags,
    And he has gi'en her kisses twa;
Awa she gaed, and again she cam,
    The fieriest beast that ever you saw.

"O out of my den I winna rise,
    Nor flee it for the fear o' thee,
Till Kempion, that courteous knight,
    Come to the crag, and thrice kiss me."

He's louted him o'er the lofty crag,
    And he has gi'en her kisses three:
Awa she gaed, and again she cam,
    The loveliest ladye e'er could be.

" And by my sooth," says Kempion,
    " My ain true love, (for this is she,)
They surely had a heart o' stane,
    Could put thee to such misery.

"O was it werewolf in the wood
    Or was it mermaid in the sea?
Or was it man, or vile woman,
    My ain true love, that misshaped thee?"

"It was na werewolf in the wood,
    Nor was it mermaid in the sea;
But it was my wicked stepmother,
    And wae and weary may she be!"

"O a heavier weird shall light her on
Than ever fell on vile woman;
Her hair shall grow rough, and her teeth
        grow lang,
And on her four feet shall she gang.

"None shall take pity her upon;
In Wormeswood she aye shall won;
And relieved shall she never be,
Till St Mungo come over the sea."
And sighing said that weary wight,
"I doubt that day I'll never see!"

KEMP OWYNE.

The subject of this ballad is the same as that of the
preceding, but is very differently treated.   The present
version is from recitation.   From the air to which it is
sung being similar to that of the ludicrous song of *Kempy
Kay*, or *Kempy Kane*, one would be inclined to believe
that the latter was a burlesque of the serious ballad.   Ringing these merry changes on sad metres was no uncommon
usage among the Northern Minstrels; of this Mr Jamieson
has produced several instances, in his interesting translations from the Danish ballads.—MOTHERWELL.

HER mother died when she was young,
  Which gave her cause to make great moan;
Her father married the warst woman ·
  That ever lived in Christendom.

She served her with foot and hand,
  In every thing that she could dee;
Till once, in an unlucky time,
  She threw her ower in Craigy's sea.

Says, "Lie you there, dove Isabel,
  And all my sorrows lie with thee;
Till Kemp Owyne come ower the sea,
  And borrow you with kisses three,
Let all the warld do what they will,
  Or borrowed shall you never be."

Her breath grew strang, her hair grew lang,
  And twisted thrice about the tree,
And all the people far and near
  Thought that a savage beast was she;
Thir news did come to Kemp Owyne,
  Where he lived far beyond the sea.

He hasted him to Craigy's sea,
  And on the savage beast look'd he;
Her breath was strang, her hair was lang,
  And twisted was about the tree;
And with a swing, she came about,
  "Come to Craigy's sea and kiss with me.

"Here is a royal belt," she cried,
  "That I have found in the green sea,
And while your body it is on,
  Drawn shall your blood never be;
But if you touch me tail or fin,
  I vow my belt your death shall be."

He stepped in, gave her a kiss,
  The royal belt he brought him wi',
Her breath was strang, her hair was lang,
  And twisted twice about the tree;
And with a swing she came about,
  "Come to Craigy's sea and kiss with me.

"Here is a royal ring," she said,
  "That I have found in the green sea;
And while your finger it is on,
  Drawn shall your blood never be;
But if you touch me tail or fin,
  I swear my ring your death shall be."

He stepped in, gave her a kiss,
  The royal ring he brought him wi';
Her breath was strang, her hair was lang,
  And twisted ance around the tree;
And with a swing she came about,
  "Come to Craigy's sea and kiss with me.

"Here is a royal brand," she said,
  "That I have found in the green sea;
And while your body it is on,
  Drawn shall your blood never be;
But if you touch me tail or fin,
  I swear my brand your death shall be."

He stepped in gave her a kiss,
  The royal brand he brought him wi',
Her breath was sweet, her hair grew short,
  And twisted nane about the tree;
And smilingly she came about,
  As fair a woman as fair could be.

EARL RICHARD.

The locality of this ballad—Barnisdale—will bring to the remembrance of the reader tales of Robin Hood and Little John, who, according to the testimony of Andrew of Wyntown,

> " In Yngilwode and Barnysdale,
> Their oysed all this tyme thare travaile."

Whether the ballad is originally the production of an English or of a Scotch minstrel, admits of question; certain, however, it is, that it has been received into both countries at a pretty early period. Hearne, in his preface to "Gul. Neubrigiensis Historia," Oxon. 1719, vol. i. p. lxx., mentions that *The Knight and Shepherd's Daughter* was well known in the time of Queen Elizabeth. In Fletcher's "Pilgrim," Act IV., Scene 2, a stanza of the same ballad is quoted. The English version of this ballad is given in the "Reliques of English Poetry," vol. iii. There are various copies of it current in Scotland. The present version, obtained from recitation in one of the northern counties, is out of sight the most circumstantial and elaborated that has yet been printed. It possesses no small portion of humour, and appears to be of greater antiquity than the copy published in the Reliques. In one of the recited copies of this ballad, Earl Richard endeavours to shake the lady's conviction of his identity by using the same means as the Gaberlunzie man, who sang—

> " I'll bow my leg, and crook my knee,
> And draw a black clout owre my ee,
> A cripple or blind they will ca' me."

But the eyes of love were too sharp to be deceived by such witty devices, for, as the ballad has it, when

> " He came hirplin' on a stick,
> And leanin' on a tree,"

the lady, with a hasty voice, in the face of all the court, immediately cries out—

> " Be he cripple, or be he blind,
> The same man is he !
> With my low silver ee."

Earl Richard's unbridegroomlike behaviour on his wedding night, and his agreeable discovery on the morrow, will remind the ballad reader of the gentle Sir Gawaine,

who, when reluctantly turning round to caress his loathly
bride, much to his joy and contentment found her trans-
formed into a most lovesome lady.—MOTHERWELL.

EARL RICHARD once upon a day,
  And all his valiant men so wight ;
He hied him down to Barnisdale,
  Where all the land is fair and light.

He was aware of a damosel,
  I wot fast on she did her bound,
With towers of gold upon her head,
  As fair a woman as could be found.

He said, "Busk you, busk you ! fair ladye,
  The white flowers and the red ;
For I would give my bonnie ship,
  To get your maidenhead."

"I wish your ship might rent and rive,
  And drown you in the sea ;
For all this would not mend the miss,
  That you would do to me."
" The miss is not so great ladye,
  Soon mended it might be.

"I have four-and-twenty mills in Scotland
  Stand on the water Tay ;
You 'll have them and as much good flour
  As they 'll grind in a day."

" I wish your bonnie ship rent and rive,
  And drown you in the sea ;
For all that would not mend the miss,
  That you would do for me."
" The miss is not so great ladye,
  Soon mended it will be.

"I have four-and-twenty milk-white cows,
    All calved in a day ;
You 'll have them and as much hained grass
    As they all on can gae."

"I wish your bonnie ship rent and rive,
    And drown you in the sea ;
For all that would not mend the miss,
    That you would do to me."
"The miss is not so great ladye,
    Soon mended it might be.

"I have four-and-twenty milk-white steeds
    All foaled in one year ;
You 'll have them and as much red gold
    As all their backs can bear."

She turned her right and round about,
    And she swore by the mold,
"I would not be your love," said she,
    "For that church full of gold."

He turned him right and round about,
    And he swore by the mass,
Says,—"Lady, ye my love shall be,
    And gold ye shall have less."

She turned her right and round about,
    And she swore by the moon,
"I would not be your love," says she,
    "For all the gold in Rome."

He turned him right and round about,
    And he swore by the moon,
Says,—"Lady, ye my love shall be,
    And gold ye shall have none."

He caught her by the milk-white hand,
    And by the grass-green sleeve ;
And there has taken his will of her,
    Wholly without her leave.

The lady frowned and sadly blushed,
    And oh ! but she thought shame ;
Says—"If you are a knight at all,
    You'll surely tell your name."

"In some places they call me Jack,
    In others they call me John ;
But when into the Queen's Court,
    Then Lithcock it is my name."

"Lithcock ! Lithcock !" the lady said,
    And spelt it ower again ;
"Lithcock ! it's Latin," the lady said,
    " Richard's the English of that name." ·

The knight he rode, the lady ran,
    A live long summer's day ;
Till they came to the wan water,
    That all men do call Tay.

He set his horse head to the water,
    Just thro' it for to ride ;
And the lady was as ready as him,
    The waters for to wade.

For he had never been as kind-hearted,
    As to bid the lady ride ;
And she had never been so low-hearted
    As for to bid him bide.

But deep into the wan water
    There stands a great big stone;
He turned his wight horse head about,
    Said—"Lady fair, will ye loup on?"

She's taken the wand was in her hand,
    And struck it on the foam,
And before he got the middle stream,
    The lady was on dry land.
"By help of God and our Lady,
    My help lies not in your hand.

"I learned it from my mother dear,
    Few is there that has learned better;
When I come to a deep water,
    I can swim thro' like ony otter.

"I learned it from my mother dear,
    I find I learned it for my weel;
When I come to a deep water,
    I can swim thro' like ony eel."

"Turn back, turn back, you lady fair,
    You know not what I see;
There is a lady in that castle,
    That will burn you and me."
"Betide me weal, betide me woe,
    That lady will I see."

She took a ring from her finger,
    And gave't the porter for his fee;
Says, "Tak you that, my good porter,
    And bid the queen speak to me."

And when she came before the queen,
    There she fell low down on her knee;
Says, "There is a knight into your court,
    This day has robbed me."

"Oh, has he robbed you of your gold,
　Or has he robbed you of your fee?"
"He has not robbed me of my gold,
　He has not robbed me of my fee;
He has robbed me of my maidenhead,
　The fairest flower of my bodie."

"There is no knight in all my court
　That thus has robbed thee;
But you'll have the truth of his right hand,
　Or else for your sake he'll die;
Tho' it were Earl Richard, my own brother,
　And oh! forbid that it be!"
Then, sighing, said the lady fair,
　"I wot the same man is he."

The queen called on her merry men,
　Even fifty men and three;
Earl Richard used to be the first man,
　But now the hindmost was he.
He's taken out one hundred pounds,
　And told it in his glove;
Says, "Tak you that, my lady fair,
　And seek another love."

"Oh no, oh no," the lady cried,
　"That's what shall never be;
I'll have the troth of your right hand,
　The queen she gave it me."

"I wish I had drunk of your water, sister,
　When I did drink your wine;
That for a carle's fair daughter,
　It gars me dree this pine."

"May be I am a carle's daughter,
    And may be never nane;
When ye met me in the green wood,
    Why did ye not let me alane?"

"Will you wear the short clothes,
    Or will you wear the side,
Or will you walk to your wedding,
    Or will you till it ride?"

"I will not wear the short clothes,
    But I will wear the side;
I will not walk to my wedding,
    But I to it will ride."

When he was set upon the horse,
    The lady him behin';
Then cauld and eerie were the words,
    The twa had them between.

She said, "Good e'en, ye nettles tall,
    Just there where ye grow at the dike,
If the auld carline my mother was here,
    Sae weel's she would you pike.

"How she would stap you in her poke,
    I wot at that she wadna fail;
And boil ye in her auld brass pan,
    And of ye she wad mak gude kail.

"And she would meal you with millering,
    That she gathers at the mill;
And mak you thick as any daigh,
    And when the pan was brimful

"Would mess you up in scuttle dishes,
　Syne bid us sup till we were fu',
Lay down her head upon a poke,
　Then sleep and snore like any sow."

"Away! away! you bad woman,
　For all your vile words grieveth me;
When ye heed so little for yourself,
　I'm sure ye'll heed far less for me.

"I wish I had drunk your water, sister,
　When that I did drink of your wine;
Since for a carle's fair daughter,
　It aye gars me dree all this pine."

"May be I am a carle's daughter,
　And may be never nane;
When ye met me in the good greenwood,
　Why did you not let me alane?

"Gude e'en, gude e'en, ye heather berries,
　As ye're growing on the hill;
If the auld carle and his bags were here,
　I wot he would get meat his fill.

"Late, late at night I knit our pokes,
　With even four-and-twenty knots;
And in the morn at breakfast time,
　I'll carry the keys of an earl's locks.

"Late, late at night I knit our pokes,
　With even four-and-twenty strings;
And if you look to my white fingers,
　They have as many gay gold rings."

"Away! away! ye ill woman,
    And sore your vile words grieveth me;
When you heed so little for yourself,
    I'm sure ye'll heed far less for me.

"But if you are a carle's daughter,
    As weel I take you for to be,
How did you get the gay clothing,
    In greenwood that ye had on ye?"

"My mother she's a poor woman,
    She nursèd an earl's children three;
And I got them from a foster-sister,
    For to beguile such sparks as thee."

"But if you be a carle's daughter,
    As weel that I believe you be,
How did ye learn the good Latin,
    In greenwood that ye spoke to me?"

"My mother she's a mean woman,
    She nursèd an earl's children three;
I learn'd it from their chapelain,
    To beguile such sparks as ye."

When mass was sung, and bells were rung,
    And all men boune for bed,
Then Earl Richard and this lady
    In ane bed they were laid.

He turned his face to the stock,
    And she hers to the stane,
And cauld and dreary was the luve
    That was thir twa between.

Great was the mirth in the kitchen,
  Likewise intil the ha',
But in his bed lay Earl Richard
  Wiping the tears awa'.

He wept till he fell fast asleep,
  Then slept till licht was come,
Then he did hear the gentlemen
  That talked in the room

Said—"Saw ye ever a fitter match,
  Betwixt the ane and ither;
The king o' Scotland's fair dochter,
  And the queen of England's brither."

"And is she the king o' Scotland's fair
    dochter?
  This day, oh, weel is me!
For seven times has my steed been saddled,
  To come to court with thee;
And with this witty lady fair
  How happy must I be!"

ANDREW LAMMIE.

The ill-starred loves of *Tiftie's bonnie Annie* and the
Trumpeter of Fyvie have already been made familiar to
the readers of ballad poetry, by Mr Jamieson, who has
published in his collection two different sets of this simple, but not unpathetic ditty.* Neither of these sets,
however, is so complete as the present version, which is
a reprint from a stall copy, published in Glasgow several

* Vide "Popular Ballads and Songs," Edinburgh, 1806, vol. i. p. 123,
and vol. ii. p. 382.

years ago, collated with a recited copy, which has furnished one or two verbal improvements.

"The beauty, gallantry, and amiable qualities of 'Bonnie
Andrew Lammie' seem," says Mr Jamieson, "to have
been proverbial wherever he went; and the good old
'cummer' in Allan Ramsay, as the best evidence of the
power of her own youthful charms, and the best apology
for her having 'cast a leggen girth hersel,' says—

> 'I 'se warrant ye have a' heard tell,
> Of bonnie Andrew Lammie?
> Stiffly in luve wi' me he fell,
> As soon as e'er he saw me—
> That was a day !'

"In this instance, as in most others in the same piece, it
seems most probable that Allan Ramsay forgot that he
was writing of the days of the original author of 'Christis
Kirk on the Green,' and copied only the manners and traditions of his own times. If a woman who could boast
of having had an intrigue with the 'Trumpeter of Fyvie,'
was bale and hearty at the time when Allan wrote, we
may reasonably suppose poor 'Tifty's Nanny' to have died
sometime about the year 1670." This conjecture as to
the period when

> "The fairest flower was cut down by love,
> That e'er sprung up in Fyvie,"

is very near the truth, if the notice contained in the title
of the stall copy referred to can be admitted as evidence
on the point. It is this—"Andrew Lammie; or, Mill o'
Tiftie's Annie. This tragedy was acted in the year 1674."

It has been remarked by Mr Jamieson, that "this
ballad is almost entirely without rhymes; as cadence in
the measure is all that seems aimed at, and the few instances of rhyme that occur appear to be rather casual
than intentional." Though the present set is not so faulty
in this respect as in the copies which came under Mr
Jamieson's observation, it, as well as the others, has another peculiarity deserving attention—namely, the studied
recurrence of rhyme in the middle of the first and third
lines of a great many of the stanzas.

It may be stated, that the present set of the ballad
agrees with any recited copy which the Editor has hitherto
met with in the West Country.—MOTHERWELL.

At Mill o' Tifty lived a man,
 In the neighbourhood of Fyvie;
He had a lovely daughter fair,
 Was called bonnie Annie.

Her bloom was like the springing flower,
 That salutes the rosy morning;
With innocence, and graceful mien,
 Her beauteous form adorning.

Lord Fyvie had a Trumpeter,
 Whose name was Andrew Lammie;
He had the art to gain the heart
 Of Mill o' Tiftie's Annie.

Proper he was, both young and gay,
 His like was not in Fyvie;
No one was there that could compare
 With this same Andrew Lammie.

Lord Fyvie he rode by the door
 Where lived Tiftie's Annie;
His Trumpeter rode him before,
 Ev'n this same Andrew Lammie.

Her mother call'd her to the door,
 "Come here to me, my Annie;
Did you ever see a prettier man
 Than the Trumpeter of Fyvie?"

She sighed sore, but said no more;
 Alas for bonnie Annie!
She durst not own her heart was won
 By the Trumpeter of Fyvie.

At night when they went to their beds,
  All slept full sound but Annie ;
Love so opprest her tender breast,
  Thinking on Andrew Lammie.

"Love comes in at my bed-side,
  And love lies down beyond me ;
Love has possess'd my tender breast,
  And love will waste my body.

"The first time I and my love met
  Was in the woods of Fyvie ;
His lovely form and speech so sweet
  Soon gain'd the heart of Annie.

"He call'd me mistress ; I said, No,
  I 'm Tiftie's bonnie Annie ;
With apples sweet he did me treat.
  And kisses soft and many.

"It 's up and down in Tiftie's den,
  Where the burn runs clear and bonnie,
I 've often gone to meet my love,
  My bonnie Andrew Lammie."

But now, alas ! her father heard,
  That the Trumpeter of Fyvie
Had had the art to gain the heart
  Of Tiftie's bonnie Annie.

Her father soon a letter wrote,
  And sent it on to Fyvie,
To tell his daughter was bewitch'd
  By his servant, Andrew Lammie.

When Lord Fyvie had this letter read,
  O dear! but he was sorry;
The bonniest lass in Fyvie's land
  Is bewitch'd by Andrew Lammie.

Then up the stair his Trumpeter
  He called soon and shortly;
"Pray, tell me soon, what's this you've
    done
  To Tiftie's bonnie Annie?"

"In wicked art I had no part,
  Nor therein am I canny;
True love alone the heart has won
  Of Tiftie's bonnie Annie.

"Woe betide Mill o' Tiftie's pride,
  For it has ruin'd many;
He'll no hae't said that she should wed
  The Trumpeter of Fyvie.

"Where will I find a boy so kind,
  That'll carry a letter cannie,
Who will run on to Tiftie's town,
  Give it to my love Annie?"

"Here you shall find a boy so kind,
  Who'll carry a letter canny,
Who will run on to Tiftie's town,
  And gie't to thy love Annie."

"It's Tiftie he has daughters three,
  Who all are wondrous bonnie;
But ye'll ken her o'er a' the lave,
  Gie that to bonnie Annie."

"It's up and down in Tiftie's den,
  Where the burn rins clear and bonnie,
There wilt thou come and meet thy love,
  Thy bonnie Andrew Lammie.

"When wilt thou come, and I'll attend,
  My love I long to see thee?"
"Thou may'st come to the Bridge of Sleugh,
  And there I'll come and meet thee."

"My love, I go to Edinbro',
  And for a while must leave thee;"
She sighed sore, and said no more,
  "But I wish that I were wi' thee."

"I'll buy to thee a bridal gown,
  My love, I'll buy it bonnie;"
"But I'll be dead ere ye come back
  To see your bonnie Annie."

"If you'll be true, and constant too,
  As my name's Andrew Lammie,
I shall thee wed when I come back
  To see the lands of Fyvie."

"I will be true, and constant too,
  To thee, my Andrew Lammie;
But my bridal-bed will ere then be made
  In the green kirkyard of Fyvie."

"Our time is gone and now comes on,
  My dear, that I must leave thee;
If longer here I should appear,
  Mill o' Tiftie he would see me."

"I now for ever bid adieu
  To thee, my Andrew Lammie;
Ere ye come back, I will be laid
  In the green kirkyard of Fyvie."

He hied him to the head of the house,
  To the house-top of Fyvie;
He blew his trumpet loud and shrill,
  'Twas heard at Mill o' Tiftie.

Her father lock'd the door at night,
  Laid by the keys fu' canny;
And when he heard the trumpet sound,
  Said, "Your cow is lowing, Annie."

"My father dear, I pray forbear,
  And reproach no more your Annie;
For I 'd rather hear that cow to low
  Than hae a' the kine in Fyvie.

"I would not for my braw new gown,
  And a' your gifts sae many,
That it were told in Fyvie's land,
  How cruel you are to Annie.

"But if ye strike me, I will cry,
  And gentlemen will hear me;
Lord Fyvie will be riding by,
  And he 'll come in and see me."

At the same time, the Lord came in,
  He said, "What ails thee, Annie?"
"'Tis all for love now I must die,
  For bonnie Andrew Lammie."

"Pray, Mill o' Tiftie, gie consent,
    And let your daughter marry."
"It will be with some higher match
    Than the Trumpeter of Fyvie."

"If she were come of as high a kind
    As she's adorn'd with beauty,
I would take her unto myself,
    And make her mine own lady."

"It's Fyvie's lands are fair and wide,
    And they are rich and bonnie;
I would not leave my own true love
    For all the lands of Fyvie."

Her father struck her wondrous sore,
    As also did her mother;
Her sisters always did her scorn;
    But woe be to her brother.

Her brother struck her wondrous sore,
    With cruel strokes and many;
He brake her back in the hall door,
    For liking Andrew Lammie.

"Alas! my father and mother dear,
    Why so cruel to your Annie?
My heart was broken first by love,
    My brother has broken my body."

"O mother dear, make ye my bed,
    And lay my face to Fyvie;
Thus will I lie, and thus will die
    For my love, Andrew Lammie!"

"Ye neighbours hear, both far and near,
　Ye pity Tiftie's Annie;
Who dies for love of one poor lad,
　For bonnie Andrew Lammie.

"No kind of vice e'er stain'd my life,
　Nor hurt my virgin honour;
My youthful heart was won by love,
　But death will me exoner."

Her mother then she made her bed,
　And laid her face to Fyvie;
Her tender heart it soon did break,
　And ne'er saw Andrew Lammie.

But the word soon went up and down,
　Through all the lands of Fyvie,
That she was dead and buriéd,
　Even Tiftie's bonnie Annie.

Lord Fyvie he did wring his hands,
　Said, "Alas for Tiftie's Annie!
The fairest flower 's cut down by love,
　That e'er sprung up in Fyvie.

"O woe betide Mill o' Tiftie's pride,
　He might have let them marry;
I should have gi'en them both to live
　Into the lands of Fyvie."

Her father sorely now laments
　The loss of his dear Annie,
And wishes he had gi'en consent
　To wed with Andrew Lammie.

Her mother grieves both air and late,
   Her sisters, 'cause they scorn'd her;
Surely her brother doth mourn and grieve,
   For the cruel usage he 'd given her.

But now, alas! it was too late,
   For they could not recall her;
Through life, unhappy is their fate,
   Because they did control her.

When Andrew hame from Edinbro' came,
   With meikle grief and sorrow:
"My love has died for me to-day,
   I 'll die for her to-morrow.

"Now I will on to Tiftie's den,
   Where the burn runs clear and bonnie;
With tears I 'll view the Bridge of Sleugh,*
   Where I parted last with Annie.

"Then will I speed to the churchyard,
   To the green churchyard of Fyvie;
With tears I 'll water my love's grave,
   Till I follow Tiftie's Annie."

Ye parents grave, who children have,
   In crushing them be canny,
Lest when too late you do repent—
   Remember Tiftie's Annie.

---

* "Sleugh:" in one printed copy this is "Sheugh," and in a recited copy it was called "Skew;" but which is the right reading, the editor, from his ignorance of the topography of the lands of Fyvie, is unable to say. It is a received superstition in Scotland, that when friends or lovers part at a bridge, they shall never again meet.—W. M.

THE WEARY COBLE O' CARGILL.

This local ballad, which commemorates some real event, is given from the recitation of an old woman, residing in the neighbourhood of Cambusmichael, Perthshire.   It possesses the elements of good poetry, and, had it fallen into the hands of those who make no scruple of interpolating and corrupting the text of oral song, it might have been made, with little trouble, a very interesting and pathetic composition.

Kercock and Balathy are two small villages on the banks of the Tay; the latter is nearly opposite Stobhall. According to tradition, the ill-fated hero of the ballad had a leman in each of these places, and it was on the occasion of his paying a visit to his Kercock love that the jealous dame in "Balathy toun," from a revengeful feeling, scuttled the boat in which he was to re-cross the Tay to Stobhall. —MOTHERWELL.

DAVID DRUMMOND'S destinie,
   Gude man o' appearance o' Cargill ;
I wat his blude rins in the flude,
   Sae sair against his parents' will.

She was the lass o' Balathy toun,
   And he the butler o' Stobhall ;
And mony a time she wauked late,
   To bore the coble o' Cargill.

His bed was made in Kercock ha',
   Of gude clean sheets and of the hay ;
He wudna rest ae nicht therein,
   But on the prude waters he wud gae.

His bed was made in Balathy toun,
   Of the clean sheets and of the strae ;
But I wat it was far better made,
   Into the bottom o' bonnie Tay.

She bored the coble in seven pairts,
　　I wat her heart might hae been sae sair;
For there she got the bonnie lad lost,
　　Wi' the curly locks and the yellow hair.

He put his foot into the boat,
　　He little thocht o' ony ill:
But before that he was mid waters,
　　The weary coble began to fill.

"Woe be to the lass o' Balathy toun,
　　I wat an ill death may she die;
For she bored the coble in seven pairts,
　　And let the waters perish me!

"O help! O help!　I can get nane,
　　Nae help o' man can to me come!"
This was about his dying words,
　　When he was choked up to the chin.

"Gae tell my father and my mother,
　　It was naebody did me this ill;
I was, a-going my ain errands,
　　Lost at the coble o' bonnie Cargill."

She bored the boat in seven pairts,
　　I wat she bored it wi' gude will;
And there they got the bonnie lad's corpse,
　　In the kirk-shot o' bonnie Cargill.

Oh, a' the keys o' bonnie Stobha',
　　I wat they at his belt did hing;
But a' the keys of bonnie Stobha',
　　They now lie low into the stream.
Z

A braver page into his age
   Ne'er set a foot upon the plain;
His father to his mother said—
   "Oh sae sune as we've wanted him!

"I wat they had mair luve than this
   When they were young and at the scule;
But for his sake she wauked late,
   And bored the coble o' bonnie Cargill.

"There's ne'er a clean sark gae on my back,
   Nor yet a kame gae in my hair;
There's neither coal nor candle licht,
   Shall shine in my bower for ever mair.

"At kirk nor market I'se ne'er be at,
   Nor yet a blithe blink in my ee;
There's ne'er a ane shall say to anither,
   "That's the lassie gart the young man
     die.'"

Between the yetts o' bonnie Stobha',
   And the kirk-style o' bonnie Cargill,
There is mony a man and mother's son
   That was at my luve's burial.

THE END.

BALLANTYNE AND COMPANY, PRINTERS, EDINBURGH.